Diana Appleyard is a writer, broadcaster and freelance journalist for a number of national newspapers and magazines. She worked for the BBC as an Education Correspondent, before deciding to give up her full-time job to work from home, a decision which formed the basis for her first novel, *Homing Instinct*. She lives with her husband Ross and their two young daughters in an Oxfordshire farmhouse. *Homing Instinct* and her second novel, *A Class Apart*, are also both published by Black Swan.

Also by Diana Appleyard

HOMING INSTINCT
A CLASS APART

and published by Black Swan

OUT OF LOVE

Diana Appleyard

BLACK SWAN

OUT OF LOVE
A BLACK SWAN BOOK : 0 552 99933 4

First publication in Great Britain

PRINTING HISTORY
Black Swan edition published 2002

3 5 7 9 10 8 6 4

Copyright © Diana Appleyard 2002

Set in 11/12½pt Melior by
Kestrel Data, Exeter, Devon.

Black Swan Books are published by Transworld Publishers,
61–63 Uxbridge Road, London W5 5SA,
a division of The Random House Group Ltd,
in Australia by Random House Australia (Pty) Ltd,
20 Alfred Street, Milsons Point, Sydney, NSW 2061, Australia,
in New Zealand by Random House New Zealand Ltd,
18 Poland Road, Glenfield, Auckland 10, New Zealand
and in South Africa by Random House (Pty) Ltd,
Endulini, 5a Jubilee Road, Parktown 2193, South Africa.

Printed and bound in Great Britain by
Cox & Wyman Ltd, Reading, Berkshire.

To Ross

To Jo, my agent, for her calm support as always, and Linda, my publisher, for her enthusiasm, professional help and belief. Many thanks to Tess and Harold, in whose beautiful Cornish rectory I wrote most of this novel, and my old retriever Hamish who forced me out on windy, invigorating walks. Thanks too to Gill Crampton-Smith for her support and ideas, and my friend Margie for allowing me to borrow her name but not her personality. To wine expert Kym Milne, for his advice, and above all, my family – Ross for putting up with me going away with so little bad grace, my mother Pam for stepping into the breach as always and my children, Beth and Charlotte, who put everything in perspective.

Prologue

Hattie lay asleep next to Tess, curled around her like a softly breathing dormouse. She seemed to know instinctively when Mark was not there, and would creep in, taking care not to wake her, so it was only when the sunlight began to slowly filter through the curtains that Tess would feel Hattie's breath on her face, her hand like a butterfly's wing on her arm, waking to the whispered words, 'Is it morning time?'

To Hattie, this was the safest place in the world, and Tess, who had never been allowed to sleep in her own parents' bed, would not have dreamt of turfing her out. Tonight she turned and put an arm gently around her daughter, smiling into the darkness. This is perfect peace, she thought, as Hattie twitched with her vivid child dreams of sand and sea and sailing kites in a blue, blue sky.

In the morning they woke simultaneously, early. Hattie's eyes were wide with astonishment at still being at the house, without the boys, the luxury of having Tess all to herself. 'Can we swim?' she whispered. They had to be out of the house by ten. Tess lifted herself up onto one elbow and looked at the alarm clock. It was just after seven, and already the pale light was slipping into the room beneath the heavy lined curtains like a ghost, a promise of bright sun. 'Yes,' she said. Hattie squealed, and jumped out of bed.

'Come on! Come on!' She tugged at Tess's arm. 'Up now!'

She ran off into the adjoining bathroom, tanned and naked like a small brown seal. Tess thought how perfect her daughter's body was, how compact and agile, compared to hers which bounced rather too often and in the wrong places. The only women who seemed to manage to keep a body like that of a child's, she reflected, so smooth, with skin which fitted so perfectly, were forced to lead a life of severe deprivation from all things tasty. But after the holiday she really, really would go on a diet, because as usual she'd eaten too much because it had all been part of the fantasy, that she could put whatever she wanted in her mouth without worrying about the consequences. It was so irritating that the boys could eat almost constantly, like ruminants, yet remain exactly as they were.

'You're not going to have coffee, are you?'

At the foot of the stairs, Hattie's anxious little face peered upwards. She could not understand the obsession grown-ups had with having to drink coffee, which always took up so much time when there were so many more interesting things to do. Tess paused on the rush-matting stairs, striped swimming towels over her arm, and smiled. 'I'll skip it just for once. Where are your jellies?' Hattie looked around her helplessly. Hattie and shoes were oil and water. 'Why?' she said.

'Stones. Oh, never mind.'

The cases she'd packed the evening before stood like a reproach by the front door. Tess resolutely didn't look at them. They still had two hours, two hours of borrowed time before the drive home, when she would be forced to think about all the things she had to do at home, none of them nice, from mounds and mounds of washing to opening their bank statement, which would undoubtedly reveal the fact that they couldn't actually afford this holiday, and all they were doing was sliding inexorably into a bigger and bigger overdraft . . . no, she really didn't want to think about that at all. Margi had a phrase for avoiding such realities of life – 'pushing the tigers away', she described it – anything which was just too gruesome to contemplate should be simply shoved out of your aura, back into the jungle darkness. Tess looked at Hattie's smiling face, and pushed the tigers away.

'Put a jumper on,' she said, without thinking. Hattie groaned. Why were parents so insistent about jumpers and coats? She knew when she was cold, thank you, but no-one ever believed her and she was forever being muffled up into hot things she didn't want. Hattie hated being hot more than anything – more, even, than having her hair washed and shampoo getting in her eyes. More than constantly being told to wear her seat belt and having to eat broccoli, which was like having to eat a small tree.

Tess pulled on an old sailing jumper of Mark's over her swimming costume. It smelt reassuringly of him, of faint aftershave, cigarette smoke and the sharp, bitter tang of dried salt water. Then she added a pair of shorts, just in case they met anyone, which they were unlikely to do, as everyone else in the handful of whitewashed holiday cottages dotted around the tiny coastal peninsula had gone home yesterday. It was the end of the season, the end of days of damp towels and flip-flops, dripping ice creams and fresh crab bought from the shellfish stall in Polperro. The end of cloudy mornings drifting round the shops in Fowey, buying things for pure pleasure, not need, books, a pair of earrings, a small framed watercolour she would hang near the phone, to look at, and remember. The end of the sense of holiday-suspended animation, when all is to enjoy.

'OK, no jumper,' she relented.

She'd packed it already anyway, leaving out a T-shirt and pair of jeans for Hattie, socks and shoes, which were neatly placed on the end of her bed. Mark said Tess's compulsion to constantly tidy and place things in neat piles was anally retentive and a clear sign of her repressed upbringing. He liked to tease her about her childhood, so very different from his own. Tess retorted that Mark's urge to leave his belongings wherever they fell was less an expression of a free spirit unfettered by convention than sheer wilful male laziness.

She opened the door, mentally noting there was still a cricket bat of Jake's by the hatstand which had been missed in her pincerlike clearance sweep of the house last night.

The light, even so early, was blinding, and for a moment Tess stood blinking on the doorstep, feeling the warmth and the brightness flooding through her eyelids. You couldn't drive back to London on such a day. This was a day for idle pleasure, not plunging back into the cold water of real life.

Hattie ran on ahead down the path, unhindered by her bare feet. The soles of her feet were hardened by now, after two weeks of hardly ever wearing shoes.

The path meandered down to the sea past a Norman stone church, a church whose graveyard was full of fascinating, tragic stories. So many of the tombstones, tilting, cracked, moss-covered, told tales of children who had died in infancy, sometimes two or three from the same family. One morning, when Tess thought it was too cloudy and cold to sit on the beach, and Mark and the boys had gone surfing, she'd wandered through the graveyard with Hattie, the names on the tombstones touching her, like old friends whose death she mourned. Hattie, no respecter of mortality, practised jumping over the tombstones which had fallen and lay flat on the ground, and then, unnoticed, gathered flowers from different graves to make a posy for Tess. She took it hurriedly, torn between the desire not to hurt Hattie's feelings and the appalling thought of being caught in the act by the local bereaved.

Despite the sunshine, the path was already damp with the threat of autumn, small eddies of water trickling down one side which met halfway with a full-blown stream, rushing to the sea. At this point there was a bridge, its rail worn down by generations of hands, pausing to take a breather on the way back up when coolboxes, carrier bags of wet towels and cumbersome snorkels and flippers became dead weights. Hattie had disappeared from view, but Tess wasn't worried. Hattie knew exactly where she was going and would wait at the edge of the sea for Tess to come.

Most of the path was shaded with overhanging trees, but about twenty metres or so from the beach it suddenly opened up into a view which always made Tess catch her breath. It was best, today, with no-one else there, no-one to blot the landscape with their beach bags and their windbreaks. Tess was so jealously possessive of the tiny cove – even though she too was a holidaymaker she was resentful of other people, as if she alone understood the secret of its beauty. Ahead of her a green field fell away, a dusty path winding through it to a stile just before the sharp drop to the beach. She stood still for a moment. 'If this were the whole world, it would be enough,' she thought. Filled with a sudden, raging joy, she ran down the path, tempted to hold out her arms and whoop to the sky like Jake and Hattie. She climbed the stile, jumped down, and looked for Hattie.

She was sitting, a tiny figure, at the edge of the sea.

13

This morning the sea was calm, lolling gently back and forth, deep green in colour with small breaking waves like hoar frost. In all the summers they had been coming here, the sea had never looked the same – sometimes grey, a sullen, surging mass, at other times azure blue, not the inviting, glossy turquoise of the Mediterranean, but a dull, threatening blue that warned of depths of cold. Kicking off her shoes, she felt the tiny stones of the shingle prick her feet as she carefully made her way over to Hattie.

'Going in?'

'It's *freezing*.' Hattie shivered, delighted. She had plucked several slimy, olive green fronds of seaweed from the tideline and was draping them deliberately over her legs. The waves, which up till now had just brushed her toes, surged forward covering her knees and she leapt up, shrieking.

'Are you coming in?' she said to her mother.

Tess looked out towards the horizon, the dark blue line of the sea broken by a small fishing boat, its sails whipped by the wind.

'I might,' she said. 'If you will.'

'Race you then!' shouted Hattie, running forward into the shallows, kicking up spray with pointed toes, well aware Tess still had to take off her jumper and shorts. Tess pulled them off, and threw them haphazardly up the beach. Hattie by now was up to her knees walking slowly through the shallow water, pausing every now and then to peer at something, a tickly slither of seaweed or a shoal of darting small grey fish.

'I won!' she called, triumphantly.

'Don't go in too deep,' Tess warned. 'I'm just going to swim out a little way.'

The coldness of the water numbed her knees, her thighs, her midriff. But after a few seconds the numbness disappeared, as her body acclimatized to the cold.

Taking a deep breath, she dived forward. The shock was immediate, an icy rush, a roaring in her ears. Then she surfaced, shaking the water from her eyes, and turned to look at Hattie. Hattie waved back, distracted, then dropped her head to look again at the object of her fascination, a tiny chipped pink shell which lay like a jewel in her open hand.

Tucking her blond shoulder-length hair behind her ears with one hand, Tess turned and began to swim slowly, feeling the icy water become almost warm against her body, enjoying the sensation of floating above deep water, a tremulous sensation of not knowing what was beneath, an enjoyable frisson of fear. She trod water for a minute, watching the seagulls wheeling above her, catching the currents of air, dropping with folded wings until they caught the next, rising with wings outstretched, effortlessly. Tess turned and floated on her back, rocked by the slow, heavy motion of the sea, before turning to check Hattie.

She was not there.

Chapter One

The end of the holiday had felt almost like a death. It had been an Indian summer, and the approach of autumn and the long, cold run-up to Christmas seemed to Tess an unforgiving journey. If only she and Hattie could stay here, for ever, alone.

When the phone rang in the kitchen she was cleaning the night before they were due to leave, Tess snatched it up, thinking it might be one of the boys ringing to say they'd forgotten something vital, like a PlayStation game or one of their Harry Potter books. It wasn't. It was Mark, and his deep voice, though trying to be ironically plaintive, had an underlying layer of real irritation.

'Do you have to stay? We got here an hour ago, the bloody fridge has defrosted all over the floor and there are mice droppings in the bread bin. Please, please, Tess, come home. We need you.'

The feeling he alone could arouse, a mixture of unreasonable guilt, anxiety and love, wheeled within her. A sensation she had all but forgotten, in this brief time here with Hattie, rising from the pit of her stomach, making her choose her words carefully, running through sentences first in her mind, consciously thinking ahead as to how he might react. It

17

was a sensation which rose above freedom. As if only his feelings mattered.

Here was Mark with mice droppings in the bread bin. Against her better judgement she felt at fault, selfishly abdicating her responsibilities by snatching this precious extra day with Hattie in dereliction of her duties. The tigers, held at bay, were beginning to circle.

For Mark the holiday had been a pleasant enough interlude, a chance to relax and spend time with the children, but by the end of the two weeks he was itching to get back to his real life, a life where he felt confident and effective and which was far less tiring than that of being the father of three children, with their constant demands and the need to make endless, minor decisions which never pleased all of them simultaneously. He adored them passionately, but Tess knew he found being with them all day, every day, exhausting. She found it exhausting too, but she was used to it. This frustration made him snappy; towards the end of the two weeks his limited supply of patience had run dry.

For Tess, the holiday had meant so much more. It had been a chance to step back, and think. Thinking about herself at home tended to be abruptly curtailed by the immediate need to find a recalcitrant geography book or a wayward recorder. With Hattie seven and the boys both relatively settled at their secondary school, perhaps it was time she began to take control of her life and make plans just for herself, rather than letting being a mother of three with a frequently absent husband and a chaotic house to run pull her endlessly this way and that, like seaweed straining to and fro in the tide.

The chance to actually have the time to think, instead of rushing breathlessly from one minor disaster to the next and never even having time to look in the mirror some days, had touched her like a calling, a memory of something she hadn't fully realized she had lost. It was extraordinary, within these last two weeks, with the responsibility of looking after the children shared, to recognize a truth at the very core of her – that there were things she needed and indeed wanted still to achieve. The thought of leaving here, where the idea of the possibility of change had begun to crystallize, made her feel almost physically ill. She was terrified to take the hope from here, that by exposing it to the rigours of her real life with all its attendant demands, it would be rendered ridiculous, impossible, and broken.

Mark was angry, of course, that Tess hadn't driven back home to London at the same time as him, that she'd foisted on him the need to drive back with Ollie and Jake, querulous at the thought of school tomorrow, bickering about who sat in the front next to Dad, and that he would have to be the one to heave open the front door and confront the stale air of the house and mountainous post. Over the fifteen years of their marriage she had become – without being consciously willing to assume the role – his buffer from mundane but essential domesticities, and having to be the sole parent, he felt unpleasantly exposed. It took her absence to make him realize just how much of this minutiae she must absorb daily, without his ever being aware of its existence. He loathed being in the house without her.

'Can't you leave tonight? Jake says he can't find his school tie and Ollie thinks he left his piano music at school.'

'No he didn't,' Tess said quickly. 'It's in the piano stool. Jake's tie is in his sock drawer, he knows that, he's just being awkward.'

'Have I got any clean shirts?'

Tess grimaced at the phone. Why didn't he know

if he had any shirts? Couldn't he just open up his wardrobe and have a look, and if he didn't, then he could wash one and put it in the tumble-dryer. Why did men pretend to be so bloody helpless, when all life took was common sense?

But then she could not be blameless – although they began their marriage as exact equals, the realities of organizing children, home and careers had, by the nature of their myriad essential demands, forced upon her the reality of a need to compromise her ideals. Mark – whose career was the better paid and thereby deemed at the time the more important – had been able to slide, by dint of his need to sleep because he had such a busy day ahead, out of the more irksome and exhausting tasks such as seeking to entertain an exceptionally wide awake toddler at five in the morning or stuffing washing into the machine immediately prior to leaving for work via the nursery, toddler, howling, under one arm. This compromise – while valedictory in its own way – unfortunately led to responsibility. Thus anything which went wrong with either the children or the house had become, over the years and without guilt of the perpetrator, her fault. It was a responsibility which was becoming an increasingly heavy burden, especially now the children were growing up and ought to take on far more themselves, but how hard it was to persuade two boys they ought to pick up after themselves or help around the house when they had spent their young lives watching Mark subtly cocoon himself from these responsibilities. In all fairness, he did it very well – if asked directly, he would cheerfully fulfil any task she gave him – the frustration lay in the fact that he didn't actually see any of them needing to be done in the first place.

There had been a time when she had been proud to be the one who selflessly kept everything running smoothly, appreciated or not. Now it just pissed her off.

'I'm sure you have a shirt in the wardrobe, just look,' she said swiftly, seeing Hattie open the fridge and take out an almost full carton of orange juice, which Tess knew she couldn't carry, and if she didn't intervene within moments it would be all over the grey slate kitchen floor she had just swept. 'I'll have to go,' she said. 'Hattie's about to drop something horrible.'

'Will you come?'

'I haven't finished packing,' Tess said. 'I'll come soon, tomorrow, first thing, and I'll ring you when I get home. OK?'

'OK.' Mark's voice was reluctant, as if he didn't want to let her go.

'And Tess . . .'

'What?' she said, trying to make him go, reaching out with her free hand to avert sticky disaster.

'I miss you. Come home.'

Chapter Two

Putting down the phone with the juice carton firmly grasped in her other hand, Tess expected to feel guilty. She didn't. She felt only relief.

It was impossible to sensibly explain to Mark why she so desperately wanted to have one last evening at the cottage, especially one last evening on her own. With the boys and Mark here, there was always so much noise and all the constant demands of food and drinks and finding things, with meals and mess ebbing and flowing, endlessly, like the tide. Just for one night, she wanted to do absolutely nothing. She could put Hattie to bed and then just sit, with a glass of cold white wine in her hand, on the comfortable blue sofa in the living room, next to the piano, and look out over the garden which sloped away down towards the cliffs, and imagine the sea beyond. She wanted a night alone, just to think, and listen to the silence.

She also wanted to bid the house a private farewell. Tess loved the holiday cottage with a passion unreasonably greater than their London home, where you couldn't move in the narrow front hall for falling over skateboards and Mark's squash racket which should have been in the cupboard under the stairs but never was. Her feelings for their London home, once an intense love affair, had dwindled into the mundane familiarity of a tired marriage. Driving towards the rented Cornish cottage where they had spent the past eight summers, she felt the cares and responsibilities which made up the geography of her life falling away, like so many tight and restrictive clothes.

Turning through the gateway, under the overhanging chestnut tree and then stopping on the untidy gravel in front of the door, its blue frame outlined by faded pink climbing roses, she felt each summer as if she was coming home. Leaving the cottage, and the profound sense of calm it gave her, felt strangely as if she was leaving a part of herself behind.

Here, even when the children were babies and at their most mind-numbingly time-consuming, she was able to rediscover who she really was. A person she was sometimes frightened she had lost.

When they had been shown around the four-storey terraced house in Clapham, desperate to escape from their one-bedroomed flat as Tess was pregnant with what would turn out to be Jake, they saw only the house's good points. The high ceilings, moulded cornices, oak floorboards and the basement kitchen with an ancient powder-blue Aga, seemed to Tess the epitome of a spacious family home, and one in which they could not fail to be happy. What they hadn't noticed, in that first flush of love, was the damp, the ancient wiring and the narrowness of the corridors – if you passed anyone in the hall you had to flatten yourself against the wall, like a silent-movie star walking along the outside of a train. Nor had they anticipated just how quickly three bedrooms would become too few, or how very small the rooms actually were, that all sound echoed throughout the tall house and the fact that they would spend their lives perpetually going up and down the stairs like a loop of toy penguins.

Tucking one foot beneath her on the sofa, Tess mused that the realities of their home – it was far too small for the five of them and very much in need of an overhaul they could neither afford nor be bothered to give it – were strangely at odds with the way she had felt just before the holiday, when Mark had suggested they ought to think about moving. She could see the logic of what he was saying, but aside from the fact that they had no money to pay for a larger house, she had also felt a stab of fear. At the time she had reasoned she felt this way because she was always so worried about money that the idea of taking on a bigger mortgage was laughable, ludicrous – but now, with the space in which to question herself honestly, she could see that the fear came from taking such a major step forward into their future. Mark said that if they did stretch themselves, they probably wouldn't have to move again until the children left home, years and years away. When he said this, Tess had felt as if her life had been trundling down a series of passageways which she had thought would go on for ever, only to turn a sharp corner and find an end. Was that all there would ever be? Her life mapped out until there was no more?

And their home, tatty as it was, bore the imprint of so much of their lives together – the red-wine stain under the rug in the living room, stigmata reminder of a particularly boisterous Christmas party, the indelible grubby bit on the carpet in the bathroom where their cat, Nigel, regularly landed after entering through the tiny bathroom window. This was his main source of ingress and egress, primarily because nobody could be bothered to wait for him to leave by a normal exit, such as a door, because this was a cat with 'saunter' down to an art form. In a house where everything happened at breakneck pace, the idea of a cat with no concept of hurry-up simply could not be tolerated.

Mark didn't like Nigel because he jumped up onto the kitchen work surfaces, and wove muddy pawprint patterns around boxes of cereal and bottles of milk. The children spent a great deal of time covering up the evidence of Nigel's misdeeds from their father, such as removing disembowelled shrews from bedroom slippers and desiccated cat crap from behind the sofa.

To get his own back on the cat which had also won the battle to sleep on Hattie's bed, despite Mark's insistence that it would sleep on her face and smother her – a concept Hattie pooh-poohed because she said she'd jolly well know if she had a cat on her face, even if she was asleep, thank you very much – he half-closed the top bathroom window so Nigel couldn't quite get his neutered dumpy ginger body in. This meant that Tess, the lightest sleeper in the house, was frequently woken by the sound of a bicycling cat who was jammed neither in, nor out, a feline Pooh Bear.

In attempting to justify a move they patently could not afford, Mark said he was fed up with the litter in the street, the lack of space and the sporadic vandalism to their cars. Broomfield Road was a pleasant, wide, tree-lined street in a quiet suburb of South London – not smart, being three streets away from the Common and perilously close to the border with a far less salubrious area renowned for high-rise flats and drug-dealing, but hardly on the cutting edge of crime. Tess occasionally left the back door unlocked for Ollie and Jake to come in after school, if she wasn't back from work.

Mark, in a conversation which had taken place the night before she left for Cornwall with the children, said he could not understand why she didn't seem enthusiastic about moving, ideally out of London, to a house with a proper garden, not a yard and a patch of grass hardly big enough to satisfyingly swing Nigel. If he put up with the commute, then the money they'd get for Broomfield Road should pay for something far more substantial, four bedrooms even, with a garden, in the country. Surely she wanted to live free from the fear of youths in sportswear interfering nightly with their cars? He'd be the one who had to travel, after all, because it would hardly be worth Tess continuing her job at the gallery, so handily placed for Hattie's school: it would be financially counterproductive if you added in the cost of commuting and child-care. He had been so enthusiastic about the plan, his handsome face animated at the prospect of an exciting change, his idea. She didn't want to express misgivings, did not want a row just before leaving for a family holiday, but her unwillingness to match his enthusiasm frustrated him. After fourteen years of marriage, he had delicate antennae for her opposition, voiced or not.

And if she did agree to move, where would that leave her? Mark rationally pointed out the benefits it would bring to their lives, a less hemmed-in childhood for Hattie, a removal of numerous dangerous influences on the boys, Jake especially, the chance to plan a garden and even get the dog the children longed for. He would be able to actually do something useful and relaxing with his weekends, spend time outdoors, instead of endlessly ferrying the children in the car from one organized activity to another, with their only open space in which to run free the parks or the Common, along with all the other families who couldn't afford a weekend country cottage.

And, as he said, she was always complaining she had no time for herself – this could be the solution. But what, thought Tess, would be my life? Where could I work, in the country? Did he mean time for me to become a proper wife and mother, organizing the house and spending my time mulling over seed catalogues? Waiting for Mark to come home for

26

intelligent adult conversation, no Margi or Vanessa, endless Radio Four and muddy walks? She shuddered. What she could see – and what Mark would never admit to himself – was that this would be a chance for him to develop interests which would carry him into retirement. His career gave him such a big, colourful life it consumed all his energy, and all he sought outside it was peace and a chance to recharge his batteries before tackling the next crisis. Home for him was something to escape to. For her, it was something to escape from.

Her life, rather than being played out like Mark's on the wide stage, did feel a bit like standing in the wings handing everyone else their props and costumes. She could hardly complain about the quality of her life – a pleasant job at the gallery which fitted in with Hattie's school hours, friends, the children, the house – but a void was beginning to make itself felt inside her, a void that had previously been filled by the demands of keeping small children alive and safe. She was bored. Before, she would have said she'd kill for boredom. But now, at almost forty, with the children at least marginally capable of looking after themselves, she had the chance to find something more exciting, more challenging, to do. Which meant she was hardly willing to begin freewheeling towards a peaceful retirement. She'd only just got back on the damn bike.

Nursing her glass, Tess slowly lifted it until her lip rested against the chilled rim. Then she tipped it up, and took a long, satisfying gulp. Perhaps she was being unreasonable. Maybe she was trying to make a decision on purely selfish grounds. The children might be happier – Hattie probably would, but she had severe reservations about the boys, they would miss their friends too much and Jake especially now had a far more invigorating social life than she and Mark. What would she do with two teenage boys in the

27

country, with no skatebowls or Multiplex cinemas? No wonder country people took up killing things. There was nothing else exciting to do.

Above all, if they moved out of London, she would lose her emotional-support network. Close friendships rely inevitably on a shared need, and that need would be lost. No Margi, who lived just two houses away, and Vanessa, who lived in the only double-fronted house at the smart end of the road, nearest the Common. When Tess first saw her, she had reversed her car into the one behind, got out without even looking at the bumper, flicked a scarf over her shoulder and, running her hand through her immaculate blond hair, sauntered to her navy blue front door. Tess had found her terrifyingly glamorous, and hadn't dared smile at her when they met in the delicatessen, but eventually Vanessa had marched up to her and demanded to know if that absolutely gorgeous dark-haired boy was hers, the one who skateboarded up and down the street. Tess said hesitantly, yes, that was Jake, whereupon Vanessa said her daughter Clementine was totally in love with him and would they all come for tea?

Tess found Vanessa's home as beautiful and groomed as she was, which depressed her a great deal. She had the kind of life that Tess had flirted with wanting in the early years of her marriage – no career, a rich husband, and all the time in the world to fanny around with soft furnishings and have facials. It hadn't lasted long because, as Margi pointed out, they only enjoyed shopping, drinking coffee in Starbucks and discussing curtain material because they had the contrast of an intellectually stimulating career, even if Tess's was only part-time. Vanessa didn't have any grit in her life, just gilt. She saved herself from Tess and Margi's opprobrium by apparently honestly stating how much she envied their purpose in life and that she had absolutely no status beyond how thin she was, the clothes she bought, the exact location of her house and whether her daughters might get into St Paul's. Her gilded existence was also marred by her pompous husband who treated her like his social secretary.

Despite their differences, within months they had formed a triumvirate which could deflect most of the slings and arrows of daily life, including the problems with Margi's ex-husband and Vanessa's bleating about not having purpose in her life beyond co-ordinating fabrics and pinning her hopes on the latest non-surgical CACI facelift. How would she survive, buried in the country, without the two of them to make her laugh and feel she did have interesting and funny things to say?

She shifted on the sofa, untucking the leg beneath her and rubbing it to get rid of pins and needles. The tanned skin was beginning to peel on her shins, and the paint on her toenails, applied especially for the holiday, had chipped. She had meant tonight to be a haven in which she could make some calm decisions about what she wanted to do with her life – a change of career, perhaps, a step forward – but felt instead a growing sense of unease. Was it just the fear of going home, leaving the cottage, facing life again, having to think about moving and all that entailed? Those were concrete fears, ones she could understand. What she felt she had to face – and yes, this was what scared her – was a contradictory fear of no longer being able to hide behind the roles she had created. If she did look for herself, through a challenge as yet undecided, what might she find? Strip away these roles, and who was left? You give, and give, she thought, to make everyone else happy – but do you then give everything you once were away? Perhaps that was why so many men, Mark included, seemed selfish in always putting their own needs first, whereas women would always put their children first. Men simply had a stronger instinct for their own survival.

There was a slight chill in the room. Tess thought about making a fire in the empty grate, and briefly considered whether there would be any logs in the shed by the back door, but then remembered it was padlocked, logs hardly being a requirement for the summer.

She shivered. Outside, what had been a deep indigo sky was now black, so deeply black that she felt that if she opened the window the blackness would flow in, like molten midnight lava. The silence, which at first had seemed comforting, was now threateningly loud. It was time to sleep. She sighed. All that thinking, nothing resolved.

Finding Hattie in her bed was like the most precious gift.

Chapter Three

At first Mark found it hard to turn the key in the door. They had only been away for two weeks, but it felt as if the key had become rusty. He leant his shoulder against the door, and pushed hard. He soon discovered what was causing the resistance – a neat but towering pile of post, placed carefully behind the door by Margi, who had come every day to minister to the needs of a hungry and sulking cat. He groaned, and turned back towards the car. The doors were wide open, and inside Ollie and Jake lolled on the back seat, Ollie's blond head bent over a book, Jake's dark one hunched over his mobile phone.

'Boys!' he shouted. 'Get a move on. Come and help.'

There was a long pause, and then Jake yelled back, 'Yeah, right, Dad.' Neither of them moved. Ollie was the archetypal bookworm who, if he had nothing else to read, would stare in a fixed manner at the back of a cereal packet. Tess had once found him sitting on the loo reading the blurb on the toilet-roll wrapper. If either Tess or Mark tried to interrupt him when he was reading with an urgent warning, such as, 'Ollie, you are pouring milk over your trousers,' he would look at them as if trying to remember exactly who they were, think very hard for a minute and then say, 'Whatever,' before returning to his book. This incensed Mark, Tess less, because she had been exactly the same as a child.

Ollie was a quiet, undemanding soul without any of Hattie's bossiness or Jake's moodiness, who Tess suspected immersed himself in the comforting fantasy world of fiction as an antidote to having the meteoric and troublesome Jake for an older brother. He would be good-looking, she reassured herself, once he lost the chubbiness in his cheeks – his features were rounded and smoother than the sharp angles of Jake's film-star face, currently topped by sharp, spiky hair. Ollie and Hattie had inherited Tess's pale, creamy complexion. Jake had Mark's, with freckled, olive skin which flushed easily, the blood pumping close to the surface.

Jake had driven Mark mad on the journey by failing to respond immediately to his questions. Any attempt at conversation had to be repeated at least twice, increasingly fortissimo. Then he would either say, dismissively, 'Yeah, right,' and go back to looking out of the window, twirling the bootlace he wore on his wrist round and round, or he would simply look at him blankly. When he had failed to elicit a civil response from a simple enquiry about the whereabouts of his school uniform, Mark tried to whip round to give him the full benefit of a bellowed 'Will you answer me!' and then had to swerve to avoid a people carrier which pulled out suddenly in front of him, driven by a harassed-looking mother and containing what appeared to be the contents of a small orphanage.

'Bloody women!' Mark shouted. Jake snorted.

'Good job Mum's not here. She'd lynch you.' Mark smiled at him through the rear-view mirror, relieved by at least some form of communication from the Planet Teenager.

'Good holiday?'

'Cool.' Jake relaxed his mask of detached boredom and smiled back at his father, before taking his mobile from his back pocket and staring intently at the screen. He had no more money left to text, as Mark and Tess had agreed on a strict budget each month. He'd used his money up by the end of the first week of the holiday, even though the signal had been useless, he'd had to go to the top of the road, half a mile from the cottage, just to get any cones at all. Thank God his parents – unlike his friend Nick's – never read his messages.

Tess had intimated that by travelling back without her, Mark could have some rare time on his own with the boys. He loved them intensely, but these days it seemed to be primarily an infuriated intensity, as they were just so uncommunicative, in their different ways. He seemed to have more of a verbal relationship with the cat.

Whenever he and Tess did venture to ask Jake to do anything, such as carry a pile of jumpers upstairs, the ensuing reaction was like asking him to regrout the shower. Groaning, he would flop down on the nearest chair with the words, 'I'll do it later, OK?', the 'OK' on a rising note of anguished hysteria. The age of instant response had long gone. Ollie was far more amenable, but he lived in such a dream world it was hard to make contact, and he was so easily distracted from what he was asked to do – a simple request to make his bed would lead to him finding a forgotten comic, and half an hour later Tess would find him immersed in the *Beano*, lying slumped on his bed with his duvet at half-mast. Thank God both boys were forced to play sport at school, or, Mark conjectured, they might eventually lose the art of motion altogether. He often caught himself saying things to them he had sworn never to say to his own children, but the wheel, of course, came full circle.

As he lifted the post to one side and opened the door fully, Mark was startled by the sudden appearance of

Nigel. 'Bloody hell!' he said, jumping back. He'd forgotten that the cat would be there. Why couldn't he use the flap like he was supposed to, instead of lurking behind closed doors? They'd spent a small fortune buying a collar which automatically opened an electronic flap, which the sales blurb assured them would be safer vis-à-vis crime – although Mark was hard pushed to work out how a burglar could enter through a cat flap anyway. But Nigel, in a very Nigel-like manner, had totally failed to grasp the technicalities of the new device. For the first few days he sat within the electronic beam of the flap, bemused by the constant opening and shutting of his door. There was no way he was going through that, thank you very much. A cat with a capacious rear like his could end up with a nasty nip. Far more effective, he knew, was to sit by the front door and yowl very loudly, or risk life and limb by heaving his elderly body through the bathroom window.

'Yo, cat.' Nigel, spotting Jake and Ollie in the Discovery, jumped inside nimbly for such a large animal, and, purring, arched his body against Jake's sweatshirt, rubbing his face against him. Jake closed his eyes and breathed in his familiar smell of hot radiator and cat food. That friend of his mum's, Margi, had been feeding him while they were away and by the look of his overstuffed body, he had eaten a lot more than usual. 'Yo *fat* cat,' Jake said, with affection. Nigel gave him a withering look. He tolerated Mark and Jake, liked Ollie to the extent he would condescend occasionally to sleep on the end of his bed, but his real passion was Tess and Hattie. Mark, unreasonably, given the evolutionary scale, was jealous of this and took it out on the cat by trying to ban him from the house. Nigel, however, usually got his way by cunning and stealth.

'Boys! For fuck's sake, get *out* of the *car*.'

Jake and Ollie looked at each other.

'Keep your hair on, Dad. Chuck me the keys.'

'Why?'

'I want to get the CD out of the machine.'

Mark groaned. He had, for the sake of harmony, allowed Jake to choose the music on the way home, which meant they'd spent the entire journey listening to a monotonous high-pitched whine, interrupted by scratching sounds and a continuous tone on a rising note, like someone trying to tune an old radio. The music, if it could be called that, kept stopping, and then starting again for no real reason, as if someone had wandered out of the room and shut the door. Jake showed no real appreciation of what to Mark was aural torture, save the occasional nodding of his head.

'Catch!' Mark walked out of the front door and lobbed the keys at Jake, who caught them expertly. Mark began lugging the mountain of luggage out of the boot. Ollie put down his book and looked about himself vaguely, while Jake carried the CD into the house.

'Don't strain yourself, mate,' Mark said, as Jake walked past him, the CD tucked under his arm.

'I won't. Thanks.'

'There's bugger all to *eat*,' Jake called up into the hall, after Mark had moved everything visibly portable from the car into the hall. If possible, there seemed to be even more stuff now than when he packed the car, once it was spread out on the floor. He looked at it helplessly. Where did it all go?

'And I don't know how to tell you this, but there's water all over the kitchen floor.'

'Frigging hell.'

Mark had a blinding flash that while Tess had been checking all the windows were shut and the bins had been put out, he had gone around pulling out plugs, and feeling mightily efficient in the process. It was just possible that he had removed one plug too many. He was working out how he could possibly blame one of the boys for this, when Jake appeared up the stairs, his too-long hugely baggy jeans sporting a two-inch tide-mark.

'It's really wet down there,' he said, helpfully.

'Well, mop it up, then,' Mark replied. Jake regarded him as if he had said, 'Please put on this skirt and play netball.'

'No way. There's loads of it. It's like a *swimming pool*.'

'Don't be a twit. It can't be that bad.'

'It is. No joke, Dad. Come and see.'

Reluctantly, Mark followed him down the stairs, ducking his head to avoid the beam which crossed the stairwell halfway down. When they first bought the house, Mark, who was over six foot tall, bore a permanent red mark across his forehead from for-getting to duck. It made getting a cup of coffee an unnecessarily dangerous affair.

The culprit was indeed the fridge. They had recently bought a double-door American-style affair, which Mark and the boys adored as it had lots of gadgets like an ice-maker and chilled-water dispenser. Tess had agreed to spend so much money on a functional house-hold item only because Mark had been able to make the business pay for it, as he could argue he needed it to keep white wine chilled. Mark was such a golden boy at the moment, the other directors had agreed. It had stood, for the two weeks they were away, help-lessly leaking water from the freezer side and knowing there would be hell to pay when they came home.

'Where's the mop?'

'Don't ask me,' Jake said. 'I'm not a girl.' Mark aimed a swipe at his head.

'It must be in that cupboard. Go and look.' Jake gave him a defiant look, and then changed his mind,

36

spotting the beginnings of rage on his father's face. If his dad did lose his rag, he could really go off on one.

'OK, OK. No need to get so eggy.'

Mopping the floor, Mark felt increasingly annoyed with Tess. Why had she insisted on staying behind? OK, they had had to take two cars because he'd had to drive down a day late because of a meeting, but that wasn't his fault, Tess knew how busy he was at the moment. It would have been far easier to have driven back in tandem, and then she could have sorted this lot out while he got on with the mountain of work in his study, and made a start on the million emails which would be lying in wait for him.

He had a sudden mental image of his computer upstairs, bulging with electronic messages which might flood out and smother him with words. He had wanted to take the laptop with him to Cornwall, so he could get on with some sales figures for a new vineyard he had taken on in Hungary before they went away, but Tess had banned him. This was a holiday, she said, not an alternative work venue. Mark knew she was right, but she didn't fully appreciate how much he had to do, how it never stopped, especially now he was a director. Their first Aussie director. Quite a daring measure for such a traditional old-school-tie importer of quality wine, situated in the heart of Piccadilly.

He had been brought into Merry's originally to boost the New World business, and because the other directors realized they needed young blood if they were to survive in what was becoming an increasingly competitive market. The supermarkets now controlled most of the trade, and they dealt primarily with them, far more than the small chains of retailers or individual, family-run off-licences. At the time they had needed a maverick, and Mark certainly fitted that bill with his earring and strong Australian accent. The earring had long gone – when he reached thirty, Tess put her foot down and said he looked less daring, more comical. The accent too had faded, smoothed into a hardly discernible lilt, and many people today mistook him for American. He no longer stood out in the way he had done when he and Tess first met, his spiky edges smoothed, his rebellious ideals all but smothered by the siren call of success, of making money, providing. Sometimes he too wondered how much of himself he had lost.

In the ten years he had been with the firm, this last year as a director, he had all but doubled their sales figures. To Mark, this success was immensely satisfying but also frustrating, too. If he could make so much money for the company, might he not be better setting up as a wine consultant on his own? The shares and bonus he had been given last Christmas had been handed over with so much benevolent smugness, like the initiation rites into some secret male club. The money, although desperately needed and hardly a huge sum, made him feel uncomfortable. The board contentedly voted themselves more and more money off the back of everyone else in the company, who worked at least as hard if not harder than they did. He hated the feeling of belonging to a club, being owned. But setting up on his own would be both risky and expensive. And with Jake and Ollie both at an independent school – although Ollie thankfully on a scholarship – not to mention their mortgage, he could not justify such a leap in the dark.

Tess brought in money too, but it was hardly live-on money. Keeping everything afloat sometimes seemed like a great weight grinding him down, and there were so many moments when he felt like chucking it all in and taking the family home, back to Australia. Tess did not appreciate, he thought, just how much responsibility and shit he had to bear – and how, at times, he felt like getting up from behind his mahogany desk, marching out of the oak-panelled office, down the old stone steps, out of the portico, past the liveried doorman and running, running, until he left the city behind and his feet hit sand and he could hear the sound of the sea. No more politeness, no more diplomacy and having to bite his tongue when the new managing director Rupert, who was a lazy bastard and the son of the former chairman, appropriated his achievements. One day, one day. Instead he quelled his rising frustration, had another cup of coffee and picked up the phone.

He paused, mid-mop. It was happening again, a heightening of his blood pressure, his heart rate increasing, making him feel slightly breathless and dizzy. He stopped, stood upright and straightened his back. The tension, which he'd felt draining away from him while he lazed about on the beach, searched for crabs with Hattie and taught the boys the finer points of body-surfing, was coming back. An ache started in his neck, and rose slowly into his head, giving him what felt like the beginnings of a migraine. He really must find time to do some sport – take up squash again, there was a young guy at work who'd play with him. He was forty now. Heart-attack time.

As he rubbed the small of his back, he thought of Tess. And smiled. God, he missed her. She would be feeding Hattie now, or maybe they'd be having a bath together. He was envious of Tess's relationship with Hattie, envious of her relationship with all the children. They were so open, so easily intimate. He couldn't be that intimate with them, even with Hattie. He still tried to hug the boys, but Jake especially spurned his physical contact. When Hattie was a baby he used to have baths with her, but he couldn't now –

it would look weird – whereas Tess and Hattie still bathed together often, with Hattie floating on Tess's tummy like a little fish. Skin on skin, the innocent intimacy of family. Skin on skin to him meant making love with Tess, and that was becoming too rare as well.

Sometimes he felt so physically lonely, a rocky outcrop surrounded by a sea of love he could no longer touch. Reassurance had to come from making, not giving, love.

All too often he felt that Tess made love to him out of politeness, as if she had something far more vital to do but could just spare him these ten minutes or so as long as he was quick and didn't do anything surprising. Passion was becoming a memory, although he had never lost his longing for her, nor did he want anyone else. Often he felt he just got in the way of her orderly life, like an awkward household gadget left out in the hallway which refused to be tidied away. She and the children seemed a complete unit, he was the outsider. He longed to be longed for, and Tess's calm practicality and lack of passion for him made him even more irritable. When was the last time they had made love anywhere but in bed, at night? What he could not see was that the bad temper and the stress he brought home from work made her want him less. She had so much to do that the last thing she needed was an adult with needs, too. He tended to go to the bottom of the pile.

What they should have, he thought, was more time alone together, but how could they have that, with three children in too small a house? Nor could they justify the expense of holidays on their own.

The house felt wrong without Tess, empty and cold. She made the house. The one thing he hated more than anything was coming home and Tess not being there.

'Is there any bread?'

Ollie wandered down the stairs into the kitchen. 'Try the bin,' Mark said.

'Nope,' Ollie said. 'Hey, what the hell are all these little black things?'

Mark leant the mop against the Aga.

'What? Oh, Jesus,' he said, looking over Ollie's shoulder.

'They're mice droppings. Put it down.'

'Yuck.' Ollie ran his hand under the tap. Nigel sat, swishing his tail, in the centre of the wooden table.

'You,' Mark said, pointing the handle of the mop at him, 'are totally fucking useless. We spend hundreds of pounds each year pouring cat food into your fat body on the understanding you divest us of mice. What do you do while we're away? Have some kind of cat party? Watch videos? Hang out with the boys? Drink my drink?'

Nigel looked at him balefully, and began slowly licking his back paw, yawning.

'I'm going to sell you and get a decent *trap* that doesn't *eat* and *shit* behind the *sofa*,' Mark said. The boys grinned at each other. No way. That cat had Mum's protection. It wasn't going anywhere.

Mark badly needed Tess. He really didn't want to clean mice droppings out of the bread bin. He'd been driving for five hours on a busy motorway, his head ached from five solid hours of dance music, he was hungry and he really, really needed a drink. It was all too much, and work tomorrow.

Jake's voice floated down the stairs.

'I can't find my tie, Dad.'

'Sodding *hell*,' Mark said, and, rooting in the wine stack, pulled out a bottle and uncorked it.

'It's only six o'clock,' Ollie said, with raised eyebrows.

'I really don't care if it's six o'clock in the morning. Where's the number of the cottage?'

*　　*　　*

He hadn't meant to whine, but he did subconsciously recognize that what he wanted to do was make her feel guilty. After all, the kitchen was her domain and things had gone wrong here that he, unfairly, had to try to fix. But on the phone Tess didn't sound apologetic – in fact she sounded almost defiant and cut him off very quickly, saying Hattie was about to drop something. What he really wanted was sympathy, but he hadn't got it, and he felt unreasonably peeved when he put the phone down. He knew he was being childish, but he couldn't help himself. Tess had a joke that whenever she was going out with friends for the evening – which she did rarely – he always found something he needed her to do urgently just before she left. Or, even if he wasn't physically there and he knew she was going out, he would ring her with a request to find something or make a call for him. If he was really honest, in his heart of hearts, he hated her going out without him.

And there was nothing to *eat*. He poured the greyish water from the bucket into the Belfast sink, leaving a film of grit on the white porcelain. Then he carried his suitcase upstairs to their bedroom, leaving the rest of the suitcases and clobber downstairs. Tess, as usual, had left the house tidy, but there was something very different about everything – the air felt dead, unused. Tess would have opened windows, but Mark couldn't be bothered. What he really wanted to do was lie down on the bed and drink his wine before making a start on his emails. But the boys had to be fed.

Crashings and bangings came from the direction of Jake's room. Mark made a swift decision to leave unpacking even his suitcase to Tess. He followed the source of the noise downstairs.

'What exactly are you doing?'

Jake was pulling out a hoard of stuff from under his

42

bed – tennis rackets, old training shoes, magazines, CDs, a deflated football.

'Can't find my rugby boots.'

'Just leave it. Mum will sort it out when she gets back. You won't be playing rugby on your first day, will you?'

'You're really useless, Dad.'

'Thanks. So who pays your school fees?'

'No dis, Dad. Point taken. What are we going to eat?'

'Get your brother. Chinese.'

'Wicked.' Jake grinned happily.

The pile of dirty foil cartons stood on the table, next to an empty bottle of red wine. The tap, which hadn't been turned off properly, dripped into the sink. Nigel, who realized no-one was going to remember to feed him, picked delicately at the remains of Peking duck with beansprouts. It definitely wasn't tuna-flavoured, but it was almost edible. The mop still rested against the sink, and the freezer door, which hadn't been quite closed, shone a thin line of white light onto the quarry-tiled floor, as the defrosting process slowly began again.

Upstairs from the kitchen, a lamp had been left on in the TV room, and from outside through the open curtains the blue screen of the Sky digital menu could be seen, playing to an unseen audience. Five suitcases, heaps of coats, three sandy pairs of wellington boots and numerous plastic bags lay at the foot of the stairs in the hall, next to a football. Ollie had tried to get his sports bag together, but he couldn't find his rugby shirt and the white pumps he had to have for PE. He knew his mum had washed them in the machine, but he didn't know they were sitting, dry and pristine, on the top of the boiler in the utility room by the kitchen. Jake had given up immediately when he couldn't find his rugby boots, but had found his tie.

The light from the hall chandelier, a housewarming gift from Tess's parents, lit the stairs up to the first landing. A crack of light glowed from under Ollie's and Jake's bedroom door. Ollie was asleep on top of his duvet, still in his sweatshirt and jeans. His school uniform, neatly folded by Tess, had fallen off the chair at the bottom of his bed and lay, creased, on the floor. His fingers were stained black at the tips with the polish he'd rubbed with a cloth on his shoes, but he couldn't get a shine and had given up. His baseball cap lay on the floor by his bed, and his thick blond hair, unwashed, was flattened and dark with sweat, as Mark had felt cold and turned the heating on full, and his bed was next to the radiator. The Philip Pullman book he had been reading lay face down on the duvet next to his outstretched hand. Jake lay on his bed, still awake, headphones clamped to his ears, the tinny whine of music faintly escaping. He was very worried about tomorrow. He had some history homework he had completely forgotten about and he was going to be *lynched*. And where the hell were his boots?

The cat paused by the doorway, and then glided up the next flight of stairs. The door to Tess and Mark's bedroom was open, but there was no-one there. He withdrew his head and sauntered towards Mark's study. Mark was sitting with his back to him, his head buried in his folded arms. A second half-full bottle of red wine stood next to the computer, by an empty glass, stained with a blood-red line. The Internet connection, unterminated, pinged and whistled to itself. The cat jumped up, and walked deliberately over the computer keys before pressing his face against Mark's hand. Mark flinched, then raised his head. The time on the computer screen said 12.27. He yawned, stretched and pushed the cat away. Only six hours until he had to get up. His mouth felt sour, his stomach bloated. Nigel gave him a disdainful look, then jumped down and headed back towards Hattie's empty room.

While Tess slept warm and happy, Mark lay awake until dawn in a bed which felt empty and cold. Just as he was drifting off to sleep, the faulty car alarm in the Discovery went off, like an air-raid siren sounding the all-clear into the chilly morning light. His only consoling thought was that Tess would be home today, to make everything better.

Chapter Four

Frantically looking about her, Tess scanned the length of the small beach. There was no sign of her daughter, and as she trod water, she called, 'Hattie!' Her voice was caught by the wind, and carried away, on a falling note, up the empty shoreline.

Underneath her, the water rose and fell. A small wave, spray curling, hit her in the face, filling her mouth with bitter salt water, blinding her. She began to swim back towards the beach. But while it had been so easy to swim away, the current lifting and carrying her further with each stroke, swimming back was like fighting an immovable force. After every stroke she raised her head again and searched the beach, the water, looking for Hattie's bobbing head, her blond hair caught up in a topknot. She had slipped into a dream, and any moment she would wake, and Hattie would be there, laughing at the edge of the sea.

She was only twenty yards from the shore, but still she could not see her. As she swam she called, lungs stinging, her eyes raking the shingle, the slope beyond up to where the path turned by the big rock. All she could see was the haphazard pile of clothes she'd flung away as she waded into the water, now only feet from the dying surf. How could she have been so stupid, so irresponsible? How could she swim away from Hattie, knowing she could easily get out of her depth? How could she rely only on previous experience, that it had never happened before, that Hattie was too scared of getting out of her depth, that she never lasted more than ten minutes in the sea, anyway, it was too cold?

Her feet struck the bottom, painfully, against the rocks. The water pulled back against her thighs, making her stumble. She was wading as fast as she could, getting near the shallows, the water was just over her knees, and still she could not see her.

Tess stopped, and called her name again. Hattie couldn't just disappear. Walking through the shallower water, she forced herself to look down, to search for her. She loved all her children, but Hattie was something more, the child she and Mark had thought they might lose, whose first year of life had been a struggle, a child who might have been taken but who had not, but now . . . What? What could have happened?

She had to stop and think logically. If Hattie had been pulled out to sea by the current, then it would have brought her in again, she would be here – or perhaps, perhaps she had been carried out and then brought back into the small cave, on the far side of the beach, a shallow cave cut off from the rest by a little peninsula of rocks, the rocks where Mark and Hattie had searched for crabs with Hattie's new net, bought for a pound with her holiday money from the village store. It was a pathetic little thing with yellow netting already coming away from the bamboo handle. Mark said it was a waste of money and had made Hattie cry. But, so like him, he was sorry he'd upset her and spent almost all of the next day with her, crouching over pools filled with slime, abandoned seaweed and dead fish which Hattie picked up with glee but which Mark made her throw away, and they'd tried to prise mussels and limpets off the rocks, nearly succeeding as the white gluey stuff stretched then snapped back, and Hattie's cry of triumph turned to frustration.

Tess scrambled over the rocks, forcing herself to look down into the water, almost black, which lapped up towards the back of the cave. Her eyes became used to the gloom. There was no dark shape moving there, nothing. Tess turned, and waded as fast as she could back through the shallow water. There was just nowhere else, nowhere else she could be. Should she swim out, search under the deeper water? Get help?

She hesitated, then ran up the beach towards the path, the sharp stones cutting her feet. 'HATTIE! HATTIE!' It was colder now, despite the early sun, it wasn't going to be a fine, bright day as the dawn had promised. It was going to be chilly, the weather had turned.

As she reached the beginning of the path, which bent round the rock and then rose towards the stile, she stopped. There was something glinting among the stones. Tess stooped down to pick it up. It was Hattie's hairband, a pale yellow ring of elastic with a gold band. She had used it to stretch and pull Hattie's hair into a topknot this morning, while Hattie pulled away and complained but Tess said she'd get her hair in her eyes otherwise.

Tess reached out and touched the cold stone of the rock. When she turned, she would see the path, at least fifty metres of it, leading up towards the bridge. She had only been minutes, five at the most, in the water, and Hattie, even running, could not have got so far if she'd decided to go back to the house. Tess paused, her heart beating as if it might choke her. She had to force herself to look.

Hattie sat, swinging her bare feet on the stile. She was holding something tightly clenched in one hand, the other resting on the top rail of the fence.

'I've got a present for you! It's brilliant! But you can't see it yet,' she called.

'Why?' Tess said, making her voice calm.

'It's a secret.'

'When can I?'

'When I've washed it properly. It's the best thing ever.'

Tess walked slowly up to her, her wet feet drying, becoming dusty.

'Hattie?'

'Yes?'

'I love you.'

'I know. You always say that.'

Agilely she turned, and hopped down off the other side of the stile.

'Hang on. I've got to get my clothes.'

'I'll be fine,' said Hattie, and ran away from her up the path.

Tess gathered up her clothes, and pulled them on over her wet swimming costume. The sea water had run into her crotch, and felt unpleasantly damp. Mark's jumper stuck uncomfortably to her breasts. The hair she hadn't pulled outside the jumper dripped down her back. She walked back up to the house, the frantic pace of her heart slowing back to its normal rhythm.

From inside, she heard the sound of running water. Hattie had dragged a stool over to the sink in the kitchen, and was standing leaning over on tiptoe, intently washing a greeny-blue object.

'What is it?' Tess stood behind her.

'Not now!' Hattie said. 'You'll have to wait. Go and do something.'

Obediently, Tess turned, went up the stairs and

began to make her bed. There was a calm logicality about her movements, the practical considerations of the day beginning to run through her head like subtitles – get Hattie changed, find a plastic bag for their wet swimming costumes, load the remaining suitcases into the car, check to see all windows were closed, read the electricity meter, check in the airing cupboard to make sure none of the towels left were theirs. She and Hattie really should have a shower, or they'd be salty and sticky in their clothes in the car. She pulled the sheets and blankets – how much more comforting they were than duvets – up the bed.

There was a small hollow halfway up the bed, a small indent where Hattie's body had lain, like a footprint. Tess reached out to touch it, smoothing away the dent with her hand. It might have been the sun slanting through the window, but it felt warm. Slowly, she leant forward. She put out her hands, and her face came to rest against the warm patch, a warmth which smelt of Hattie, of the washing powder Tess used for her pyjamas and the bubble bath which was all hers and not for boys that she'd been given for her birthday and had brought with her in her special holiday bag.

She heard Hattie's footsteps on the stairs.

'What are you doing, Mum?'

'Making the bed.' Tess lifted herself up, turning her face away from Hattie, and wiped her eyes. Hattie missed nothing.

'Why are you crying?' she said. 'I've found the bestest shell in the world. It's either for you or Miss Webster at school. I haven't decided yet, so you have to be extra nice to me on the way home. Can I have some sweets?'

'You're a monster. We'll see.'

'I hate it when you say that. Does it mean yes or no?'

'I said, we'll see,' Tess said. 'Now let me finish off up here and then we have to go. We're late already.'

'OK.'

It was time to go home. Hattie was safe, all was well. She followed Hattie down the stairs, with a heart still sinking.

Chapter Five

'Look, I don't care if your grandmother makes you sleep with an electric blanket. You have to go. Get in the car.'

'But I *fry*,' Jake said, plaintively. 'I'll wake up in the morning and there'll be nothing left of me. Just glue.'

'Oh, for Christ's sake.' A pulse was beating beneath Mark's eye. He had to drive the boys up to Yorkshire, Tess had gone to the hospital already. He desperately wanted to be with her, and couldn't see how he could spend even an hour away from Hattie, who had no idea of what was going on, and drive these two for hours up the motorway. It was just a year after Hattie's birth, a year filled with trips to the hospital, blood tests and scans. A year Mark would never, ever, want to repeat.

Of course the boys were worried too, in their own way – Ollie had even offered to let Hattie take his floppy rabbit into hospital, a rabbit so unhygienic it was verging on the radioactive. Tess had melted at the offer, and said that Hattie would, as long as they could wash it in the machine first. But Ollie had been very frightened about this. It was his rabbit, and he knew how it smelt – it had taken him years of loving to achieve that smell. If it went in the washing machine, who knew what might come out? It might be a different rabbit. It might not be – and he couldn't bear this thought – *his* rabbit. He withdrew the offer. Jake showed how worried he was by being even more difficult than usual.

Tess thought she could cheerfully give him away at the moment, and feared that he and Mark might physically come to blows. Even at eight he was tall for his age, with the promise of Mark's height and broad shoulders. He would be a godsend to the girls, but good luck to them.

He had all of Mark's insouciant attitude and fearlessness, but coupled with this and his mocking sense of humour was a lack of sensitivity about other people's feelings, which worried Tess. He had Mark's charm, too, and his wicked smile which made one side of his mouth turn up at the corner. Yet it was a charm he used primarily as a weapon to get what he wanted. He expected love, but didn't feel that he had, necessarily, to love back. Being able to control his temper was not one of Jake's strong points, and at one stage they had had to battle to persuade the headmaster of his primary school to keep him, because although he was naturally very clever, he was also insufferably lazy with the boredom threshold of Attila the Hun. He was also, like Attila, partial to the odd scuffle and had last term been involved in a fight so serious he had broken another boy's nose. Tess had been appalled to realize that Mark was secretly impressed. She was outraged.

In Jake, Tess was worried to recognize the same restlessness and anger which must have driven Mark when he was young, led him to leave his homeland and his broken family, and travel the world. Would providing him with a stable, happy, family home quell the anger which might have been born within him? Their life together appeared to have quelled the demons within Mark – only very occasionally did the dark violence erupt. Most of his drive and aggression was now channelled into his career.

Ollie, gentle soul that he was, was tactile and loving with Hattie when they'd first brought her home, Tess white with fear, reeling from the possibility there was something seriously wrong, which there couldn't be, how could there, she looked so perfect? The hand of God which she trusted to keep her safe had turned, and handed her a wild card when Hattie was born. Mark, who'd been buffeted by far more insecurities and fears in his life, had taken the news that Hattie had a heart problem with equanimity and squared shoulders. Jake, on the other hand, acted as if they had brought home an unexploded bomb.

'What's it for?' he had said, peering into the Moses basket where Hattie's face peeped out, still pink and crumpled from the birth, but not pink enough, slightly yellow with jaundice and with a faint blue line around her mouth. She had to go back into hospital in two days, and had only been allowed home for a short while.

'Do we have to keep her?'

'Don't be ridiculous. She's your new sister.'

'I'd rather have a bike.'

The seven-year-old Jake cast another despairing glance into her cot – and she was a sickly girl, too – picked up his skateboard and walked out of the house, slamming the door loudly behind him. Mark told Tess he'd come round, but Tess wasn't so sure – she and Jake had a relationship which seemed to balance permanently on a knife edge and she wasn't sure this wouldn't tip him over. Like Mark, he constantly wanted to be the centre of attention, and when he wasn't, he would do something so awful he would force everyone to concentrate on him. Little Ollie coped with Jake by giving in most of the time, and spent his life trying to avert one of Jake's moods.

*   *   *

Tess had bought them some new books and drawing pads for the journey to their grandparents while Hattie went to hospital. Jake had lost his pad, and as they reached the outskirts of the city, he grabbed Ollie's. Ollie said, mildly, 'Please give it back.'

'Oh, just give me a go.'

'No,' Ollie said. 'It's my new one from Mum. She gave you one too.'

'Can't find it. Give us a go.'

'No. Dad, Jake's pinching me really hard.'

Mark, trying to negotiate the turning onto the motor-way, flicked his eyes from the road into the back via the rear-view mirror.

'For Christ's sake, Jake. Find something to do.'

'I'm bored. Can we have the radio on?'

'No. Just shut up.'

'Mum says shut up is rude. Is it rude, Dad?'

'Shut up.'

'It is. Ollie, gimme a go.'

'All right. But don't push too hard on my felt-tips. If you push too hard you're dead,' he said, bravely.

'Yeah, right. As if you'd dare.'

'Ow! That really hurt!'

Mark, his face tense with fury, turned round suddenly, making the car swerve across a lane, into the path of a huge lorry, which blared its horn.

'For God's sake!' he shouted. 'Why, just for once, can't you be nice to each other? Any more of this and I'm going to put you both out on the hard shoulder and leave you.'

'You can't,' Jake said. 'That's against the law. I'd call the police.'

'Good,' Mark said. 'They might keep you.'

Ollie, who hated being shouted at, felt tears welling in his eyes. They brimmed, and fell down his cheeks. He tried to swallow a sob.

'Ollie's blubbing.'

'No I'm not,' he said, wiping away the tears with the back of his hand. He badly wanted his mum. He didn't like going to his gran and granddad's, although they were very kind. Their food was weird. It wasn't like food at home, predictable food you knew was coming, like chicken nuggets and pizza, but it came all covered in wet stuff – gravy and sauces like parsley, and Granddad said you had to finish everything on your plate but Mum didn't mind. Their house was very hot, too. Like a furnace, and there were loads of ornaments everywhere so you couldn't run about. The one good thing they had was a big garden with lots of tall trees. Ollie didn't know how long they'd have to stay there, it was all to do with Hattie and her heart. As Tess had left earlier that morning, Ollie had hung onto her neck and said, 'Please let me stay. I will be very good. I can make my own sandwiches and tidy my room and everything. I won't make a mess. You won't know I'm there. Please.' Tess had melted at the sight of his pleading, kind, round face. She hugged him and said he would have a lovely time. He wasn't sure about that at all. That was like being told to have a lovely time in a museum.

'Don't worry, they'll be fine,' Jean said, as she and Mark stood awkwardly on the doorstep. She'd been baking a chocolate cake for the boys when they arrived, and Mark saw her through the glass panel in the front door, taking off her apron and wiping her hands on a tea towel as she walked into the hall, patting her short grey hair into place. A narrow wooden ledge ran all the way around the hall, halfway up the wall, on which were lovingly placed china ornaments and decorative plates. Mark winced.

'They'll be right as rain. Oh, do come in. Just have a bite to eat before you go back. It's such a long way.'

Mark didn't want to stay, he wanted to dump the boys and get off as quickly as he could. He couldn't erase the memory of Hattie's face out of his mind when he'd last seen her that morning, strapped into the car seat while Tess packed cuddly toys around her.

'If you don't mind, I'd like to get back.'

'Of course,' Jean said. 'You get off then. Don't worry about the boys at all, they can stay as long as you like. We'll play it by ear. Here's some sandwiches for the journey.' She handed him a small parcel wrapped in silver foil.

'Thanks.'

Mark turned back to the car, then something made him stop. Jean was still standing on the doorstep, her stoical expression gone. She was crying. Mark walked back, and she hugged him.

'We're thinking of you,' she said. 'It'll be all right. She's a tough one, is Hattie.'

Tess knew she mustn't cry, but when the nurse was booking Hattie in she felt her throat constricting and her voice beginning to break. All they were asking her was Hattie's address and the name of her doctor and they were being so kind and so gentle with her she really mustn't embarrass them and let herself down, not to mention worrying Hattie, who thought she was going on some kind of exciting adventure. She was used to the hospital now because she often came in for tests, and she enjoyed helping Tess pack a suitcase with her favourite pyjamas and picture books and all her best toys.

'I'm sorry,' Tess said, reaching down into her handbag for a tissue. 'It's ridiculous, I know, but we've just been so . . .'

'Don't worry,' the nurse said, putting a hand on her arm. 'Everyone's always nervous, it's only to be expected. The doctor will try to see you later on today, to explain what's going to happen and how long Hattie will be in. What a lovely big teddy. Is that yours?'

'Yes,' Hattie said, happily, squeezing it. Tess shifted, trying to get some feeling back in her bottom. They were sitting, like Baby Bear, on tiny child-sized chairs in the waiting room of the children's ward. The walls were painted with colourful murals, and toys and children's books lay about the floor. It had a cheerful atmosphere, which almost, but not quite, masked the air of neglect.

Hattie screamed when they pricked her heel for the blood test. Tess had tried to make her cot inviting by filling it with her toys, and putting up cards friends had sent on the bedside table. She had own overnight bag, as she wasn't sure where they'd stay – they only lived ten minutes by tube from the hospital, but Tess didn't want to leave Hattie at all, if she'd had her choice she would have slept underneath the bed.

By tea-time Mark still hadn't come and Tess was exhausted, exhausted by having to force-feed Hattie with her food. The only thing which seemed to settle her was her night-time bottle of milk. A child was screaming further up the ward, and Tess felt worn out by the emotion, not just her emotion, but the collective emotion of all the other parents on the ward, every child a story, every parent living the reality of a nightmare. At half six the nurse came and suggested she try to settle Hattie, as it was unlikely the doctor would be able to come that night. Sitting on a hard plastic chair, Tess read Hattie a favourite story about Charlie Beaver, trying to make things normal. Hattie clung to her. She didn't want to go back into that cot and be separated from her. Just as Tess was trying to lie Hattie down, Mark walked in.

Immediately, most of the nurses on the ward paused in what they were doing to watch him walk past.

He took one look at Tess's drained face, and lifted Hattie out of the cot. She instantly nestled her face into Mark's neck, a small pink hand reaching up and twirling itself into his dark hair. 'Darling,' he breathed. With the other hand, he reached out and took Tess's hand. Mark looked at her and smiled.

'Go and get a coffee. I'll sort Hattie out.' Tess nodded, and walked away. At the end of the room by the swing doors, she turned. Mark was sitting with Hattie in his arms, oblivious to everything around him. Hattie's eyes were closed, ecstatic, as Mark rocked her gently backwards and forwards in her pyjamas, singing, Tess guessed, the special song that was for Mark and Hattie. It was an Aboriginal song he'd learnt from his nanny. The words meant nothing to Tess, but it had a plaintive, haunting quality that made her want to cry. He hadn't sung it for the boys. He had saved it for Hattie.

The consultant was very brusque. He obviously had very little time: his business, after all, was saving lives twice daily. He told them Hattie had a very small hole, which they knew, that the chances of mending it were good, they'd use a kind of gauze patch, there might be a tiny residual hole but it wouldn't in any way affect the working of her heart as this hole was doing, leaking blood from one chamber to another, putting pressure on her lungs and endangering her life. But it was open heart surgery, there was no getting round that, and there was always the possibility of something going wrong. But it was a very slim possibility, the odds looked very good indeed. It would take about five hours, then she'd be on a ventilator in intensive care, so they might as well find something to do while the operation took place. They could stay with her until she'd had the anaesthetic.

Tess and Mark slept the night in a single bed in a

part of the hospital reserved for parents. It had been like sleeping in a prison cell, tiny and airless. They made love and Tess, despite all her expectations, slept like a child. Mark didn't, and by six in the morning was sitting drinking lukewarm coffee in the hospital canteen, before wandering outside for a smoke. He stood by the large grey hospital bins, looking out across the narrow London side street. It was a drizzly, damp, overcast day, and all around him people were getting on with their normal lives, walking to the tube, café staff putting out rubbish, shopkeepers unwinding awnings. In front of him a taxi driver sat, waiting for business, reading a newspaper.

Before they went down to theatre a nurse took Hattie's pyjamas off and put her into a green theatre gown. She wasn't allowed to have breakfast, and she'd been given her pre-med early, before Mark and Tess went in to see her. She was drowsy and not really aware of her surroundings.

As she was lifted onto the trolley which would take her down, Tess took her favourite moose from the cot. It was a weird-looking thing, with big furry antlers and a ridiculously long nose. It was known in the family as Kissamoose, because bedtime with Hattie always involved the ritual of giving first her a kiss, then her moose, and it slept lying across her chest. Tess tucked it in next to Hattie, who looked up at her with eyes blurred.

At the door of the anaesthetic room, Tess hesitated. Beyond, through an open door, she could see the consultant waiting, theatre nurses, the operating table, oxygen cylinders and a metal trolley covered in gleaming steel instruments on a dark green cloth.

'It's OK,' Mark said. 'You stay here. I'll go in with her. Take Kissamoose.'

'We'll count together, shall we?' the anaesthetist said. Hattie held tightly onto Mark's hand, and her heavy-lidded eyes never left his face. Mark smiled at her. 'Come on, Hat. You can count now. One, two, three . . .' Hattie's voice, little more than a whisper, started to count. 'Daddy, very . . .' She squeezed his hand. Her eyes closed. 'You can leave her now.' Mark looked down at Hattie, and fought an overwhelming urge to pick her up and run away with her to somewhere he could make her safe. Instead, he smiled reassuringly at the anaesthetist and walked out.

Tess was sitting in the corridor on a wooden bench. He sat down next to her. He put one arm around her shoulders, and pulled her to him.

'You'll never know,' he said, 'how much I love you.'

Tess leant against him, her blond hair lying like a curtain against his navy blue jumper. As was his way, he gently put his hand into the hollow at the back of her neck, feeling the softness and warmth. He put his mouth against her hair.

They walked through a nearby park, and sat down on a bench, looking out over a lake, watching ducks flying in to land, bracing their feet forward and holding their wings outstretched like little landing aircraft. They had coffee in a café. They talked about Hattie, and how annoying and lovely she was. Mark said that right from the moment she was born he felt quite differently about her, compared to his feelings about the boys. He was so proud of them, but he was so glad to have a daughter, he could openly show the huge tide of love he felt within him, hug her and kiss her. With the boys, even though he hugged them, he felt a constriction, that he must not smother them. They would always be OK, they were boys. They were tough, they were like him. With Hattie he felt as protective as he did of Tess. It gave him a clear male role, and a purpose.

They walked back through the streets near the hospital with their arms around each other and when

61

they returned, the consultant told them it had gone well and they could see Hattie, who was now in intensive care. She was still unconscious and on a ventilator, but she was a good pink colour. She was wired up, eyes closed, little chest rising and falling rapidly. They stared at her in wonder.

'Can we touch her?' Tess asked. The nurse lifted the sheepskin cosy over her chest. Mark hesitantly reached into the clear plastic cot, and gently stroked her hand. The hand stiffened, and then curled around his finger. Even in the depths of unconsciousness Hattie instinctively knew she would be safe, because her father was there.

Chapter Six

Driving home from Cornwall, Tess thought that the awful feeling of helplessness she'd felt when Hattie was lost had been exactly the same way she had felt when they were first told about Hattie's heart. It was that moment of disbelief, when everything around you stopped and even familiar objects took on a surreal image. The sharp reminder of our fragile mortality.

Mark had left for the office by the time they reached home. Hattie slept most of the way back, tired from the fresh air and the sea, her head pressed against the seat belt, which left a vivid red mark on her cheek. She held the one-antlered Kissamoose firmly in her sleeping arms. The mono-antler was the result of a tussle between the moose and one of Jake's teddy bears, unfairly armed with a small plastic sword. Tess had had to intervene in this battle which had been played out by the boys over Hattie's shrieking head. Being the younger sister of Jake was enough to enable you to withstand most things in life, Tess thought. Like civil war. Thank God for Ollie the peacemaker.

She manoeuvred the car into their residents' parking space. In front of her the skip was still there, as it had been for what felt like years, as next door were in the process of renovating their house. They only got the occasional glimpse of a builder, and Mark's theory was that they were doing it all themselves, armed only with a teaspoon. Gradually the skip had filled up with the detritus of everyone else's lives – an old mattress, a Silver Cross pram without wheels and, one ghastly night, a dead dog. Hattie had had nightmares about that for weeks.

Tess switched the engine off and leant forward, her elbows resting on the steering wheel. Hattie slept on, undisturbed by the sudden deafening silence in the car. As they got nearer to home, Tess had driven past the increasingly familiar landmarks, expecting to feel comforted, but quite the opposite had happened. She felt discomfited, in a peculiar way, as if she were driving through a foreign country. Everything was so familiar, and yet not. She looked up at their house. It was exactly as they had left it – the slightly peeling paint of the front door, the chipped stone step and a Coke can in the tiny front garden which Mark had lobbed out of the window of his car in the week before the holiday, in protest at the children's habit of littering it with empty fizzy drink cans and sweet papers. Their house, indisputably. But not yet home.

Tess shook herself. Get real, as Jake would say. It was high time she got back to normal, tackled the day-to-day demands of life and stopped all this soul-searching, as if she in reality had any time whatsoever to do anything with her life which didn't involve loading and unloading the dishwasher, getting the children out of bed, feeding them and then getting herself to the gallery, wearing clothes. That was her life. Not some vague possibility of something new, as yet unexplored.

Hattie woke, opening one eye and then the other.

'Are we home?'

'We are.'

Hattie's face, to Tess's horror, crumpled into tears.

'I don't want to be home. I want to be on holiday.'

'I know,' Tess said, reaching over and undoing Hattie's seat belt. 'So do I. Come here, you chump. It'll be Christmas before you know it.'

'How long?'

'About three months.'

'How much is that in days?'

'About a hundred,' Tess hazarded a guess.

Hattie frowned. 'That's an awful lot.'

'Yes, but there are nice things in between.' Tess racked her brain. 'Bonfire night. And Halloween. And your nativity play,' she ended, lamely.

Hattie regarded her with some disgust.

'Halloween? Our school doesn't even let us talk about witches. Too scary.'

'Who says?'

'Miss Webster. She says we shouldn't be thinking about horrid things like that. Or werewolves.'

Hattie, screwing her face up in disdain at anyone being so pathetic as to be scared by werewolves, clambered over the handbrake and snuggled onto Tess's knee.

Werewolves were a particular fascination of Hattie's. She had made Tess buy her a werewolf outfit for her sixth birthday, a tricky request because most toy shops including Hamley's and the Disney Store didn't quite run to werewolf outfits, preferring less threatening characters such as Scooby Doo and Tweety Pie. Tess had had to improvise with a black cloak, a pair of grey plastic gloves covered in ghastly ginger synthetic fur and a set of false pointy teeth. Hattie had been thrilled, and wore them all day, to Mark's amusement. He and Hattie shared a keen sense of the ridiculous, and ganged up together to frighten Tess with horrible tricks like voice-activated spiders which suddenly dropped down in front of her face when she walked into the kitchen.

Most of Hattie's friends turned up for her birthday party wearing pretty dresses. Hattie was dressed as the bride of Dracula, which provoked some doorstep tantrums. The boys thought the werewolf hands were really groovy and Tess became accustomed to the sight of Jake playing his saxophone in them or Ollie sitting mildly reading a book, his legs draped over one arm of the armchair in the snug, one long pointed hairy finger flicking over the pages.

Hattie didn't go back to school until next Monday, and Tess also had time off until then, so at least she had half a week to sort out her uniform and try to get her homework finished. Hattie went to the Church of England primary school round the corner from their house, which had educated both Jake and Ollie. It was a much sought-after school, its catchment area adding greatly to house prices and precipitating many families to move into the area for that specific purpose. The children wore a uniform, discipline was strong and the results were actually better than the private school a mile away, a fact which made many of the parents secretly gloat. Not only could they assuage their socialist principles, they could get a private school education in a middle-class area for nothing. Tess found this attitude rather nauseous but there was no denying it was an excellent school and they couldn't afford the fees at Collingwood Prep anyway.

Jake's greatest strength lay in his sporting ability, and it was mostly for this reason that they had opted to fork out money they could ill afford for an independent boys' day school when he moved on to secondary level. The alternative in their area, a huge and intimidating comprehensive, seemed to place little or no emphasis on competitive sport and Tess reasoned that unless Jake was allowed to beat the hell out of other boys on the rugby or football pitch, he stood a pretty good chance of beating the hell out of

66

them behind the bike sheds. That, and girls. Even by the age of eleven, Jake had attracted a small coterie of ardent female admirers who rang him at all hours of the day. He seemed to treat them all with equal disdain, but Tess was very worried that it was only a matter of time before he discovered their possibilities. And he was unlikely, on current showing, to meet with much opposition. Attending an all-boys school with a rigorous sporting agenda might just delay the process a bit. She hoped.

Tess bent her head and rested it against Hattie's hair. It smelt of L'Oréal 'No More Tears' shampoo and also, more faintly, of salt and sun. Another age, already gone.

'Come on. Let's get on with it,' she said, more to herself than Hattie.

'Not yet,' Hattie said firmly. She knew that once in the house she would lose Tess, lose her to all the things she would have to do with precious little time to sit and have a cuddle. Her mother was much more short-tempered at home than she was on holiday, and even at seven, Hattie was beginning to question why it was always Mummy who rushed around at home while Daddy spent quite a lot of time asleep. Tess countered these queries by saying that Daddy worked very hard indeed, and he deserved to have the odd lie-down on the sofa.

Opening the car door, she swung Hattie's knees around so she could tip her onto the pavement. As she did so, Hattie stuck her feet out in front of her, revealing the fact that she had no shoes.

'Oh, for goodness sake. Where are they?'

'In the back.'

Tess turned and looked at the hell that was the back seat of the old Volvo. In the half-hour before Hattie had fallen asleep, she had munched her way through most of two packets of crisps, a small tub of Twiglets

67

and a carton of apple juice. Most of the contents of one packet now lay like crispy confetti on the seat. Pages of her pink furry notebook had been ripped out and strewn around, covered with felt-tip drawings of lopsided dogs, cats and hearts. The felt-tips themselves were scattered on both the seat and in the well. None had tops. Tess, who spent her life attempting to impose order on chaos, groaned. She had spent over half an hour packing the car, large suitcases in the estate boot, wet items like their wellies and swimming costumes from this morning in plastic bags and all the clothes which needed washing in a separate bin-liner. Yet Hattie, in the space of just half an hour, had imposed her own little universe of mess upon Tess's best laid plans.

She reached over and fished Hattie's shoes out from among the debris. But Hattie had gone, dancing up to the front door on tiptoes, hopping over puddles and wet leaves as she went. Climbing out of the car, Tess thought how grey their street seemed after the sharp sunlight and vast skies of Cornwall. She had always thought it had a certain charm – not smart but nice enough, the area having a pleasant villagey air. It was a wide street, with trees planted at intervals along the pavement, but looking at it now with eyes focused by absence, she was struck by its shabbiness – the untidy front gardens, the litter, the peeling paint and in the house next to them which was divided into student flats, the broken bike left forgotten, leaning against a wall by the door.

The only house which could be described as smart was Vanessa's, with its two perfectly cylindrical bay trees standing to attention at each side of her navy blue front door, and window boxes which vomited trailing geraniums in the summer. Tess and Margi had been secretly pleased when these geraniums were mysteriously beheaded one night, because they were a constant reproach to both of them that they didn't make more of an effort to beautify the outside of their houses. Vanessa pointed out trenchantly that she didn't work like they both did and therefore had literally nothing else to do but whisk about wearing gardening gloves and fiddle with compost, so why beat themselves up about it?

Maybe it was the weather, or the fact that the trees were beginning to lose their leaves, but there was a general air of neglect Tess hadn't noticed before. A plastic carrier bag blew past her as she stepped from the car, and by their gate was a mound of chocolate-brown dog muck. The weather had begun to turn as they had left the cottage, greyish clouds scudding across the blue sky, a wind ripening, but back here in London it felt even colder. Tess pulled down the sleeves of Mark's jumper and felt the chill breeze lift her hair, still stiff with salt water. She touched her hair, tweaking the ends. Already the cottage seemed a million miles away, another life. And yet she was not quite home. In limbo, a foreign place.

Hattie rattled the knocker and shouted 'Hello!' through the letter box.

'There's no-one there, darling. Daddy's at work and the boys have gone to school.'

'Nigel's in,' Hattie pointed out, reasonably.

'I don't think you could expect him to answer the door.'

'He might if we got him a butler's outfit.'

'Perhaps for Christmas.'

Turning the key, Tess pushed open the door. It didn't open fully, and, peering round, she saw why. The post was still in a pile behind the door, where Margi had left it.

Inside, all was devastation. It looked as if Mark had simply tipped the car up and left everything where it fell. Wellingtons, Mark's golf clubs, Jake's saxophone and an assorted range of coats and suitcases lay jumbled in the hallway. Over the bottom of the banister hung Jake's school blazer. Ollie's sports bag lay spilling out a rugby shirt and tracksuit bottoms by the door, as if he had attempted to pack it, and given up. Balanced precariously on the dado rail which ran the length of the hall was a half-drunk cup of tea. On the hall table, next to the phone, lay a piece of toast with a bite out. Tess surmised that this morning's attempt to get the boys off to school might not have gone like clockwork. Of course Mark had to get off to work, but bloody hell, did he have to leave everything to her? He had had all of last night to at least make a start on the unpacking.

Hattie vaulted the mess and bounded up the stairs, shouting for the cat, eager also to see if her fish had survived Margi's ministrations. Margi didn't allow her two girls to keep pets because she was out at work all day, and each summer argued with Tess that she might not be the best person to do the pet-nurturing thing while they were away. But Tess said she didn't know anyone else well enough to force such a vile job upon them, apart from Vanessa, and she didn't want Vanessa in her house while she was away because she might take pity on her and call in the interior designers.

Margi's worst pet-care experience had come when she had accidentally not closed the top of hamster Fluffy's cage adequately, resulting in Nigel exacting his revenge upon a small furry edible creature which for a year had been making faces at him from behind the safety of his bars. This had been a close call, but Margi rose to the challenge magnificently, nipped out and bought another hamster virtually indistinguishable from Fluffy. Hattie had not noticed, although she did remark that Fluffy must have missed her a lot while she was away, because he no longer tried to bite her when she lifted him out of his cage for a cuddle. The only firm evidence of Fluffy's demise was a scaly tail and a minute kidney found a week later by Tess under Mark's wardrobe.

Tess bent down and picked up the post. She needed both hands to carry it downstairs to the kitchen, pausing to note that the TV in the snug had been left on, and that for some reason all the cushions from the sofa were on the floor. With the car keys in her mouth, she kicked the front door shut with her heel, and walked slowly down the steep wooden stairs, spotting cobwebs as she went. Even though she had left it tidy, how very dirty the house seemed.

In the kitchen, she flicked on the electric kettle and instinctively reached out to warm her hands on the front of the Aga. It didn't feel very warm. She checked the thermometer on the front. It was running at below half power. Sulking again, Tess thought. They were supposed to be such reliable things, but hers – which was admittedly pretty old – seemed to be permanently suffering from pre-menstrual tension with a temperature which soared and dipped for no apparent reason other than pique. And the floor felt sticky underfoot. The mop lay propped against the sink. It was hardly like Mark or the boys to mop the floor. She felt like Inspector Poirot, on the trail of some mysterious domestic crisis. Not that she really wanted to know. She knew about the bread bin, and that was bad enough.

In the middle of the table, a note leant against the empty vase which usually held roses. Tess loved fresh flowers, thinking that at least they diverted attention away from the urgent need for redecoration. The note said, 'Back late tonight. Can you pack a bag – poss going away. Will ring, M.'

No, 'Sorry about the mess,' thought Tess, crossly. But then Mark wouldn't notice the fact that the house looked as if it had been vigorously burgled. Neither Mark, nor the boys, nor Hattie, ever noticed that things lying on the floor needed to be picked up. Sometimes Tess wondered why she kept on tidying up after them, whether any of them would notice if she simply stopped, and everything piled up so high they would all have to tie themselves together and use crampons to get to the front door. Maybe she was only doing it for herself, rather than for the romantic notion she harboured in her heart that the whole family noted and appreciated her efforts to create a comfortable, clean environment for them to live in, with food in the fridge, clean underpants and socks in their drawers and games bags left packed for them at the foot of the stairs.

Often, when she was tidying up, Tess kept herself going by imagining someone, a domestic expert – possibly her mother – watching her, hugely impressed and thinking 'What an organized person she has turned out to be,' as if she would blitz the entire house, make every bed, straighten piles of books, empty the wash basket, fold all the towels and sheets neatly in the airing cupboard, and then walk down the stairs to riotous applause and a cast of judges holding up cards saying '10'. Funnily enough it never happened, so she generally rewarded herself instead with a cup of coffee and *Woman's Hour*.

Flipping through the post, she swiftly divided it up into Mark's business letters, catalogues, bills, bank statements and non-frightening items such as postcards. The bank statements she hesitated over, then put them in the kitchen drawer. She couldn't face them just yet. But she would be the one eventually who had to look at them – Mark loathed anything to do with money and left it all to her. There was a postcard from Mark's father from Singapore, addressed to all of them. He was on holiday with his girlfriend – nearer

Tess's age than his own – and sent them all his love. A dangerous thing, Mark's father's love, she thought. He wrote that he might be able to drop in at Christmas as he had some business meetings in the UK. Tess made a mental note to mention it to Mark, who she knew would shrug and say, carelessly, 'Sure, whatever.' His attitude to his family – a younger brother working as a journalist in Australia, his father and his glamorous mother who had made the astonishing decision to take only her younger son with her when she left – had many years earlier hardened into one of studied indifference.

When he and Tess first met, he was only intermittently plagued by their chaotic lives, with the occasional late-night phone call from his mother whose career was now on the way down. At almost fifty, she was still beautiful, but instead of presenting a network show now fronted a regional programme and lived in terror of losing both her job and her looks. When Tess and Mark married she was living with a man of thirty-two, who claimed to be a sculptor without ever actually appearing to sculpt anything. They had not made it to the wedding, a fact for which Mark was profoundly grateful, as his mother had a tendency to drink quite heavily and be flirtatious. Tess's parents would not have been impressed.

He had loved his mother deeply as a child but had switched off that love a heartbeat after the moment she left with his brother. She rationalized the decision at the time by saying that Mark was about to take important school exams and it would be better for him to stay where he was, with his father. She had been offered an exciting new job presenting a network news show in Sydney. The real reason, he knew, was that he would have been cumbersome emotional baggage, unlike his biddable younger brother. She just didn't have time for him. So he had stayed with his father in

Melbourne, his heart broken without any visible sign. His father's parents tried to step into the breach but at twelve, he was too old to be mothered by anyone but his mother. He and his father, Mike, soldiered on, more brothers than parent and son, as his father began to drink a little too much and make an increasingly bizarre series of business deals which left him more and more in debt. Mark got used to pulling off his father's shoes on the sofa and covering him with a blanket, until the large, filthy, empty house began to close in and he, too, left. To Mark's father this was the ultimate betrayal and it was only with the encouragement of Tess that Mark had made contact again with him. Mark's departure for Europe had shocked him into appreciating the scale of his decline and today his father was once more a wealthy entrepreneur, although in quite what Tess could never establish. If you pushed him, he would say vaguely, 'Import, export. You know, darling.' Very, very charming and still handsome, but not to be trusted. When he first met Tess he straightened his tie and murmured to Mark, 'Very pretty girl. Every man for himself.'

Jake adored him and they emailed each other constantly, with Mark's father offering to take him on a range of expensive and unsuitable trips. They had never been able to afford to take the family to visit him or Mark's mother in Australia, but Jake especially was constantly asking when they could go. In arguments, he often threatened to leave and live with Mike. Thank God, Tess thought, he did live thousands of miles away.

When Tess's parents and Mark's father met at their wedding, it was like introducing two different species. Mark's father, suave, tanned and expensively dressed, looked to Tess's mother so like a movie star she was lost for words. Derek, her husband, an accountant, had him down immediately as a conman. The night before their wedding, at the comfortable, unostentatious stone hotel where the reception was to be held, Mike ordered bottle after bottle of champagne while Derek mentally totted up the cost and blanched. Tess's parents were not given to the art of the flamboyant gesture. Having a glass of wine with their evening meal during the week was seen as an act of reckless daring.

Meeting Mark's father had not in any way allayed the fears they held about Tess marrying Mark – he was a charming boy, very clever, and clearly far more responsible than his father, but he was so foreign, his life so outside the sphere of their existence, they could not help but worry. Yet Tess was clear-eyed enough about her background to note that they had accepted Mark, as a foreigner, far more easily than they would have accepted a working-class boy from their own part of the world. Even so, her father had quizzed him very carefully about his future prospects.

The gulf between her and Mark's upbringing had been one of the many things which made him so attractive. Her own home had been so safe, so conventional and so lacking in drama she found the chaos of his life fascinating. He seemed so worldly, so lacking in fear. While Tess spent her life worrying about what other people thought of her, Mark didn't give a stuff, and he found the class divisions of England both hilarious and incomprehensible. Being with him was like closing your eyes and jumping off a waterfall.

Just one nasty moment had come the evening before the wedding, when, two bottles down, Mike had tried to persuade her father to invest his carefully collected and managed savings in one of his business deals. She had felt Mark immediately stiffen, an expression shadow his face, a childhood memory, a wince of 'Oh God, what next?' But her father had extricated himself with his usual tact and diplomacy, and the crisis passed.

Mark, in turn, was fascinated by the sheer normality of her background. When he first went to stay at her parents' home he had marvelled at their routine, the way that meals happened on time, the tidiness of the house, the lack of drama. After he had been almost literally put to bed by Jean – not with Tess, she was in her old room, her parents would not have approved of them sleeping together although of course they knew they were living together in London – with a cup of tea for him to take to bed and a hot-water bottle between his sheets, he had lain awake and felt such a deep sense of loss he could have cried. It was there and then, subconsciously, he had resolved to marry Tess. Not only was she beautiful, clever and sexy, she would know how to build a family for him. A real family which wouldn't be taken away from him.

Among the holiday post was what looked like a circular, in a clear plastic wrapper. It was addressed to 'The Occupier', and normally Tess would have chucked such letters straight in the bin – usually they were attempts to persuade you to take up a new credit card or the sort of catalogues which sold back-door mats which would magically divest your pets of mud. Tess flipped it over idly, and saw it was a brochure for the Courtauld Institute. Behind her, the kettle clicked off. She put the brochure down on the table, and made herself a cup of tea. One of the tiles was coming away from the wall behind the Aga. She could ask Mark to fix it, but then it would become another of the great long list of household jobs waiting for him to do, which never quite got done. He pointed out, quite reasonably, that he didn't want to spend all weekend with a drill in his hand, or up a stepladder, but then neither did he want to employ anyone else to come in and do them either. All over the house was evidence of this policy of negative action. Most of the time Tess no longer noticed the hole in Hattie's wall where her doorknob banged, or the ceiling wallpaper hanging down in their bedroom.

'Do you want some orange juice?' she yelled up the stairs to Hattie, before spotting, through the still-open door of the freezer, that it was empty. No trip to the corner shop for Mark then, last night.

'Yes, please,' Hattie yelled back.

'Sorry!' she shouted. 'It's milk or water.'

There was silence.

'Coke?' Hattie bellowed from her bedroom.

'No chance. We'll have to go to the supermarket.'

Holding her mug, she took a grateful sip of hot tea. Her mind felt numb from all that driving, her back stiff and her right foot still mentally pressed down on the accelerator. Sitting back down at the table, she ripped open the plastic envelope. 'Have You Ever Thought of a Postgraduate Degree?' ran the headline. 'Not bloody likely,' Tess thought. How on earth could you have time to run a house, a job and study too? Margi and Tess teased Vanessa about the part-time courses she kept starting with huge determination, as the thing which really would bring meaning to her life. So far she had tried life drawing, film studies and the latest was creative writing. None of them lasted more than a month because she found the twice-weekly lectures too tying.

Tess dropped the brochure on the table, and listened to the thumping sound of Hattie pulling her holiday bag upstairs. This was a bag filled, not with clothes, but with a witch's cloak, a pink feather boa, bubble bath, four teddies, crayons, a large ball of Blu-tack and a heavy metal rocking-horse moneybox full of foreign coins from Mark's frequent trips abroad.

The phone rang. Tess started, put her tea down and picked up the Rover phone which was lying on the table.

'Hi. It's me.'

'Hi.' Tess cradled the receiver against her cheek. Now she was home.

'OK journey?'

'Fine.'

'Did you see the note?'

'Mm-mm. When might you have to go?'

'Tomorrow. I'm sorry it's such bad timing, but we've got a bit of a crisis. The Hungarian white tastes like piss, apparently.'

'Not ideal.'

'Not unless you have a penchant for drinking over-priced urine, admittedly.'

'How were the boys this morning?'

'Awful. How do you manage it without having to kill them? We couldn't find anything and Jake was still in fucking bed ten minutes before we had to go. I left him and made him get the tube.'

Tess grimaced. She shouldn't feel sorry for Jake, he deserved it. But it was his first day back. He would have been late.

'What do you need for tomorrow?'

'Enough stuff for a week. I think it's quite cold, so put some jumpers in, will you?'

'I'll try. But I have to unpack all the rest of the cases as well, you know. And go shopping. There's no food.'

'Let's eat out.'

'I meant for the children.'

'Oh, bugger the children. Take them to McDonald's. What about us? I'm not going to see you for a while. Let's splash out.'

'We can't really afford it. Not after the holiday.'

There was a pause. Mark's voice changed.

'Fine,' he said, coolly. 'We won't bother.'

'No,' Tess said quickly. 'That would be a much better idea. I'll get a babysitter. Francesca will come.'

'Italian?'

'Great. I'd better go now, I need to get on.'

'Don't go yet.'

Tess pictured him, his feet up on the desk, biro in mouth, behind his desk piled high with invoices and catalogues, an unlikely figure with the open collar of his shirt turned up, framed against the dark oak panelling of the office.

'I have to.' She smiled at the phone.

'Did you miss me?'

'For one night?'

'I missed you. It was fucking cold in that bed. I couldn't sleep.'

'Me neither,' she lied.

'What are you doing now?'

'Sitting at the kitchen table surrounded by bills, wondering which area of chaos I am going to tackle first. What did you eat last night?'

'Chinese. It was crap. I've got a stomach full of squirrels.'

'You fared better than Nigel. He's got terminal diarrhoea. Why did you leave the cartons out?'

'Tess, give me a break. He shouldn't be up on the table anyway. He ought to spend the night out, like a normal cat. From now on he goes out every night.' Tess pondered anew why all men seemed to have two deeply held beliefs – that all pets are insufficiently disciplined by the rest of the family and there are never enough sharp kitchen knives.

'Do you want me to book the restaurant?'

'Please.'

'What time will you be home?'

'Seven-ish.'

In time for the children to have been fed and the house tidied, Tess thought. He had done this when they were little, carefully timing his return from work so he could get the nice bits of helping at

79

bath-time and reading stories to appreciative, warm, sleepy children. Not tea-time, when she often felt like going out and leaving them to it. Hattie in particular was a very picky feeder and meal-times blended into one long nightmare.

'Fine.'

'Oh, and the Disco's got a faulty alarm. Could you book it in while I'm away?'

'I'll try. I take it you'll need a lift to the airport?'

'Yup.'

'Seven-ish then.'

'Love you.'

'And you,' she said, absently.

She drained the last of her tea, and, after rinsing the mug under the tap, went upstairs to tackle the suitcases. Upstairs in the hall, she noticed the answerphone light was flashing. She pressed the button, then upended the suitcases and started to divide the huge mounds of washing into piles, coloureds, whites and hand wash. Margi's cheerful voice filled the hall.

'Welcome home. Hope the fish are still alive. They were awfully hungry, greedy little buggers. You don't feed that cat enough, either. However much I gave him he yowled for more.' Nigel rubbed against Tess's leg as she listened, squeezing himself past her like a fur-covered Zeppelin.

'I have to see you soon. Tons of news while you've been pottering about playing happy families. Vanessa's had her face peeled and they're buying a house in France, which is great because we can force her to let us poor friends use it, can't we? And I – are you ready for this – have found a man. See, I told you it was explosive stuff. Ring me *immédiatement*.'

Tess smiled. Her life, like fish food floating down through Hattie's tank, was beginning to settle back to normal.

Hattie wandered downstairs, trailing her feather boa and wearing a pair of Tess's platform boots.

'I think my fish are having baby fish,' she said happily. 'Nigel's done a poo by my bed. It's very runny. Can we go swimming? I need at least *some* treats before *hideous* school.'

Chapter Seven

'The microwave's dinged.'

'Get it out for me, would you?'

'Get it out yourself. I'm doing something else.'

'Like homework, you loser.'

'I'll get it.' Tess clicked open the door and retrieved Jake's steaming micro-chips. 'Here.' She held them out as Jake, on his motorized scooter, whined past.

'Do you have to?'

'Need to get the hang of it again, Mum,' Jake said, as he executed a stylish lap of the kitchen table where Ollie sat, exercise books spread out around him on the battered wooden surface. Tess reached out and moved a mug of orange juice away from his geography textbook.

'Can't you do your homework upstairs?' Tess asked. 'And Jake, take that thing outside, will you?'

'Pissing down,' he said. 'Sorry, raining.'

'It's too quiet upstairs,' Ollie said. 'Can't think.'

'I can't do this.' Hattie, who was sitting on the opposite side of the table to Ollie, held out a photocopied sheet of paper, holiday homework, to Tess. 'These muddled sentences don't make sense.'

'That's the point,' Tess said, looking at them. But Hattie was right. They didn't. 'You'll have to add an "and" to that,' she said.

Hattie took up her sharpened pencil and began laboriously to write, her tongue squeezed out of the corner of her mouth like a tiny rosebud.

'Jake, what about your homework?'

'Ain't got none.'

'He's lying,' Ollie said.

Jake scooted behind him and, reaching over, picked up Ollie's pencil tin.

'Give it back!'

'Oops, sorry!' Jake let the tin fall to the floor. Pencils, a rubber, pencil sharpener, Caran d'Ache crayons and a protractor clattered out onto the floor.

Tess, who was loading the dishwasher, turned angrily.

'Jake, pick *all* of it up. Now. And apologize. Come on. Francesca will be here in a minute.'

Ollie looked up from his books and grinned. 'Francesca.' He made a whistling noise and looked pointedly at Jake, who reddened.

'So?'

'Nothing.' Ollie grinned again and looked down. 'No reason.'

'Just fuck off, will you?'

'Jake!' Tess put her hands on the back of the carver chair at the end of the table and glared at him. 'Don't you dare say things like that!'

'Dad does. He says them all the time.'

'Dad is a grown-up. Anyway, he doesn't.' Even as Tess said this, she knew she had lost the argument. Mark didn't see the need to moderate his language in front of his children.

'Fuck,' said Hattie, happily, to herself. 'Look, Mum, I've finished.' She held up a book with large, loopy pencil sentences which danced just above the lines. Tess scanned the page.

'That's brilliant, darling.' She reached down and gave Hattie a hug. Ollie and Jake exchanged glances.

They shared the theory that Hattie got an unfair amount of attention. The doorbell rang.

'That's Francesca now. God, Hattie, you haven't even had your bath.'

'Don't want one.'

'But you haven't had one since this morning. The sea, remember?'

'Was that this morning?' Her eyes were wide. Tess knew exactly how she felt. It seemed an age away, an age filled by unpacking eight suitcases, putting on five loads of washing, trying to clear the boys' bedroom, galloping round the supermarket and picking them up from school as a special treat, instead of making them walk home or get the tube.

'Jake, let Francesca in, will you?'

'Do I have to?'

'Yes,' said Tess, firmly. Groaning, he dumped the now empty chips carton on the table, on top of one of Ollie's exercise books.

'Yuck,' Ollie said, and pushed it away.

'Hi.' Tess heard Francesca's shy voice from the hallway. Jake said nothing, standing back wordlessly to let her in. The next moment he reappeared, thumping down two steps at a time into the kitchen in his heavy black trainers. 'Don't leave Francesca standing there,' Tess hissed at him, then called up the stairs, 'We're down here.' Francesca's long thin legs in thick black tights ending in clumpy platform-soled boots appeared down the stairs.

'Francesca!' Hattie leapt up from the table and hurled herself at the teenager.

'Hello, Hats.' Francesca caught her as she leapt into her arms. Francesca was Hattie's absolutely favourite babysitter, because she let her stay up after eight o'clock and could be blackmailed into reading her at least two stories. Hattie also thought she was very beautiful, which she was, with long pale brown hair, caught up in a spiky bun with a glittery bulldog clip at the back of her head. She had creamy, pale skin with a light dusting of freckles on her nose, and hardly ever wore make-up. Francesca was Margi's elder daughter.

Tess glanced at Jake. He was studying one of Ollie's books with unreasonably focused attention, his cheeks, beneath the holiday-tanned skin, flushed. Tess noticed that Francesca was stealing looks at him as she unwound the huge pale blue scarf from around her neck. God, Tess thought. He's only fourteen. What would it be like when he was sixteen? They'd have to paint a black cross on the front door.

'Francesca, you couldn't bear to bath Hattie, could you?'

'Sure, no problem. Come on, little bear.' Hattie snuggled happily into her neck, and waggled her fingers at Tess as she was carried away up the stairs.

'I'll be up in a sec. Boys, could you clear this lot? Ollie, I'd really prefer it if you worked in your room. Go on.' Sighing, he gathered up his books and slid them into the carrier bag he used instead of the briefcase Tess had bought for him. Jake was fiddling with his scooter.

'Could you go and put that away? And if you do have homework, please could you get on with it. *Now*.' Tess attempted to inject a note of menace into her voice.

Jake looked up, and smiled his heartbreaking lopsided smile at her. How gorgeous he is, she thought, despite that awful haircut, spiky all over with a longer tuft at the front, like Tin-Tin. Ollie longed for the same cut as well, but Tess hadn't let him, yet, although she knew it was only a matter of time. He had such lovely thick blond hair with a wave in it, like Tess and Hattie. With his round glasses, he'd look like a little bristly mole if he had his hair cut like Jake's.

After Hattie had had her bath, Tess climbed into her

water, topping it up with more hot. It would be so nice to have a second bathroom, she thought – having just one with three children was hell, she couldn't leave any of her moisturizers or bath oils out because Hattie made potions with them. The boys, especially Jake, were such unhygienic creatures and never rinsed the bath out. And now Jake bought all these horrid cheap hair products, such as violently green hair gel. There wasn't an inch of space on either of the window ledges and Mark was beginning to complain that Jake was using his razor, too, even though he didn't really need to shave. Before the holidays he had shaved a gap in his eyebrows, which made him look really odd.

Tess slid her shoulders down under the water, and tipped her head back to soak her hair. She should really have had a shower as it was quicker, but lying in the bath was somehow more comforting. She flipped her feet, and felt the water wash up her body. She examined her stomach. Too big from holiday indulgence. Most of the time she managed to keep reasonably thin by rushing around so much, and often she didn't eat until the evening, because she could never be bothered with lunch. It was easier to work through and then she didn't feel guilty at leaving at three to go and pick Hattie up from school. And, she admitted, it was an excuse to finish early.

The job had seemed such a godsend when she first found it after a long break to have the boys and Hattie, as the gallery, situated in a triangle between the convergence of the two main roads through Clapham, was halfway between home and Hattie's school. But now it was boring her. It was a pleasant enough place to work and the gallery owner – who hardly ever came in during the week unless they had an exhibition with one of their more popular artists or there was an excessively rich client to fawn over – left her pretty much to her own devices. She enjoyed the relationships she had built up with their handful of artists, especially the younger ones, listening with endless patience to their tales of tangled love lives and financial crises. It gave her a window into a very different world.

It was a small, traditional gallery with a loyal band of clients whose needs Tess now knew inside out. They trusted her implicitly when she rang to say she had found something she knew they'd like, and the profits of the gallery ticked over steadily, if unspectacularly. Bruno liked to think he was the one who found their new young artists, but more often than not it was Tess, who attended as many of the art college shows as she could. She had an excellent eye for what would sell, but far more than that, she knew how to nurture the egos of both their artists and clients. She knew she had good people skills, but that was mostly because work was a doddle compared with trying to maintain the peace at home between three warring, strong-minded and clever children.

Now Hattie was not quite so dependent on her, perhaps she could consider going back to work fulltime. But not in the gallery, she thought. Maybe what she needed was a complete change of scenery, a totally new challenge. A fresh start.

The front door banged. Blast. There was Mark, and he would want a bath, too. She reached forward and ran the tap. All the hot had gone. Next door, she could hear Francesca beginning to read Hattie's story, the story she could hear over and over again, about the pink polar bear who lived on a lonely ice cap, until one day a blue bear came sailing past on an identical iceberg. The two collided, and they fell in love, ending their days singing together, their voices echoing out into the frozen wastes.

Tess lifted one leg out of the water and soaped it. Her legs needed shaving again. Life was just a series of tasks, really, she thought. Tasks she never seemed to reach the end of – you finished one lot and then, bang, there was another. What kept her going, as she loaded the washing machine or drove the children to school in a baggy old jumper and no make-up, was the conviction that tomorrow would be different. Tomorrow, she would be more organized and put on lipstick before school. And she would definitely book a facial. Definitely. Even if she had to make the time. Always tomorrow and tomorrow, tantalizingly and encouragingly, the prospect of an entirely new her.

She lay back and closed her eyes. She and Mark hadn't done much singing together, lately. On holiday his primary desire seemed to be sleeping. She knew he was tired and she knew his career at the moment with all the new responsibilities was stressful, but surely, on holiday, he could have spent at least one whole day with her and the children. He was with them, but only in short bursts – after a morning's sailing or surfing with the boys, he would lie down on the blue sofa in the living room and sleep for the rest of the afternoon. It was like holidaying with a hibernating tortoise. Tess knew he had to give more and more of himself to his job, but that inevitably meant he gave less and less to them. And the bits they did get were often the grumpy bits that no-one else would ever want, anyway.

Maybe it was her fault. Maybe she wasn't loving enough towards him, and spent too much of her time with the children, ministering unto their needs. Well, not loving, let's be frank. What he wanted wasn't the odd gentle hug, it was sex. Sex, with all the trimmings – silk knickers, perfume, the full romantic works. Mark, in moments of anger, said it would take very little for her to make herself sexy for him, but she argued that she didn't see why she had to dress herself up like a performing elephant at the end of an exhausting day just to get him in the mood. Mark also said in the same argument she did far too much for the children and they were in danger of becoming idle and spoilt. What he meant, she thought bitterly, was that she spent too much time looking after them when she should have been looking after him, which she point-blank refused to do because he was an adult, for God's sake. Not a child. Margi had once pointed out that this was the flaw in most men – they never grew out of childhood and spent the rest of their lives searching for a version of Mummy willing to strap herself into restrictive lingerie. One of the first things Margi had done when she divorced was chuck out all her suspenders and buy a pair of very warm fleecy pyjamas.

She sighed. She couldn't win. If she did too much for the children, she was spoiling them. If she did make them get on with things themselves, Mark complained about the hellish mess they created cooking, or attempting to tidy up, which simply meant piling everything up into vast tottering edifices which collapsed when you closed the door. Yet, she thought, splashing her face with the bath water, if she wasn't physically here, then they would have to be more self-sufficient. Everyone would have to be more self-sufficient. Mark included. She soaped between her toes thoughtfully. Back to Sotheby's? Too terrifying, and as what? She could go into their administrative department, but that was hardly creative. The problem was she had no specialist knowledge. Her degree was too general, she should have taken a postgraduate course, but by then she felt she had had enough of education. Her parents were fed up with paying for her too, and thought it was high time she got a job.

'Tess! Unlock the door.' Mark's deep voice bellowed through the woodwork.

'I'm in the bath.'

'Well, get out. I want to get in.'

Muttering to herself, Tess heaved herself out of the water, and reached for a towel. Hattie had taken the only dry one, all the others were still in the wash. She opened the door hesitantly, although Francesca would still be in Hattie's room, Hattie wouldn't have let her get away with just one reading of the polar bears.

Mark slid round the bathroom door. He was wearing the linen navy shirt he'd been in when he left the cottage, and a pair of cream-coloured chinos Tess knew didn't have a button because she hadn't sewed one on. He looked crumpled and tired.

'Thank God you're back.' Tucking the towel more firmly around her, she held out her arms to him. Dramatically, he let his head droop until it rested on her damp naked shoulder.

'Totally tired out,' he said, in a tiny little-boy voice. She stroked his thick dark hair, just beginning to fleck with grey above his ears. Jake and Ollie had recently carefully cut out Sunday newspaper ads about hair dye for men and left them thoughtfully by his plate at the breakfast table.

'Not an awfully good day?'

'Not awfully,' he said, into her shoulder. His breath was warm against her body. 'The shit has finally hit the fan about Hungary and Rupert is threatening to come with me. I cannot travel with that wanker. He'll balls everything up. I will have to kill him.'

'Don't do that,' Tess said. 'It might be bad for your career.'

'I don't want to go away again. I want to stay here with you.' Slowly, he reached down and untucked the towel so it fell away from her body. 'A naked person,' he said. 'How shocking.'

'Shush,' she said, giggling. 'I thought you were knackered.'

'Not that knackered.' She tried not to shiver as he

90

ran his cold hands up from her waist, until they came to rest underneath her breasts.

'The water will get cold.'

'Sod the water,' he said, moving her backwards so her bottom came to rest against the edge of the sink. She yelped as bare flesh met chilly porcelain.

'I do love you . . .'

'But,' he said, his mouth pressed to the base of her neck. He raised it to kiss her, in a long-practised gesture.

'But,' she said, laying her fingers against his lips, 'but I haven't cleared the kitchen *or* made Jake get on with his homework.'

Mark took a step away from her, the hand which had been reaching down to undo his trousers falling to his side.

'And they are all *much* more important things. I see.' He smiled, but the smile didn't quite reach his eyes.

'Mark, I'm sorry, look—' She reached out to take his hand.

'Awfully sorry,' he said, ironically. 'Gone off the boil now. I'm not some kind of sex toy you can switch on and off, you know. I have feelings.'

Tess reached down to pick up her towel. 'And Francesca's here too.'

'And you're worried I might drive you to such heights of intense pleasure you would be compelled to make the moose noise?'

Tess looked at him beadily.

His eyes, which had been glazed with lust, regarded her closely. 'You've put on a bit of weight,' he said.

'Oh, fuck off,' Tess said, grinning. 'Don't be so childish.'

'Me, childish? What do you mean, childish? Where's my rotating shark, anyway? You know I can't have a bath without Humphrey.'

Tess reached up and took Hattie's grinning shark

down from the bathroom shelf. Swiftly, she wound it up and then set it loose in the bathwater. It whirred towards Mark, flipping its tail. He caught it. 'Hello, Humphrey,' he said. 'Perhaps you'll play with me. Everyone else appears to be closed.'

Tess bent down and without thinking picked up the shirt, trousers, underpants and socks he had left lying on the floor. Bundling them up into her arms, she reached down with her free hand to open the door. At the door, she turned. 'By the way,' she said, over the top of his clothes. 'You've put a bit of weight on too. Around your middle. It's rather sweet. Like Mr Bumble.' Then she quickly shut the door behind her.

'MUM!' Hattie's voice wailed through the wall, as she heard the bathroom door close. 'I need a kiss goodnight.'

She padded into Hattie's room. Hattie was sitting up in bed, a peremptory princess, Francesca sitting obediently at the foot of her bed, the storybook still open on her lap.

'Kiss,' Hattie said, leaning her cheek up to Tess. Tess leant forward, and pressed her lips against the smooth, sweet-smelling skin of Hattie's cheek. 'Night, darling.'

'Make Daddy come and kiss me.'

'I will. Thanks, Francesca. Has she done her teeth?'

'Yes,' said Hattie.

'No,' said Francesca.

Hattie made a face at Francesca.

'Hop out and do them once Daddy's out of the bath.'

As Tess climbed the stairs to their bedroom to get dressed, she heard Mark yell.

'Why is there no frigging hot water?'

She ran very fast up the stairs, then leant out of their bedroom door, shouted, 'What?' as if she couldn't hear, and closed the door swiftly.

Chapter Eight

In her dream, Hattie was chasing a ball. She kept nearly catching it, then the wind caught it and lifted it up again, skyward, so she had to dance in the air, and the wind caught her too and she rose, and rose, like an angel. There was bright sunlight, and the sound of the sea, and a horse, a beautiful white horse, galloping towards her. She stretched her arms towards it, wanting to feel the softness of its coat and its warm breath whispering on her face. She smiled, and stretched her fingertips towards it. The horse's skin was soft, but not furry, smoother, more like human skin. It was comforting, as she felt its breath on her cheek, like the touch of a soft mouth. As it bent its head towards her, the horse's silvery mane brushed against her face.

Mark rested his lips against Hattie's cheek. With one hand he reached up to stroke the hair off her forehead, and lifted the bedclothes higher up towards her chin. One of her outstretched arms felt cold, and he lifted it, and gently placed it back under the duvet. He was sitting in the armchair next to Hattie's bed, an armchair Tess had inherited from an ancient aunt who had collected antiques. It was probably quite valuable, and Tess had wanted to put it either in the TV room or on the landing, but Hattie, as was her way, had longed for it so vociferously they had given in. Now it was covered with Hattie chaos of books and Beanie Babies and drawing pads. Mark had moved them aside to sit down, craving the peace the sleeping child brought.

What a bloody mess.

He had been looking forward to seeing Tess all day. Even in just the space of a day he had missed her, and he held the prospect of going home to her like the quiet joy of an unopened present. She and the children – well, Ollie and Hattie anyway – made everything bearable, especially when he had had such a nightmare day culminating in a row with Rupert, who thought they ought to cut their losses with the Hungarian vineyard. Mark had argued that the vineyard, a small, family-run business, had employed extra workers especially with money it could ill afford at the prospect of such a lucrative new contract for them and they could not, in all fairness, leave them in the lurch. He argued that if he could take a wine consultant out with him, he might be able to improve the quality and bring it up to a standard compatible with British tastes. Eventually Rupert had reluctantly agreed but said he would go with Mark 'to make sure things were done properly', which was the last thing he wanted. Rupert was a hectoring, public-school type who usually tried to get what he wanted by bullying people into submission. The meal with Tess would be a chance to chill out and talk the thing over.

Many an unbearable day at work was made bearable by the thought of returning to Tess, sitting facing her over the table in the kitchen, glasses and bottle in front of them, watching the skin next to her mouth curve into a smile as he made the day's disasters funny. Then she would reach across the table, her feet on his, take his hand, and press it to her mouth, while he watched her thick blond hair fall across her cheek.

Holding Tess was like holding Hattie – a moment in time, the world paused and the shit fell away.

He could never imagine what his life would have been without her. When he met Tess his career was taking off, but he was drinking far too much and he could so easily have gone into the same freefall as his father. She showed him what an arse he was being and she and the children gave him the strength and confidence to succeed. Around him, all the time, he saw marriages falling apart, work colleagues having affairs, screwing up their lives and losing their children. He couldn't understand it. But then maybe he was unique in having a wife like Tess. He was so proud of her, of her beauty, her quick intelligence, her lack of fuss, and the fact he could introduce her to anyone and know she would never be out of her depth. The job at the gallery was perfect – it meant she had something to keep her mind occupied, and the hours didn't conflict with looking after the children. If only she had more time for him. If only he could find some way of reawakening the passionate Tess, the Tess who used to make love with him all the time in all manner of inappropriate places – before Jake was born. Children, he thought bitterly, with their nightmare waking times and sudden appearances when you were damn sure they were riveted in front of *Toy Story*, were like God's little contraceptive joke. Now she was so organized, and calm, with lists for everything except horny sex with him. It worried him a great deal that he seemed to need her far more than she appeared to need him.

One night on holiday she had started a conversation about possibly doing something different. That was fine, but, as he pointed out, they couldn't cope with two of them in high-powered careers which involved travelling, it just wouldn't work. She had agreed, and he hoped she had shelved the idea. Life was just fine as it was, if he could only persuade her to move out of London. They were well out of the baby stage with the children and they should have far more time to be together. Perhaps they could take a holiday on their own. He'd suggest it – maybe Paris, like the fantastic drunken weekend they'd had there before Jake came along. Once this work problem was sorted out.

Hattie stirred in her sleep, her lips moving. Her chin was lifted at an unnatural angle, her little hands bunched into fists and pressed up against her chin. Even in sleep she looked bossy. Mark had no fears for Hattie. Unlike Jake. His troubled mind shifted to another worry. Jake didn't seem able to concentrate on anything. His report for the summer term had been dire, he was incapable of answering a civil question and he seemed permanently full of a seething, suppressed rage. Tess could not see that they needed to crack down on him far more firmly. He was getting out of control, and Tess was just letting it happen.

One day on the holiday, Mark had hit him. He hadn't meant to. They were sailing and Mark had shouted to Jake to catch the rope as the boom swung towards Ollie's head. Jake had deliberately ignored him as he was in a mood about being told off at breakfast, and the boom had hit Ollie, square on the temple, leaving a bump. Jake had stood up to Mark immediately, shouting, 'It was an accident. An accident! Why do you always get on at me? He's the prat who didn't duck,' and Mark had smacked him with his open hand. It was an instinctive gesture, unpremeditated, a reaction to the anger that suddenly boiled up in him and then spilled over. The blow was a release, and instantly Mark felt his rage gone. But it had been a hard blow, harder than he had intended. Jake fell sideways, crashing down onto the narrow wooden seat at the side of the boat.

He jumped up again immediately.

'Jesus!' he shouted, into the wind. 'You hit me, you *bastard*!'

Mark stood over him. Ollie's face was white with fear. The wind blew hard into Mark's face, catching the untethered sail, which whipped out away from them, turning the small boat towards the shore. Mark reached out to catch the rope and secured it in a quick figure of eight, shouting at Ollie to grab the tiller.

Jake, already as tall as his father's shoulder, stood in front of him, breathing fast. His face was wet from the spray, his cropped hair glistening with drops of sea water, and small trickles ran down his cheeks into his blue kagoul. His lips were set in a tense, hard line, Mark's eyes in his face, flinty with anger. Mark reached out to put a hand on his shoulder. He pulled away.

'Don't ever touch me again.' He spoke quietly, menacingly.

Mark let his hand fall. Then Ollie cried out, 'Dad, we're heading towards the rocks!'

Mark spun round and wrenched the tiller from Ollie, who was paralysed with fear.

With one deft movement, he turned the boat back out to sea. When he looked up Jake had moved, and was sitting, his shoulders hunched, in the prow. Ollie knew to leave his brother alone. It was a cloudy day, the horizon obscured by a thick sea mist. Jake stared into the grey nothingness. The prow of the little boat rose and fell, slapping into the water, creating a wash of spray which hit his upturned face, salt water mingling with the salt water of his humiliated tears.

When they returned, dripping and exhausted, Tess met them in the little hallway of the cottage. She was so pleased they had had an outing together, the three of them, her men doing manly outdoor things. She and Hattie had enjoyed tidying the house together, and they'd made a cake which was currently deflating like a balloon on the kitchen table, to welcome them home.

She walked out of the kitchen, rubbing her floury hands on the side of her jeans, when she heard the door bang.

'Did you have a lovely time?'

Jake threw his sopping wet kagoul on the floor and, pushing past Tess, ran off up the stairs. She turned to Mark, her face a question.

'Don't ask,' he said.

Tess waited until their plates of linguine were put before them before she began her opening salvo. She'd thought about it as she dressed, worked out how she was going to introduce the idea of her going back to work full-time or studying – yes, studying – for a proper degree which could propel her into a new career. She would approach it jokily, saying how very little she had to do at the gallery and at home, and how they could do with the money. But almost as soon as she opened her mouth, Mark said, 'The last thing I want to do is leave,' looking so pathetic she had to let him explain the situation to her all over again. She really envied Mark his career – she could see the downside, all the political in-fighting and having to cope with Rupert's ego, but there was a fascinating creative side to it too, and Mark was so passionate and knowledgeable about wine. It was such an infinite subject and so personally pleasing – most of his foreign trips took him to beautiful countries and usually involved long lunches with delicious food and intelligent people. When he complained she pointed out to him what it must be like to be the sales director of a ball-bearing company.

It was their favourite restaurant near to home, inexpensive and cheerful, with the best fresh pasta with sauces of delicious vongole, or, Tess's favourite, delicately flavoured blue cheese. Mark ordered a bottle of Barolo, the most expensive wine on the list but, as he said, they would be so in debt after the holiday another twenty quid wouldn't make much difference.

The decor was wonderfully naff, with red and white checked tablecloths, and one entire wall painted with a mural depicting an idyllic Italian coastal resort, vines dripping with fat bunches of grapes and ludicrously turquoise sea. Mark and Tess had been going there so long the waiters no longer bothered to put on their 'Mamma Mia' Italian accents and spoke to them in their native south London.

She let him do most of the talking while she murmured sympathetically. He seemed so worried, felt so responsible about the failure of the wines to sell, as if it was all his fault. He clung to the hope that they could send a wine consultant out, to try to sort out the blends and attempt to make the wine more palatable to English supermarket tastes. Mark had a friend, a fellow Australian, who was the best in his field. He was expensive, but he just might be able to turn it round. Mark was so honourable in his business dealings, and he always identified with what Rupert would see as the 'little people', the workers, and thought about what any business deals would mean to them. He felt especially responsible for the small vineyards, who relied on his firm to turn a profit, and he was forever arguing their case with the other directors, who tended only to see the bottom financial line. Mark was immensely popular with most of his clients, because dealing with him was not only profitable, but fun. He could always be relied on to stay up late, drinking, talking and joking.

Tess tried to appear enthusiastic and interested, but couldn't concentrate. She kept hoping to find the right moment to change the subject. But as soon as there was a pause in the conversation, either Mark started off again or one of the waiters leapt forward brandishing Parmesan or phallic pepper pots.

Mark paused, mid-rant, catching Tess's distracted expression.

'I'm not exactly gripping you tonight, am I?'

Tess started and looked at him guiltily. She stuck her fork into the linguine, and twizzled it around.

'I'm sorry. I just – I had something to say but it doesn't matter. It can wait. What could you do? Tell me again.'

'I'm sorry, I'll shut up. Enough about me and my boring fuck-ups.'

He put his fork down, and, placing his elbows on the table, put one hand over hers. He felt tired, depressed, and the thought of getting on a plane to Budapest first thing in the morning was just too much to contemplate. At least Tess could make an effort to humour him. All she had to do tomorrow was get up and make sure the boys got off safely to school, and then the rest of the day was hers, with only Hattie to look after. She complained that seeing to the house and coping with her part-time job was draining but, Jesus, she ought to try being him for a while.

She took her hand out from under his.

'You aren't boring me. Don't be silly. It's just I have something to say and you haven't given me a chance.'

Mark leant back and hooked one elbow up onto the back of his chair.

'Shoot. Only not Jake. I can't face the subject of Jake tonight.'

'It isn't Jake. It's me.' As soon as the words left her mouth, she regretted them. This wasn't the best time to broach the subject of a new career. Mark was too distracted and bad-tempered, he'd only see faults and problems when what she wanted to feel was optimism and hope. And if he did disagree, they had no time to sort it out. She should have sounded it out on Margi or Vanessa first, the sympathetic audience of sister-hood.

'You, what? It's Ollie's piano teacher, isn't it? You're running off with him. I bloody knew it. The *bastard*.'

'Spot on,' she said, smiling. Ollie's piano teacher was a thin man like a pencil, who she knew fancied her. He sweated profusely when she was in the room, which made him look like a sweaty pencil.

'No, I was just thinking about a bit of a change.'

'Oh?' He raised his eyebrows. 'A *bit* of a change? Are we talking using a new brand of toothpaste or running off to run an orphanage for baby yaks in Tibet? Big change or little change?'

'Oh shut up,' she said. 'I'm serious.' He rearranged his features into a suitably solemn expression. 'Sorry.'

She took a deep breath. 'I'm thinking of giving up the gallery.'

He smiled, relieved. 'OK,' he said slowly, turning the idea over in his mind. He decided he quite liked it. 'The pay hardly makes much difference, does it, and that lazy puff takes advantage of you. He might have to actually turn up for work sometimes. Why not do nothing for a while, think about what you want to do? We can just about manage. And it might give you a bit more time to . . .' His voice tailed off, as he knew what he had been about to say would not be well received. He took a quick drink of wine. What had immediately occurred to him was that she could tart up the house and then they could start looking for properties outside London. It could work rather well.

Tess's eyes narrowed. Aha. He was going to turn this into an opportunity to try to get her to do what he wanted her to do – i.e. all the nightmare redecorating jobs around the house they'd ignored for ages, like the hole in Hattie's wall and repairing the peeling wall-paper on the stairs and their bedroom so they could put the house on the market. She had not agreed to move, but already he was acting as if the decision had been made. There was no way she was going to spend her time doing all the mundane things they'd been putting off for years. Hardly a fresh start. Bloody men. Right. He was going to get it now.

'I was thinking more about a kind of complete change of direction. Going back to college. To take a teaching degree, then, maybe, lecturing. In History of Art, of course, but I need much more specialist knowledge to get anything really interesting. No-one's going to fall over themselves to offer me a job if all I can offer is a twenty-year-old degree and a bit of part-time work in a minute gallery.'

Mark looked genuinely startled. 'Where the fuck did this come from? Lecturing? Studying? Why? It isn't one of Vanessa's mad plans, is it? We can hardly afford it.'

Tess had known he would be shocked. Even though he was proud of the fact she had a degree, he took a robust view of further education. Having succeeded without one, he had an Achilles heel about graduates, especially the Oxbridge types. When pissed, he could often be heard going on about the benefits of the university of life.

Tess tried to keep calm, although she felt like stabbing him. He had hit on the immediate drawback to the plan, which was the fact that they couldn't afford it. That was the one problem she hadn't liked to dwell on, and although she knew she was being deliberately ostrich-like she had already decided, to herself, this was what she really, really wanted to do. Mark was being very selfish. She could also see him mentally running through all the inconveniences it might mean to his life.

She ploughed on, while Mark regarded her with a kind of volcanic calm. 'I feel I'm wasting my time at the moment. Hattie doesn't need me so much, and it would do the boys good to fend for themselves a bit more. It would mean a lot more time out of the house, but if you all did a bit more then I'm sure we could manage.'

'If this is a slight change I'd love to know what's a hell of a change.' Mark let his half-wound forkful of pasta drop onto his plate. He knew he ought to be supportive and encouraging, why shouldn't she re-establish a career, but did it have to be now? Now when he was so incredibly busy and under so much pressure, and it would mean she would be out of the house and there might not be all the benefits at home he knew he took for granted. And what about their plans to move? He struggled for a moment with his finer feelings. Selfishness won.

'Where are you going to do all this and how the hell are we going to pay for a degree?' he said, unfairly. 'This wouldn't mean a salary, not for at least a couple of years. Courses cost thousands, don't they? And what do you need another degree for? You've got one, for Christ's sake, which is more than I have, and it hasn't made any difference to me. You're always on about Vanessa doing arty-farty courses for no reason.' He laughed, trying to lighten the mood. 'I'm not being an Aussie chauvinist shit, am I? Look,' he said, reaching out to try to hold her hand. 'I don't mean to sound negative, but have you thought it through? Surely there are jobs you could do which don't involve you having to study as well? What about us? I want to be able to spend more time with you, not less. And the move . . .'

'That isn't the point,' Tess said. 'Mark, listen to me for once. This hasn't got anything to do with you, or the children. It's about me. Don't make me feel this is selfish. That's like me saying to you that going off to Hungary tomorrow is selfish. It's just part of your job, and I accept it. I just feel – and I was thinking about

103

this a lot on holiday – that I need to have something challenging in the future, not just ticking over doing the same old thing. I'm bored, Mark. I need to try something else.'

'Bored?' Mark looked incredulous. 'Bored?' He was cross now, levity gone. 'Bored, when I'm working my arse off to pay for the boys' school fees, working twelve-to-fourteen-hour days, away in godforsaken countries half the time and so knackered at night I can hardly get into bed? And you have the life of Riley nipping off to the gallery to make a few phone calls and chat to some neurotic artists and then – God, the strain – pick up Hattie from school? What do you think I do all day? Don't you ever stop to think what it's like for me? I'd give my right arm for your life.' As soon as the words were out of his mouth, he regretted them. But he could not see what more she could possibly want.

'You always do this. Whenever I dare to make any suggestions which might mean you moving just one bloody inch to help me it always comes down to the fact that I am being selfish and not putting the family first,' she seethed. 'It is so ridiculous! I have spent almost all of the fourteen years of our marriage putting the bloody family before myself and just this once I want to do something for myself. Yes, it might be inconvenient for you. It may well be inconvenient for the rest of the family. But frankly, I don't give a shit.' Her face was white with anger. 'The point is that surely I should be allowed to make decisions which affect my future, not yours, without having to seek some kind of approval from you. It's ridiculous. I am telling you what I plan to do. You are not my father. I don't have to ask your *permission*.'

'It isn't approval!' Mark said, trying to keep his voice down. 'It's making decisions together, what's best for all of us.'

'What's best for you, you mean. Thank you so much for your support.' Mark had rarely seen her look so furious.

'But we were thinking of moving,' he said. 'What about that?'

'You were thinking of moving, not us. Why does everything have to revolve around what you want? Why do you have to have a brilliant idea about moving us out into God knows where when none of us want to leave apart from you, and when I decide that there is one thing – just one thing – I want to change about my life it is suddenly all too much trouble. When endlessly, endlessly, I have made accommodation for you and your career, which meant I had to all but give up mine, and what am I left with? Half a crappy job, never any money and a child potentially heading for disaster despite the thousands we spend on him. Isn't that any of your responsibility? It must be so lovely just to breeze through life with nothing ever being your fault.'

She hadn't meant to be so heated. She so rarely lost her temper but now, buoyed up by the independence of the last few days, she thought why bloody not? Why should he be the one to always lose his temper and shout and win arguments simply by dint of being the most vociferous and dramatic? Most of the time she refused even to raise her voice, hating the children to hear them arguing. At times, she exercised almost superhuman control over her emotions. She was tired, tired of being so calm, so organized, so fucking reasonable.

'For Christ's sake, calm down. I really do not need this tonight.' Mark tried to take her hand, but she snatched it away.

The restaurant was all but empty, and the two waiters, who had been leaning idly against the bar, polishing cutlery, were listening intently. They were

105

normally so happy together, these two. Some married people came in here and hardly spoke to each other. Mr and Mrs James talked all the time.

Tess stood up, abruptly.

'Stop telling me what I should and should not do. You do not own me. If I want to go back to college I will. OK?'

'Just sit down,' he said. 'For Christ's sake, Tess, please. Look, I'm tired. You're tired. We're both knackered after the holiday and I have to go away. Just leave it until after I get back, we'll think about it then and make plans. OK?'

'Not OK.' Tess didn't obey orders and sit down. 'I am getting really tired of being told what to do. By you, by the children. By fucking everyone.'

Then she reached down, picked up her handbag, pulled her coat off the back of the chair and walked out without looking back.

'The bill, sir?' One of the waiters moved swiftly forward.

'Thanks.'

Tess had hardly touched her linguine. Mark thought for a moment, and then reached forward with his fork and tasted it. Tess was right. It was really very good, even though it was cold. He took a drink of his wine. Twenty quid, after all, and there was still a bit left. He wasn't going to rush out after her. What the hell was she on about, overreacting like that? He hadn't said no, definitely, had he? It was very unlike Tess to be so irrational. Maybe she was getting her period.

He paid the bill with the credit card most likely to work. Outside, it was raining. The restaurant was only two streets from their home, not worth a taxi. There was no sign of Tess. He began to walk, his shoulders hunched in his jumper. He hadn't brought a coat, as it wasn't really cold. Tess had the key, he hoped she would leave the back door open for him.

It was all so unlike her. He stopped, and looked up the street.

Row after row of houses, all the same, behind them people switching off the TV, bickering about who would put out the cat, switch out the lights, check the children. The glow from an orange street lamp reflected in a large puddle in front of him, a puddle half filled with rotting leaves and gritty with mud. On the main road behind him the traffic rumbled on, not one steady sound but a jumble of noises, engines, horns, car doors slamming, shouts. He looked at his watch. It was only ten o'clock. They'd told Francesca they'd be back at eleven. He shivered. This bloody city. He'd found London so exciting when he first arrived, everything a possibility. He looked up, feeling the rain stroking his face. It wasn't even proper rain, just drizzly stuff that made you marginally damp without being in any way invigorating. He had a sudden mental image of home.

Home. The light so bright it was blinding. The vast skies, the sea, the warmth, the 'no worries', the laid-back attitude, the vastness of the country which went on for ever and ever. He had sworn never to go back when he left, he found it so small-minded, so parochial despite its geographical size, but now – maybe they ought to consider it, take Jake out of this environment with so many temptations on offer, give all the children a life outside these rainy streets, hemmed in by identical houses and all this obsession with money, which car you drove, what job you did, where you holidayed, which area was upcoming, how much your house was worth, which school your children went to – so much pigeonholing, and all revolving around status and class. It made no sense. He swallowed, as if he had a bitter taste in his mouth. All he wanted – if Tess was adamant about staying in Britain – was the chance to live somewhere they could breathe, where he didn't have to inhale enough pollution to stun an ox. Maybe moving would fill the gap for Tess too, if only he could make her see the sense of it. She'd been brought up almost in the country, after all.

He stepped over the puddle, slowly heading for home. Perhaps he'd just walk for a while. Tess might get worried, and then, when he returned, she'd be relieved to see him. They could make up, maybe even make love. He badly wanted to make love to her. It was his way of making everything better.

When he arrived home, the back door was unlocked. Downstairs, the house was in darkness. Francesca had obviously gone home. Putting on the light in the hall, he walked down the stairs to the kitchen. He took a bottle of cold New Zealand white wine out of the fridge, Tess's favourite, took two glasses out of the cupboard and the corkscrew out of the drawer in the dresser. He headed back up the stairs, clicking off the light.

Slowly, he climbed the stairs to the top of the house. The only light on the first landing came from Hattie's room – she always slept with a night light. The boys' room was in darkness, amazingly, for ten o'clock at night. He walked up the next flight. The door to their bedroom was closed. Using his elbow, he tried the handle. Fucking marvellous. It was locked. They'd put the lock on so they could make love in safety when the boys were small, as they had a habit of tearing into their bedroom like whirlwinds first thing in the morning, which rather interrupted his rhythm. But now, the lock was almost never used.

He stood, fuming, by the door. He didn't want to bang on it because that might wake the boys and Hattie, although all his clothes were in there. He'd booked a taxi for tomorrow, to save Tess a journey, and he needed to leave at six. He was debating what to do when he saw his bag standing next to the banisters. It was zipped up, and looked plump, as if packed. Next to it hung a suit and a shirt, and on the floor were carefully laid a pair of underpants, socks and shoes. He smiled ruefully. Even in anger, Tess was methodical.

He'd have to sleep on the sofa in the TV room. He wandered back down the stairs, and on the way, paused by Hattie's door. He put the wine bottle and the glasses down, and went in. At least there was one female in this house who loved him unconditionally. He looked down at Hattie. He loved her so much his heart might burst.

He slept in the chair, next to her, waking with a start of alarm as the taxi driver banged on the door at six. He left hurriedly without saying goodbye to anyone, no-one awake to say they would miss him.

Chapter Nine

'It's like *Educating Rita*, isn't it?' Margi took a large gulp of white wine. 'You'll fall in love with your tutor and Mark will feel he's no longer your intellectual equal.'

'I hope he's better-looking than Michael Caine.'

'Might be a woman.'

'More likely to be,' Tess said, picking up one of the prospectuses which littered her kitchen table. She had just put Hattie back to bed for the third time, because Hattie was convinced that any moment Francesca would walk in because Margi was here, and she couldn't bear to miss her. It was like trying to put a boomerang to bed.

'Although,' she added, 'I can see the attraction of lesbianism at this present moment.'

'Why?' Margi said, her eyes glittering at the prospect of dissent. Tess and Mark's happiness was something of a cross to bear.

'From the spiritual side. From the point of view of having someone who understands your motives and doesn't feel they have to be the one on top all the time, figuratively speaking. It would also be handy to have someone else to load the dishwasher and know which cycle to put the coloureds on.'

'But sex . . .'

'You're obsessed with sex. Come on. Tell me all.'

Margi smiled wickedly, running her hand through her short black hair, newly cut into a feathery Winona Ryder elfin style. Tess thought it really suited her, but maybe that was because she had quite an angular face, with a sharp jaw. It wouldn't suit her so well, with her rounder features, and anyway, her blond hair was her best asset. If she cut it all off, it might not be so blond. Mark liked her hair long. No. She had to stop defining herself by what Mark liked. Was she becoming incapable of making any decisions by herself?

'He's called Rowan.'

Tess snorted. 'Not Rowan, really? Is he in a boy band?'

'Jealousy will get you nowhere. He's Irish and he's thirty-two, and he's a dentist.'

'Margi, forgive me for being obtuse, but how on earth did you meet a dentist in Temple Bar? Or is he a client? I thought that was forbidden.'

Margi grinned naughtily. 'It is. He is.'

'Margi, that's terrible. Have some more wine.'

'Thanks. He's got in some kind of legal tussle with his landlord – he's only here temporarily for a year or so – he part-owns, I think, a practice in Dublin, but he wants to specialize in orthodontics and he's over here doing a course at the Royal London.'

'Orthodontics,' Tess said, 'aren't very sexy.'

'They are, believe me, they are. Anyway, we don't talk about dentistry much. Or anything, come to that.'

'A true meeting of minds. A richly spiritual and intellectual experience?'

'Excellent shagging, actually.'

'Hattie. If you come down those stairs just one more time I will make you sleep with the light off.'

Hattie's little face crumpled. 'I've had a bad dream,'

111

she warbled. 'I dreamt Daddy and Nigel were killed in an aeroplane crash.'

'Nigel doesn't do long-haul flights, you know that,' Margi said, soothingly. 'It's his ears.' Hattie looked at her bewildered.

'Silly Margi,' Tess said. 'Do you want some water?'

'Yes, please,' Hattie said, pathetically. 'Or hot chocolate with whipped cream and hundreds and thousands on the top?'

'You chancer,' Margi said, getting up from the table and sweeping Hattie into her arms. 'You are a seriously adorable monster. Listen, I'll put you to bed this time and you can tell me on the way all the things you did on holiday.'

As Margi carried the sleepy form upstairs, Tess could hear her saying, 'First we went up in a hot-air balooon, and then Daddy taught me to windsurf, and we caught a huge octopus in a big net and then . . .'

Five minutes later, Margi reappeared. 'That child has the art of prevarication down to a T, doesn't she?'

'Past master.'

'Should the boys be asleep?'

'Unlikely,' said Tess, looking at the clock. It was half past nine.

'They're watching *Friends*, not that I'm one to sneak.'

'They're supposed to be doing their homework. Jake is, anyway, Ollie's done his. I told Mark we were asking for trouble letting them have a TV in their room.'

'At least it's only *Friends*. I caught my two watching *Bridget Jones's Diary* the other night. I'd hired it for me, the little swines.'

'It's OK, isn't it? I haven't seen it, I missed it at the pictures.'

'OK if you don't mind rampant sex, enormous pant jokes and Hugh Grant at his most wicked.'

'It sounds distinctly appealing.'

'It is,' Margi said. 'But not for sixteen- and thirteen-year-olds.'

'Colin Firth's in it, isn't he?'

'Oh yes.' They both paused and stared into the mid-distance. Then Tess shook herself.

'Go on,' she said. 'You were saying before we were so rudely interrupted.'

'As soon as Rowan walked through the door of Sarah's office I just thought, "My God." He's about five foot eight, not tall, but quite broad and with this incredible thick black hair and the most evil smile and blue, blue eyes. Like Paul Newman. Only much younger,' she added, hastily.

'And?'

'And he said he'd seen me at Henry's Bar. You know, the one round the corner from work.'

'A place for orthodontists to hang out too?'

'Apparently. Anyway, he said he'd be going there tomorrow lunchtime and I might see him there.'

'And what about the Hippocratic oath, or whatever you lot have?'

'Bollocks to that. I haven't had sex for over two years.'

'So you did it in Henry's?'

'Nearly.'

Tess gulped her wine down the wrong way and choked.

'What?'

'His flat is only two streets away.'

'Let me get this straight. You met an orthodontist for only the second time and you immediately went with him to his flat which is being repossessed by an irate landlord in a bitter legal battle?'

'You're making it sound awfully complicated.'

'How silly of me.'

'No, I said I ought to see the scene of the crime, so to speak, and he said yes, what a good idea and I didn't have to be back in the office until half past two and he had a free period. So we went to have a look.'

'And what was it like?'

'No idea. We only got through the door when he started kissing me.'

Tess put a hand on her arm. 'Margi,' she said. 'You are a very dear friend. But don't you think it is just slightly peculiar that a man you barely know starts to kiss you within minutes of getting you into his flat? No coffee? No "Come and look at my roof garden"? Don't you think – and please don't take offence – that we are talking rapist here?'

Margi looked shocked. 'Did I say he kissed me? No, I kissed him. I couldn't help it. He was so gorgeous. Those eyes. That body. The youth of him. It was all very innocent.'

Tess began to laugh. 'What then?'

'We went to bed, obviously.'

'And?'

'Heaven. Just complete heaven. I mean, proper, full-on sex when you roll about the bed and fall on the floor and then you move to the chair and you keep tripping over bits of furniture and laughing and the next minute you're in the bath and the lights are going on and off.'

'Tell me you are exaggerating?'

'Well, a bit. Anyway, it was fantastic, just the best sex I've ever had and I'm seeing him again tomorrow.'

'You're going out?'

'Are you mad? Staying in for more of the same, I hope.'

'So this is going to be a meaningful relationship, is it? Are you going to progress to a stage where you leave the flat and perhaps meet up with your friends? You know, the middle-aged ones who have dinner parties and haven't had sex in the bath for twenty years?' Oh Mark, she thought. I was mean to you.

'Why?'

'What do you mean, why? So it's a proper relationship. Not just sex.'

'Tess,' Margi said, carefully. 'Why on earth do you think I want a proper relationship and not just sex? I have had enough of relationships to last me a lifetime. I cannot tell you how happy I am on my own with my girls. We are a completely self-contained unit, happy as clams. No stupid bugger is ever going to storm back into my life, dropping his underpants on the floor for me to pick up and demanding I pack his overnight bag for him, complaining I spend too much money on my daughters and peeing on the toilet seat. All I want is sex with a man who makes me feel I am still desirable and will allow me to justify spending lots of money on clothes because I want to keep looking good. I am never' – she hit the table for emphasis, making the wine glasses jump – 'never again going to tiptoe around any bloke's ego and think what I'm going to say before I say it and take his needs into consideration all the time and not stay in the bath too long and know he'll moan when I want to go out on my own at night. I never want to feel that anxiety again, the way my heart used to turn over when I heard Martyn's car pulling up outside, the immediate panic at trying to work out exactly what he was going to find fault with that evening.' She shuddered. 'Never again. At last, I am in charge. I am invulnerable as long as no-one gets too close.'

'But what about the future? It's all very well now, when you're in your early forties, but what about your fifties? Or sixties? What then, when the girls have left home and you're on your own?'

Margi sat back in her chair and laughed. 'What a lovely supportive friend you are to help me look on the bright side. I shall take up a nice mixture of choral singing and mountaineering. I shall travel the world in

115

an eccentric hat and not give a bugger what anyone else thinks. You are so old-fashioned, aren't you? You really believe in all that sticking-at-it-in-for-the-hard-slog crap, don't you? Look, I am happier than I have ever been since Martyn walked out. He was just an energy-user-upper. Just one look at his face when he walked through the door in the evenings and I felt drained, as if he was sucking all the life force out of me. He radiated negative ions. We don't have to have a man, you know. At any cost.'

'Absolutely,' Tess said wryly. 'Hence Rowan.'

'Rowan,' Margi said, 'is icing. Decorative, pleasurable, tasty, but not essential to the cake. Is that a good analogy? At least, that's how I aim to keep him. Anyway, what was all the fuss about this course?'

Tess looked at the prospectus for the Courtauld Institute sadly. 'I don't think I'll bother. It is going to cause too much friction. I don't think I've got the energy to fight the battle.'

'Bollocks,' Margi said. 'Where's a biro? We need to fill this application in immediately. Just think of all the young men.'

'I don't need young men. I haven't the energy for Mark, let alone anyone else. Anyway, I'm doing this for me, not to find another man. Honestly, you're like Mark. Everyone seems to think I have some ulterior motive for wanting to do this course. Like Mark thinks I must want to do it because I am bored with our marriage. The children, bless them, think it's great that I want to go back and become a student again but are worried who is going to make the tea, and my mother thinks it is a silly fad and I will come to my senses. She keeps telling me that of course men are selfish but we can't change them and trying to force them to take a more active role in family life will only end in tears. She even said that aiming for a more demanding full-time career will "emasculate" Mark. God.'

116

Margi paused in her examination of the form, and, looking up, followed Tess's gaze to a picture of Mark holding Hattie in his arms, pinned to the cork notice board covered with notes detailing dentist's appointments and unpaid bills. It was a photo taken the previous year in Cornwall, during a blinding heatwave. Mark was naked but for a pair of navy windsurfing shorts. Hattie's eyes were closed, ecstatic, her blond hair streaming out behind her as he swung her round. Margi felt a flash of jealousy. Christ, he was good-looking. She mentally chastised herself. Forbidden territory. Don't even go there, Margi girl. Although it was very hard, occasionally. No point anyway. For one, she loved Tess too much and any fool could see that Mark had eyes for no-one but her.

She picked up the pen. 'OK, darling, here we go. Student days beckon. You'll have to buy some new clothes. I cannot tell you how envious I am. It'll be like reinventing yourself. You'll start taking Ecstasy and going to clubs.'

'Hardly,' Tess said. 'But it might be fun. I think it is time for a new me. I'm rather bored by the old one. Do you think I should get my hair cut?'

'Maybe,' Margi said, and then felt guilty. It would make her less beautiful. She really wanted Tess to do this, she needed an injection of confidence. And it would make life so much more interesting all round.

117

Chapter Ten

An argument over the ownership of a bar of chocolate was raging when the phone rang. She picked it up, motioning frantically at the boys with one hand. There was a pause, and then an ear-splitting roar of noise, before a transatlantic voice said, 'Go ahead, please, caller.'

'Hi, it's me.'

'Hi, you.'

'Will you shut up, you two?' Tess shouted.

'What?'

'It's the boys. They're having a stupid argument. Hang on.'

Tess leant forward, stretching the phone cord to its limits, and slammed shut the door to the snug. Immediately, without an audience, the row ceased and Ollie and Jake settled back down to watch Eminem on MTV.

'How's it going?'

'Better than I thought. I seem to have persuaded Rupert there's hope yet.'

'Excellent.'

'And you?'

'What?'

'How are things at home?'

'Fine. You know. Hattie's missing you. She's made you a drawing and she wants to know if you've met any werewolves. Hang on. Here she is.' Hattie hurtled down the stairs, followed by Nigel with a pink ribbon in his tail.

'Hello, Daddy.' Hattie's voice was full of love.

'Darling.'

'Is it cold there?'

'Very.'

'Where are you sleeping?'

'In a hotel.'

'Not in a castle?'

''Fraid not.'

'Daddy?'

'Yes.'

'Are vampires in real life?'

'No. Just in stories.'

'What about werewolves?'

'I haven't seen any yet.'

'Could you bring me one home?'

'Tricky, Hat. But I will keep my eyes peeled. Promise. I don't think they travel well, though. Coffins.'

'OK. And Daddy . . .'

'Yes?'

'I came top in spelling. I beat Alicia Williams.'

'Brilliant. Put your mum on, will you?'

'OK. I love you.'

'I love you too. Bye.'

Hattie made a loud kissing noise into the phone. Tess tried to take the phone off her but she clung on.

'Daddy?'

'Hat, this call is costing quite a lot of money.'

'I'm making Nigel a Barbie girl.'

'Oh, good. Put Mum on, please.'

'OK. Love you.' Tess took the phone.

'She's no idea where Hungary is. Actually, I don't think I know either.'

'It's really rather scenic. Mountainous. Look . . .'

'What?'

'I'm sorry about what I said.'

'I'm sorry I locked you out. Where did you sleep?'

'With Hattie. I fell asleep on her chair. Thank God the taxi driver knocked loudly on the door.'

'What's the hotel like?'

'Basic. Dour.'

'No five-star meals?'

'Hardly. Tess . . .'

'Yes?'

'I miss you. I miss you all the time. I missed you sleeping in the chair and I missed you in the taxi and on the aeroplane and I especially miss you here sleeping in a double bed with a mattress the consistency of concrete. We'll talk, properly, when I get home.'

'No more moving guff?'

'Not if you don't want it. No more college? We just . . .'

'The dishwasher's totally broken. When you switch it on it just pretends and makes a noise but no water goes in. Can I get a man in or buy a new one?'

'Whatever. Buy one. That old thing doesn't wash plates anyway, just dribbles on them. Did you get the Disco fixed?'

'Not yet. I haven't had time.'

'Try and do it before I get home.'

'If I can.'

'Do you miss me?'

Tess thought hard. No.

'Very much,' she said. 'And I'm a witch for shouting at you in public.'

'We can't go to that restaurant again. What will Luigi Mamma Mia think of us?'

'Just that we're a normal married couple who fight sometimes.'

'But we aren't normal, are we? We're happy.' Mark's voice had a pleading edge.

'Most of the time.'

There was a noise in the background behind Mark, a male voice. 'I've got to go for dinner. Give my love to the boys.'

'Do you want to speak to them?'

'No,' Mark said, quickly. 'I should be home on Sunday at the latest. I'll ring tomorrow if I can. Will you be in?'

'Of course,' Tess said. 'Where else would I be?'

'I'm not sure, these days. Can you promise not to make any decisions to go trekking in the Himalayas or take up lion-taming while I'm away?'

'Ha, ha. On the contrary. I'm just off to lash myself to the tumble-dryer before blackleading the fireplace. Don't worry. I know my place.'

Mark laughed. Uncertainly.

Chapter Eleven

Tess's mum, as she had told Margi, had not been Mrs Positive.

'What do you mean, you've decided you're going back to college? At your age?'

'Thanks, Mum. I'm hardly geriatric at nearly forty. Anyway it's university. Not college. I'm going back to do an MA for a year and then a postgraduate teaching diploma for another year.'

There was a long pause. 'Well it *sounds* very exciting. But who's going to look after the children while you study?'

Tess sighed. Trust her mother to zoom in on the fly in the ointment. First Mark with the money, and now her bloody mother picking holes. 'I've found another mum at Hattie's school, Clara, who will keep her at her house until I've finished, and give her tea. Hattie is very excited about it. Hopping. Can hardly wait.'

'And what about the boys?'

'They are old enough to get themselves home and make their own meal. They're thirteen and fourteen, for goodness sake. Think of all the millions of full-time working mothers out there. They cope. Why should my family be any different? I've been the odd one out of most of my friends, apart from the very rich ones, only working part-time.'

'But this isn't work, is it? Work, I could understand. But why do you need to do this other degree first? Why don't you just go back to your old job if you've got so much time on your hands?'

Tess thought for a moment. This was the hard one to explain. The real answer, if she was brutally honest, was that she was scared. By going back to university she could ease herself into a new experience, not immediately plunge into something she might not like. Going back to college would give her the building blocks of confidence, from which she could then launch a new career. Of course she had worked at the gallery, but it was very small, very safe. It didn't really matter how much of a success she was because no-one saw. Now she needed the hunger of a real challenge. Thinking about it so hard over the past few days, she had realized that to stop trying and stop pushing meant you began the slow process of dying. Children were one thing, but she couldn't live her whole life through them, no matter how much she loved them. Nor could she live through Mark, carried along like one of those little feeder birds, pecking off the crumbs of his success. It had to be for her, by her.

Margi, however, with her gimlet eye, while being largely encouraging and the catalyst who actually made her fill out the forms, had also made her feel uncomfortable by pointing out the simple truth – that doing a course like this meant all the fun, intellectual stimulation, the chance to meet new people and broaden her horizons, without any of the responsibility of a new job. That would come later, when she felt ready.

'I really want a change of direction, and I can't just walk into a new career, Mum. Not after I've had so much time off with the children. The gallery hardly counts, it's just admin and I'm bored of it. I need to move on.' She stopped herself from pointing out the obvious – that her mother was hardly an expert on the world of work, her experiences being primarily limited to running the charity shop in the village and sitting heavily on various committees.

'What does Mark think about it?'

'He's perfectly happy,' Tess said firmly. 'Why shouldn't he be?'

There was another pause. Tess caught herself grinding her teeth. Jean let out an exhalation of air. Tess held the phone slightly away from her ear. How could her mother make her feel this bad with just a handful of words and *air*? It was ridiculous. She had expected to get support, her parents had always been very big on education, instead she was getting this tight-lipped approbation, as if what she was planning to do was some kind of indulgent whim.

'Look, Mum, it's a brilliant opportunity. It's something I've always wanted to do, really specialize in one area of History of Art. Then, once I qualify, I can apply for lectureships which will fit in perfectly well with the children and I'll have the same holidays as them. It's perfect.'

'But it's going to make your life very complicated, isn't it? And the children need you so much, especially Jake. With Mark away so often . . . I'm sorry, darling. I know you think I'm old-fashioned but I do think children need one parent they can rely on to be there. I'm only trying to be practical.'

'Oh for God's sake, Mum! They're not babies. They're perfectly capable of looking after themselves and in all honesty it will do the boys good to take more responsibility for themselves. I've mollycoddled them far too much, you're always telling me that. It will also do Mark good to come home to an empty house occasionally. It's high time he took more responsibility for things in the house. I've supported him in his career for years and now it's his turn to do his bit to support me. I'm not asking for the earth.'

Jean snorted disbelievingly. 'But you can't have it all ways, can you? You can't expect him to have a job like his which means he has to work long hours and be away from home, and then in the same breath expect him to be home dead on six every night so you can do your studying. I'm sorry, darling, but it doesn't really wash.'

'Whose side are you on?' Tess said, crossly.

'The children's,' Jean replied shortly. 'Why don't you wait at least until Hattie is at secondary school?'

'Because . . .' Tess said. Because what? Because she had the bit between her teeth now and Mark's opposition had meant she bloody well was going to do it, he wasn't going to dictate to her how she ran her life. And now she had the hope, the shining light inside her as if she had opened up a corner of a grey, overcast sky and been literally blinded by what lay beyond.

'Your generation seems to expect to be able to have everything, but something has to give. It worries me that a lot of the time it is the children that suffer.'

Tess exclaimed angrily, 'Oh hang on . . .'

'I don't mean in your case. You've made a brilliant job of bringing them up but part of that has involved sacrifice on your part, of course it has. I know you think I don't see things and I don't understand, but you can't think the children can look after themselves now because they can't.'

'So I have to wrap myself in a hair shirt until they're all ready to leave and then finally I can do something marginally interesting with my life?'

'And bringing up a family isn't a challenge? Honestly, you lot today make me livid. Do you think my generation didn't see raising a family as our career?

We did, and I don't see why I should apologize for making you my career. Being a mother wasn't seen as the pathetic option it seems to be viewed as today, as if any young girl you pull in off the street can look after your children better than you can. Almost every time I go to the supermarket I see children running amok and screaming for sweets and being given in to, because giving in to them is a lot easier when you haven't got the time for proper discipline. No-one seems to have the courage to stand firm any more.'

'Come on, Mum. Don't tell me that if you were in my position now you wouldn't have wanted to have had a career? You always said you wished you had gone on to train as a teacher.'

'I know. But I had you instead, and I don't feel I missed out. It was just unfortunate we couldn't have any more children after you, but I've filled my time perfectly well with charity work and helping out. That's what gets lost these days, helping others. Why don't you think about doing something like that, instead of all this me, me, me?'

'Remind me to ring you again next time I want to be made to feel completely selfish and worthless, Mother. I can't see why what I am planning is not perfectly logical and sensible and will benefit us all in the long run. Even if it does pinch a bit at first. Please, Mum. Say it's a good idea.'

'If it is what you have set your heart on, you know I will support you. If you need me and Dad to come down and lend a hand, of course we will.'

'I know, Mum. But we should be able to manage. It just makes me a bit cross that the minute I ask anyone to put themselves out for me I'm made to feel I am being selfish.'

'Welcome to womanhood,' her mother said, and laughed. 'I'm just trying to see this from Mark and the children's point of view, that's all. He works very hard

126

for you all, you know. Don't take away or belittle that reason. Men need to be appreciated too.'

'I know.'

'Just be careful,' Jean said. 'That's all I'm saying. Don't make him feel his nose is pushed out. Men are funny things, their feathers are easily ruffled.'

Chapter Twelve

The letter came in April telling her she had a place. Tess hid it. She had a special place for hiding things, an old wooden salt box which stood next to the Aga. If she didn't police it, it would quickly become filled with all kinds of rubbish – menus for the Indian takeaway down the road, reminders about non-payment of oil bills, letters from the children's schools about concerts and plays long past. The letter arrived in an envelope with 'Courtauld Institute' clearly marked on the front, and she opened it with a beating heart. The first sentence began, 'We are pleased to inform you . . .' She put the piece of paper down on the kitchen table, and stared at it. Success. Success after three different interviews, a specimen essay she had sweated blood over and a wall of silence from Mark. Now here was the indisputable proof she was going to do something against his wishes. The subject had lain more or less dormant since the bitter argument back in September. Perhaps he thought it was just going to go away if he didn't talk too much about it.

Mark had brought an inflatable sheep home with him from Hungary. He gave it to her wordlessly, and she looked at it, quite overcome.

'You shouldn't have.'

'I know. I just couldn't resist it.'

'And all those women who get Chanel perfume or expensive jewellery from the duty-free shop.'

'It was an impulse buy,' he admitted. 'I was looking for something for the children in the toy section and there it was. You refuse to move to the country, so I shall bring the country to you.'

'Do you really think,' she said, 'that one inflatable sheep – cute though it is,' she added hastily, 'is going to make me change my mind, chuck in all thought of advancing my career and agree to bury myself in the country?'

'Yes,' he said. 'At least, I hoped. Betty and I hoped.'

'Betty, is it?'

'We had a chance to get to know each other in the taxi.'

'Sorry,' she said, chucking the sheep over her shoulder. It squeaked as it bounced. 'It's going to take rather more of an incentive than that.'

'I shall have to move on to Plan B,' Mark said.

Ollie and Jake emerged from the kitchen stairs.

'Why did you buy Mum a sheep?' Ollie said.

'Cool,' Jake said, grinning. 'Different present.'

Hattie hurtled down from her room. 'What did you get me?'

'He's waiting in the car.' Tess looked at him, alarmed. 'What?'

'Joke.' He reached down to his bag. 'Boring chocolates, I'm afraid, Hat. No werewolves. None I could get through customs, anyway.'

'What about us?'

Mark delved deeper into the bag and brought out baseball caps with 'Hungary' emblazoned on the front. 'Unoriginal, but succinct,' Mark said.

Ollie put his on. Jake looked put out. 'Why do I have to get the same as Ollie?'

'Why do you always have to question everything? Now push off, all of you. I want to be alone with your mother.'

Hattie made a sick face. 'Ergh.'

'Exactly. Now go away.'

'Drink?'

'More wine? Why not?' He followed her down the stairs. Tess turned her back to him, looking for an appropriate bottle. Expensive? A celebration? Or just usual stuff?

'Crap or good?' she said, without turning.

'Oh good, I think, don't you? It's not every day your dim husband pulls off a fantastic deal.'

She spun round. 'You saved it?'

'Certainly did. Very clever person, I am.'

'I know.' She put the bottle down on the sink, and walked round the table to where he was sitting. She wrapped her arms around him from behind. 'I was a foul witch. I'm sorry.'

'I was a selfish pig.'

'You were.'

'No I wasn't.'

'Why did you say you were then?'

'I can say it. You can't. Can we compromise, then? No move, no university bollocks?'

'Not very fair. Anyway, there's no way I'd get a place until next September. Ages off. Anything could have happened by then.'

'Like me persuading you to move.'

'Hell, freezing and over?'

'Just meet me in the middle, OK?'

'I will,' Tess said, sliding the chair out so she could sit on his knee. 'As long as you meet me halfway too.'

'The way I feel at this precise moment is that I would be prepared to meet you anywhere you want, my little moose.'

On the way up, Mark stuck his head around the TV

door. 'Five pounds to anyone who can watch the whole of *Nickelodeon* before it goes off the air without moving.'

'Done,' Jake said, without looking up.

Tess picked the letter up, and held it against her cheek. A *fait accompli* now, she couldn't go back. He wouldn't be so very angry, even though she had kind of fibbed, telling him it was hardly worth going for the interviews, she was so unlikely to get in. But in six months' time, there she would be. She hugged herself. He wouldn't mind, really. Once he got used to it. Then she put the letter behind the reminder for a brace appointment for Ollie. And firmly closed the lid.

Chapter Thirteen

It was a cold winter's day, but not depressingly so. Not the kind of day they seemed to have had for weeks, when the sky was so grey and low it appeared to be just overhead, as if you could reach up and touch it, oppressive and imprisoning. Today, as Tess walked in the park with Hattie, the light was sharp and clear, their breath smoked before them, the winter sun shone and Hattie talked on and on of Christmas. Her eighth Christmas, but still she was positively radioactive with excitement.

'It's only the end of November, Hat,' Tess said. 'I don't think you can start working up to the festive season just yet. Give Father Christmas a bit of a rest first.'

Hattie pulled her mother to a stop, and fixed her with a beady eye.

'Is Father Christmas you and Daddy?'

Tess's heart missed a beat.

'Of course he isn't. He's a magical person who comes in the night.'

'How does he land on the roof?'

'Carefully.'

'And how does he get down the chimney?'

'He's very good at sliding,' Tess said, firmly.

'How do all the reindeer fit on the roof?'

'They have very small hooves.'

'Jake says he's you and Daddy. Jake says Father Christmas isn't in real life.'

Tess made a mental note to carpet Jake. What the hell was he doing, spoiling the magic of Christmas? There was a damn sight too much experience in their house at the moment, and not enough innocence by far.

'Is God in real life?' Hattie said, moving on to a different tack and swinging on Tess's hand. Tess paused, to let a woman with three small children and a medium-sized dog of indeterminate breed pass them. The woman was saying, 'For fuck's sake, Jasmin, I never said you could have them trainers.'

'Well,' Tess said, loudly. 'He is – kind of. He's not a real person, not like you and me but He's more of a being, someone up in heaven who watches over us and keeps us safe.'

'He didn't keep Princess Diana very safe.'

Hattie had been much affected by the death of Princess Diana, even though she had been only three at the time. Somehow all the grief and the trauma had pierced her three-year-old consciousness and Diana had assumed, in Hattie's fevered imagination, a kind of godly status, a mixture of the most beautiful Barbie in the world and the Angel Gabriel. Tess wondered if she wasn't far wrong.

'Can He see me now?' Hattie asked, suspiciously.

'He sees everything we do,' Tess replied, confidently.

'Even going to the toilet?'

'Hattie! I hardly think that's relevant.'

'Does He see the Queen on the loo?' Tess glared at her. 'Well, you said He sees everything. Can we play on the swings?'

Tess looked over at the play area. A group of youths were sitting on the swings, throwing a flick knife in turns at a beer can. They were smoking, and passing something around – Tess couldn't quite see what but it looked like a can. They were making a lot of noise, a kind of indeterminate roar of which 'fuck' seemed to be the most prevalent word.

'Let's go and see the ducks instead,' she said.

'Are you frightened of those boys?' Hattie asked.

'Of course not, darling. I just don't think there's room.'

'Two of them go to my school,' Hattie said.

Tess looked at her in horror. 'Do they?'

'Yup,' Hattie said. 'Who's God's wife?'

'He doesn't have a wife.'

'No Mrs God? How come Jesus was born?'

'Jesus wasn't born to Mrs God, you know that. He was born to the Virgin Mary.' As soon as Tess said this, she regretted it.

'What *is* a virgin? Am I a virgin?'

'A virgin is – nothing, darling. Look at that silly duck. He's got stuck in the reeds.'

'Why didn't we bring any bread?'

'Because I forgot.'

'You're forgetting lots more things since you started at your college,' Hattie said, with weary stoicism. 'You forgot my packed lunch on Friday, remember? And I had to do PE all week without my shorts. I had to wear just knickers.'

'No need to rub it in. You shared Alice's lunch, didn't you?'

'It wasn't the same. She had cucumber sandwiches not ham because her mum's a vegetarian. She says meat is murder. Is it?'

How lovely it is, Tess thought, to have a clever child. How lovely it is to have a child with an endlessly questioning mind, who cannot simply accept a concept but must always know the whys and wherefores.

134

'Hattie,' she said. 'Just shut up, will you?'

She had left Mark at home with the boys. Jake had wanted to go off and meet some friends to go roller-blading in Battersea Park, but he was currently under a cloud after Tess and Mark had been called in to see his headmaster, and had been grounded. He had been overheard swearing in the corridors for the second time in only a week.

That Wednesday afternoon she and Mark had been ushered into the head's study, a place of almost sepulchral calm with wood panelling and a blazing fire. The head's leather-covered table, which stood underneath a window looking out over the circular entrance drive, was piled high with papers, an antique brass table lamp balanced precariously on the edge. It was to a round table in the middle of the room, where a handful of reports lay, that he beckoned Tess and Mark.

'Do sit down,' he said, in a friendly manner, pulling up a chair.

They sat awkwardly, Tess wishing that Mark had acceded to her demands to put on a tie, if only to be polite. He seemed out of place in these surroundings, too outdoor-looking, too casual, almost too young to be a parent here. He always stuck out like a sore thumb at school events, many of the other fathers City types, wearing their 'casual' weekend country clothes of moss-green tweeds and moleskin shirts from Boden. They spoke in loud, confident voices, exchanging greetings in a look-at-me kind of way, quite at home, having been to private school themselves. They had found only a handful of kindred-spirit parents to be friendly with, and Tess felt that taking Mark to a school event was rather like lobbing a hand grenade into Evensong. She never knew quite when he might go off. It annoyed her when he reacted against this kind of group conformity – of course this hadn't been his life, but it didn't mean that everything about it was false or pretentious. He became purposefully contentious and sarcastic, as if he was the only one who had to do any real honest-to-goodness work to pay the fees. She accused him of inverted snobbery and he said she lacked the courage not to always try to fit in.

Tess wondered anew if they had been right to send Jake here. He was so like Mark, so inclined to rebel when faced with authority, yet he had so much to give – he was such a bright, intuitive boy if only he could be channelled. He couldn't learn just by rote, he needed a more creative, inspirational approach. They had first hoped that the calm, traditional methods employed by the school with their tenet, 'Discipline is not a problem here, we know the boys too well', would work, but clearly it hadn't. Thank God Jake was such a hero on the sports field, or Tess was sure they would have booted him out already.

Dr Williams made a steeple of his fingers and surveyed them thoughtfully. Tess coughed, and shifted nervously on her chair. Mark was regarding the head belligerently, in a bad mood already because Tess had insisted he come with her, although he argued he had far too much work and would have to miss an important meeting. Tess also knew how uncomfortable he was feeling. Oh God, she thought. What is he going to say? Dr Williams, with his checked shirt and corduroy jacket wearing thin at the elbows, was hardly a symbol of the British establishment Mark loathed, but he was so hypersensitive about being patronized in any way that he found it hard to relax in any situation over which he had little control.

When they had first met Dr Williams they had been surprised by his slightly bumbling manner, but behind the relaxed attitude lay a razor-sharp intelligence and an iron will.

'Jake,' Dr Williams said in a quiet, reasonable voice.

'Yes?' Tess said, raising her chin.

'We are having a few problems with him, as you know.'

'I know,' she said. 'We have spoken to him but I'm afraid he seems to be going through a rather tricky time at the moment.'

'I think he needs – how can I put this – reining in a little. The swearing is only the tip of the iceberg, I'm afraid. He's a bright boy, but at the moment it worries me that his intelligence isn't properly focused.' He tapped the reports in front of him. 'His marks bear this out. He is sliding down the class, and he shouldn't be anywhere near the bottom. Of course this is our responsibility too, and we are doing all we can to encourage and interest him. I just wondered – do forgive me for asking – are there any problems at home?' He paused, and looked directly at Tess. She thought wildly, What on earth does he mean? Does he think this is all our fault?

'Well,' she said, feeling the blood rising in her cheeks, 'I am doing a course at university which means the boys are having to look after themselves a bit more. But on the whole they've behaved really responsibly, and I can't see this would be a factor.'

'And do you know they are at home after school?' he enquired, pleasantly.

'Of course,' Tess said, stung. She didn't dare look at Mark. 'I ring Jake to check and they have always eaten by the time I get home.'

'He is bringing a lot of money into school.'

Tess and Mark looked at him in astonishment.

'What?'

'He was found with fifty pounds on him last week.'

'That's not possible,' Tess said, quickly. 'He only gets a small amount of pocket money from us, and he doesn't have a Saturday job, he's still a year too young.'

'I can only give you the evidence we have uncovered,' Dr Williams said, reasonably. 'We are finding it rather worrying.'

'What reason did Jake give?' Mark's voice was dangerously calm.

'He said it was his pocket money.'

'But why would he bring it into school?'

'Why indeed?' Dr Williams looked puzzled. 'I have talked to Jake, at some length,' he went on. 'But he could not – or would not – tell me where the money came from. He may be protecting another boy, or he may have a perfectly innocent explanation. It's very common for boys of this age to be taciturn, but I have spelled out to him that we need to know, and he has to stop bringing in this amount of money. His form tutor is working closely with him, and rest assured we will do everything we can to get his marks back up. But if there is anything you would like to talk to us about, then please do. It would be such a shame if Jake didn't perform as well as he should in his exams next year. He has so much potential.'

'So what do you plan to do about it?' Mark said. 'This is all very polite, but it doesn't seem to be getting us anywhere. We will talk to him at home, and don't you worry, we'll find out how he came by that money. And I want to know the second he steps out of line again, and what punishment you intend to use.' Dr Williams glanced at Mark's tense, angry face.

'Oh, we will keep you in touch, don't worry. We may seem to be very relaxed here, but I can assure you we will not tolerate bad manners or dishonesty of any kind.'

'I know,' Tess said quickly. 'I think Jake needs to know just how lucky he is.'

'He certainly needs discipline, which he doesn't always get at home,' Mark said.

Tess looked at him, horrified. 'That's hardly true,' she said, as calmly as she could. 'He knows where the boundaries are. He's fine at home,' she said, reassuringly, to Dr Williams.

'Rubbish,' Mark said sharply. 'You indulge him.' Dr Williams looked at them uncomfortably.

'I don't think this is the time or the place to have this discussion, do you, Mark? Thanks very much, Dr Williams. We will talk to him, and you'll let us know, won't you, if there are any further problems? This is a wonderful school, and we really appreciate everything you are doing with both Jake and Ollie, don't we, Mark?' Mark said nothing, and looked out of the window. Dr Williams smiled at her.

'Oh, Ollie,' he said. 'Ollie is no problem whatsoever. Very clever and very hard-working. One of our rising stars. Which Jake will be again, I'm sure,' he added, quickly.

'Thank you,' Tess said. He was such a lovely man, she couldn't understand why Mark had to be so rude. Dr Williams stood up to usher them out. He stretched out his hand to Tess, who shook it warmly.

Mark stood back, away from them. 'Goodbye,' he said, and, nodding at Dr Williams, walked swiftly out of the room. Tess caught Dr Williams's eye. She detected a note of sympathy.

'Thank you again. I'm sure we can sort this out.'

'Of course.'

Outside, Mark was waiting for her by the stone entrance. His mouth was set in a hard, angry line. 'Don't ever do that again,' he said, quietly.

'What?' Tess hissed back, as a group of boys in navy blue blazers filed past them.

'Shut me up in front of someone, as if I had no right to speak.'

'I didn't,' she said. 'Come on. Let's go home. All I said was that this wasn't the time or the place to have a domestic argument about whether or not I am tough enough with Jake. It's hardly relevant.'

'Of course it's bloody relevant! What that man was saying is that Jake is getting away with murder at home and he's bringing that attitude into school. You're letting him run riot – God knows what he's doing when you're not there.'

'Oh hang on,' Tess said, grabbing his arm, forcing him to turn. A teacher walked past them, and murmured, 'Good afternoon.' Tess smiled back at him, waiting for him to get far enough away before she spoke.

'What do you mean, I'm letting him run riot? What about you? Do you have no say in this matter? Why exactly is Jake's behaviour all my fault?'

'Because you are the one who always says, "Don't shout at him, Mark. Don't punish him" when he's deliberately cheeky or just won't bloody well communicate. I try my best to knock some sense into him but you refuse to back me up. And don't you think it's just a slight coincidence that we're having these problems since you decided you absolutely had to study in the library rather than at home, and even then you spend most evenings on that bloody computer?'

Tess, who was just about to climb into the car, stopped dead.

'Oh, please,' she said. 'Jake's been bolshy for almost two years now, but for heaven's sake, it's his age. Don't you remember what you were like? All he's doing is trying to establish his own independence and it doesn't help that you do nothing but criticize him instead of spending any useful time with him. What happened last Sunday? You took Ollie and Hattie to the park to fly their kites, but you didn't even ask Jake to go with you.'

'As a matter of fact, I did,' Mark said. 'But he said he'd rather stay at home and listen to his music. I am not always criticizing him, it's just that someone in our house has to stand up to him occasionally and unfortunately that person always seems to be me.'

'As if,' she said. 'Come on. We need to go and get Hattie from Clara's. We'll be late. I have so much work to do too . . .' Her voice tailed off.

'Of course. And that's what's important, isn't it? Your work. Not your family, not our son who is currently out of control but some fucking essay about some fucking dead artist. How silly of me.'

They drove home in furious silence.

Chapter Fourteen

'If you tip it up any more the whole bloody lot's going to come down.'

Mark was standing on a chair, precariously holding the top of the Christmas tree. As usual, he had bought one at least two sizes too large for the TV room, a tree more suitable as the centrepiece of the Yuletide celebrations of a metropolitan city.

'Dad, for God's sake, I'm squashed here.' Jake was pinioned behind the tree, having elected to attempt to plug in the lights. However, the size of Jake and the space available behind the tree did not equate. Mark, who was trying to put the fairy on the top, caught the tree just in time after Jake made an ill-advised move.

'You'll kill her!' Hattie shrieked, from below. Hattie was exceptionally fond of their fairy, perched on the top, who was a wispy-looking thing in a frayed green netting skirt with a garishly painted face. Originally she had had lustrous blond hair, but most of this had been pulled off by the boys when they were young and now she was partly bald, as if suffering from alopecia. Her gilt knickers had rubbed away too, a fact which had thrilled Jake when he first made the discovery at the age of six.

'Hand me up that last bit of tinsel,' Mark said. 'Ouch, these bloody pine needles are sticking in me.'

'You were the one who insisted on a real tree,' Tess pointed out.

'You didn't really want a fake one, did you?'

'No, but we could have bought one of those non-drop ones. We must be the only family in Clapham with an eight-foot tree which will be completely bald by Christmas.'

'It doesn't help if you have a yeti behind it doing the conga.'

'I am just,' Jake said, in a muffled voice, 'trying to get these bloody lights plugged in.' There was a pause. 'Sorry.'

Tess stifled an admonition. Ever since she had sat Jake down in the kitchen the evening after they had been to see the headmaster, and told him that unless he got his act together he would definitely be kicked out, he had appeared to be making a determined effort to behave better. When they had got home, after picking Hattie up from her childminder's, Mark said, 'Right. You are going to sort this out. I am sick of being the ogre,' and he had stomped off to his study.

At first Jake was sulky and uncommunicative. But Tess had pointed out that his behaviour was reflecting really badly on them, her especially.

'Why you?' Jake said.

'Because Dad says I let you off with murder,' she replied.

'Yeah, right,' he muttered, twisting his bootlace round and round. 'As if he cares.'

'He does care. Stop doing that. Look, Jake, you cannot go around sounding off and being so vile to everyone. It's incredible that you've got away with it at school. Look at me.' Jake, who was lolling on the kitchen chair, his school tie at half mast and his shirt

143

unbuttoned, looked up sulkily from beneath his thick, dark lashes.

'What?'

'I mean, you're really lucky they haven't decided to kick you out. Honestly.'

'So?'

'So,' she said, temper rising. 'So Dad and I are spending a fortune keeping you there in the first place, and the least you could do is bloody well work hard. I don't expect thanks,' he flashed the glimmer of an amused smile at her, and she had to forcibly stop herself smiling back, 'but I do expect you to try. Jake, for God's sake, you know what the alternative is. A huge comprehensive where you wouldn't get an iota of the attention you're getting at St Peter's and about an eighth of the sport. Please,' she said, leaning forward to put her hand over his, squeezing it. 'Don't let us down. Don't let me down. All we need to know is where you got the money and that you'll promise not to swear and to get your head down and do some work for a change. OK?'

'OK,' he said, giving her the full benefit of his heartbreaking smile. 'I got the money from Nick, I sold him some of my computer games.'

'But why did you need the money?'

'No reason,' he said, quickly. 'He just wanted them so bad I thought I'd let him have them. It's not a big thing, is it? I'll get them back if you want.'

'No, it's OK. I trust you.'

'I'm glad somebody in this family does.'

'Dad does, really. Just give him a chance. Come on. None of us want to fight. It's nearly Christmas. Please, we love you.'

'I know *you* do.'

'So does Dad. Really.' Jake raised a mocking eyebrow at her, and got up.

'Give me a hug, you big eejit.'

He reached down from behind, and put his strong,

tanned forearms around her. She leant back against him. 'How did you get to be so big?' she said.

'Not from your cooking, that's for certain,' he said, laughing.

'Just go away,' she said.

He ruffled her hair. 'I love you.'

'I know. Show it then.'

Ever since then, he had watched his language around the house, especially when Hattie was in the room and had even been witnessed – and this really was a first – lying on the snug floor with Hattie helping her with her jigsaws. Ollie was amazed to find that he no longer threw all his possessions onto Ollie's side of the room and – temporarily, at least – stopped pinching his headphones because his were broken. Ollie, sagely, knew it wouldn't last but was enjoying the current lull in hostilities.

This year Tess was determined to make Christmas perfect. Every year she meant to wave her womanly wand and make this *the* Christmas they would remember, but something always went badly wrong at the last minute. Last year she and Mark had had an almighty row about her buying Jake a PlayStation without asking Mark first – she pointed out he was away so much it was kind of hard asking thin air – and the year before that Hattie had fallen off her pogo stick and fractured her collarbone so she and Tess spent Christmas Day in Casualty with assorted drunks. The year before that her parents had come to stay and Mark had got so drunk he was asleep by three in the afternoon and she had to carve the turkey under the pitying gaze of her mother. But this year she was more determined than ever to be a domestic goddess with a beautifully decorated home and a fridge stocked with home-made delicacies rather than most of the contents of Marks and Spencer's Food Hall bought in a rush on Christmas Eve. Only she didn't have enough time. Maybe giving up sleep was the answer.

Not only that, she was also determined to be more sexy and had bought, with embarrassment, two pairs of lacy hold-up stockings from the underwear shop on the High Street. Maybe her mother was right and meeting Mark halfway was the answer. She had to admit she had been rather obsessed by her course of late, but it was all so new and fascinating that remembering to unload the dishwasher and buy bread had become pretty low down her list of priorities. Unfortunately they were pretty low down everyone else's list of priorities too, and the house was in danger of sealing over with grime. If only she could afford a cleaner to beat back the advancing army of dust. Not caring was probably the answer, but so far she hadn't perfected that particular art. Instead she felt guilty and caught herself hoovering at midnight.

And what was really making her and Margi livid was the way in which Vanessa had transformed her home into a *Country Homes and Interiors* wonderland, with every mantelpiece, every banister and every doorway swagged and tailed and beribboned with tartans, greenery and outsize pine cones. It was like stepping into a living Christmas card. It made the paper chains festooning her house, the work of Hattie and Ollie, look rather limp. Vanessa's children weren't allowed within spitting distance of her decorations.

'Bugger me,' Margi said, when Vanessa invited her and Tess round for drinks. 'It's like Harrods. How much did this lot cost?'

'Under a thousand,' Vanessa said defensively. 'Ish.'

'Did you do all this yourself?'

'Yes. Sort of.'

'Be honest.'

'OK, OK, I got Emmanuel from Fleurtations in Hampstead.'

'Aha! Then it doesn't count. I refuse to feel envious of anyone who has simply thrown money at the problem.'

'I don't care,' Tess said dreamily, taking in the host of candles reflected in the heavy gilt mirrors, the greenery, the bows and the cards so elegantly displayed, 'I'd just like to move in for the whole of Christmas. Could you do bed and breakfast?'

'Only if you bring your divine husbandwith you.'

'Husband? Do I have a husband?'

'Still working hard?' Margi said, sympathetically.

'He's never home. Hattie had a fit about it the other day because he had promised to come and watch her carol concert and he turned up five minutes before the end. Never mind the fact that I had to miss a lecture to be there. We were two verses into "Oh Come All Ye Faithful" when there was this great crashing at the back and Mark fell through the door. I'd saved him a seat, which was bloody hard in such a cramped hall – I had a baby practically on my head all the way through – so he had to fight his way over all these grannies' knees to get to me. Still, at least Hattie knew he had come – you could hardly miss him.'

Vanessa pressed a glass of mulled wine into her hand. Tess looked at her closely.

'You look really lovely, you know.'

'Do I?' Vanessa laughed, turning her head this way and that so her sleek blond bob fell against her unlined, glossy cheek.

'It's Botox, isn't it?' Margi said, peering at her forehead. 'Or have you gone the whole hog? I thought your eyebrows looked higher,' she added, suspiciously.

'I have not gone the whole hog, as you so rudely put it,' Vanessa said. 'I may have had a little injection, hardly anything at all.' Both Tess and Margi leant forward to examine her minutely.

'There must be an entire flock of lamb foetuses in there,' Margi pronounced.

'It's amazing,' Tess said, in wonder. 'No frown lines, no eye bags, not even any lines from the corner of your eyes. I'm sorry, but that cannot just be injections.'

'It's a lifetime of no stress,' Margi said. 'If I only had to wave my credit cards about and plan the next holiday I wouldn't have a face that looks like a screwed-up brown paper bag.'

'I have stress!' Vanessa said, sitting back on her tartan-covered chair, shocked. 'You have no idea how stressful setting up this house in France is proving. All the things I have to buy – of course, it's going to be primarily a party house, so I need at least thirty sets of everything. There is just so much to think about.'

'I may have to kill her,' Margi said to Tess, and then turned to Vanessa. 'Do you know what it's like trying to put on a merry Christmas for a family when you only stop work at seven o'clock on Christmas Eve and start again the day after Boxing Day? I have bought precisely three presents so far – and all of them came from Knickerbox because it's next to the tube. I will have to buy all the food in one go on the Saturday before Christmas Day which is like trying to buy Brussels sprouts in a Tiananmen Square uprising, and then on Boxing Day my girls will go to stay with their father and Suzi the handbag will give them ten times as many presents as I have. And while I have said absolutely positively "no" to a mobile phone for Georgina because she is only thirteen, Miss Thong-Wearing Aphid will have persuaded my git of an ex-husband to buy her one. Do not,' she said, brandishing a home-made mince pie at Vanessa, 'give me Christmas stress.'

'Did I mention the fact,' Vanessa responded, artlessly, 'that you and Tess are invited to come and stay in St Jean de Luce at Easter?'

'I take it all back,' Margi said, hastily. 'You are a martyr and a saint and your life is hell. How you manage to remain so naturally unlined is one of God's little wonders.'

'Can our families come too?' Tess said hopefully.

'Of course,' Vanessa said, tuning her headlamp eyes on Tess. 'It's got masses of room. Not that I'm boasting, or anything.'

'Eight bedrooms!' Margi said. 'Eight bedrooms and five bathrooms. It isn't a house. It's a bleeding hotel. You're not going to charge us, are you? Oh – and I want chocolates on my pillow. And a little basket of shampoo and body lotion. It's ages since I went anywhere luxurious.'

'You're not coming if you're only going to take the piss, OK?'

Margi held her hands up in front of her. 'I promise I won't. I'll even be nice to Ed and talk to him about share options and market growth.'

'Even Jake can come?' Tess said, thoughtfully, through a mince pie.

'Especially Jake, I hope,' Margi said. 'There's no way my girls would go without Jake. They are both completely in love with him.'

'Not Francesca? She must be sixteen now. What on earth would she see in Jake? I know she used to quite like him, but she must have masses of older boys after her.'

'Especially Francesca. She isn't massively worldly-wise for her age, and I don't think she can handle boys her own age. She says they are only interested in one thing.'

'Of course they are. So what makes Jake any different?'

'She says he talks to her about things.'

'How? When?'

'They text-message each other all the time. Didn't you know?'

'No. How do you know?' Tess said.

149

'I read them when she's asleep,' Margi said, licking crumbs from around her mouth. 'Don't you read Jake's?'

'He sleeps with his phone under his pillow, so it would be a bit tricky. Anyway, I wouldn't dare. I can't bear to think what I might find. I had no idea he and Francesca were close. He never mentions her.'

'Our children,' Margi said wisely, 'live powerful secret lives. We think we know them, but we don't know the half of it, and probably a good job too. Just think what we were like at their age.'

'Pretty blameless,' Tess said, sadly. 'But I might have a word with Jake about Francesca. She's too old for him. Anyway, I didn't think he was really interested in girls.'

Both Margi and Vanessa shrieked. 'Not interested in girls!' Margi yelled. 'Looking like that! God, he's like the Pied Piper walking down the King's Road. Francesca showed her friends a picture of him and now they're all in love with him as well. He has his own fan club, you know. It'll be a web site soon. Anyway, don't you think it's rather fascinating when your children start to get interested in the opposite sex? It's kind of vicarious, as if you can live through all those thrilling times again without the hassle of actually having to do it yourself.'

'You shouldn't be allowed to be a mother,' Vanessa said, pretending to be shocked. 'I can't imagine quizzing Clemmie about her boyfriends.'

'More fool you,' Margi said, taking a slug of wine. 'It's riveting.'

'Anyway,' Tess said sharply, taking a sip of warm wine and keen to avert one of their niggles at each other – in the triumvirate, Tess tended to be the peacemaker – as well as being eager to steer the conversation off the disconcerting subject of Jake's sex appeal. 'Talking about doing it yourself, what happened to Rowan? You haven't mentioned him for ages.'

'He dumped me, the bastard.'

'No!'

'He said he wasn't looking for any kind of commitment because he's over here for such a short time and he was worried I was getting too keen.'

'But you were hardly looking for commitment,' Tess pointed out. 'All you wanted was to extract his luscious young body from his boxer shorts.'

'I am afraid,' Margi said, 'he found a rather more luscious young body than mine. The secretary in the next office to mine, the minx. He came in to see me once at the office and I could tell she fancied him. Anyway she and he are currently in Ireland, if you must know, no doubt drinking Guinness on Grafton Street and laughing about my cellulite and sagging tits.'

'Oh, I'm sorry,' Tess said. 'Anyway, you couldn't really go out with someone called Rowan. Maybe you need someone a bit, you know, nearer our age.'

'I don't want to go to bed with some wrinkly old bloke! We're talking recaptured youth here,' she said.

Tess and Vanessa tried not to look offended. 'Not all men over forty are past it,' Tess ventured. 'Look at – Sting.' There was a long pause while they all looked dreamily into space. 'But it isn't just Sting's body we long for, is it? It's the fact that he's a wonderful father and so spiritually aware and thoughtful and intelligent. And faithful to his wife.'

'And rich,' Margi pointed out. There was another pause, until Margi sat back decisively. 'Nope. I'm sorry, but it's his body and face for me. Can I have another glass? That wine is totally delicious.'

Wandering down Oxford Street with a mind like an overstuffed wheelie bin, Tess reflected that Christmas had changed an awful lot since she was a child. When she was growing up, even though her parents were by no means badly off, there hadn't been this positive orgy of present-giving, with the expectation being that each child received at least thirty presents each and the festivities went on from the first week in December well into January. Already she and Mark had been to five Christmas parties including his work's party, and there were three more scheduled for this week alone. Thank goodness they would be alone for Christmas itself – her parents had said they really ought to stay at home this year as they had so many invitations from friends themselves, and Tess's grandmother was still alive at the age of ninety-five and living in a nursing home nearby. Jean didn't feel it was fair to leave her alone, even though it could have been St Swithin's Day for all she knew. Thank God, really, because the house was far too small for all of them.

From every shop came the tinny sound of Christmas pop music, so the street was filled with an anodyne blend of seasonal noise. Hattie was already beside herself, waking at five every morning, bouncing up and down on their bed whispering, 'Is it Christmas yet?' Tess was trying to get the house straight, having what she thought would be a glorious three weeks off until her course resumed.

Only it wasn't very glorious, she thought, as a small child wearing flashing reindeer antlers on her head pushed past her on the way into Benetton. Their bank statement had arrived this morning – what kind of sadistic computer would post bank statements in the week before Christmas? – revealing that they were currently massively overdrawn. They were way past their limit and Tess had had to ring and do a great deal of grovelling, explaining that Mark's seasonal bonus should be arriving any day now and that should leave them a little in credit. Only they needed all of that money to pay for her course fees, and the boys' school fees were another great dollop of money to go out at the beginning of next term. Ho, bloody ho, she thought. Merry Christmas. But how could you have a Merry Christmas without buying lovely things? Most of the time she tried not to spend money by avoiding shops, but you could hardly avoid shops when you had to buy a hundred and two presents.

So, holding Hattie firmly by the hand, she dived into Benetton. And bought her the most adorable red fleecy coat with a hood, because she did need a new coat and you could not spend your whole life denying yourself things. It was bad for the soul. Then they battled their way down Regent Street towards Hamleys. It was almost four o'clock, and already it was beginning to go dark. Light thickens, and the crow makes wing to the rooky wood, she thought. Good things of day begin to droop and drowse. Only it wasn't rooks, it was mothy-looking pigeons, and for rooky wood read Oxford Circus tube sign.

But it was beautiful, she thought, pausing by the steps to the tube, next to the grubby man selling the evening newspaper. Buffeted by crowds consumed with shopping fever – only four days left, hurry, hurry – she stopped and took in the scene. The lights from the shops spilled out on the street, every window a masterpiece of tasteless self-indulgence. Overhead, the illuminations had just flicked on – a gaudy fairy tale of iridescent light, white, gold, red, green and orange. Hattie adored the lights, gazing at them in speechless delight.

I must not spend too much money, she thought, stepping into the hallowed portals of Hamleys. We have a massive overdraft and none of the children actually need any more toys or games.

'Mind out!' She ducked as a sales assistant sent a boomerang whizzing past her head.

An hour later, she and Hattie emerged, grinning from ear to ear. In Tess's arms was an enormous stuffed fox, and she was clutching a host of carrier bags containing computer games and books for Ollie and Jake. They took a taxi home, and hugged all the way.

Hattie's face hovered an inch from her own. Tess had been dreaming about Margi's Rowan, bizarrely, as she tried to impress upon him the fact that she was a happily married woman and did not want to make love in a broom cupboard.

'Oh!' she said, startled.

Hattie's face was just beaming.

'He came,' she said, simply.

'Did he? Oh darling, have you looked?'

Hattie nodded, almost too excited to speak.

'Come on,' she said, reaching under the bedclothes to find Tess's hand, pulling her out of bed. Mark's leg lay heavily over her, and she gently pushed it aside. He didn't wake.

'Hang on a minute, Hat,' she said, levering herself out of bed. Her head was pounding considerably, probably from the bottle of champagne she and Mark had consumed on top of all the wine at Margi's Christmas Eve drinks party, which Hattie had had to attend as well, mainly because most of their babysitters were there. Tess had kept a very close eye on Jake and Francesca, but they hadn't tried to be alone – all the teenagers had stayed together, lying in various poses of abandonment in front of a video. Hattie had fallen asleep on top of Jake, who later carried her out to the car. Tess had noted that Francesca's eyes did follow him, although he hadn't bothered to say goodbye. Margi and her girls were due round for drinks at twelve, so she'd have to clear the debris which would no doubt ensue as the boys and Hattie ripped into their presents.

Downstairs, it felt cold. 'What time is it, Hat?'

'It's twenty to nine,' she said, in a definite voice. Tess looked out of the window and then at the clock. It was pitch-black outside. 'No it isn't. It's half past six. I think we had better just look at the presents, don't you, and then maybe you could read for a little while until the boys and Daddy get up.'

Oh fucketty fuck, she and Mark had been too pissed to remember to eat the Christmas cake and drink the whisky.

'Hattie, could you just nip down into the kitchen and let Nigel out? He must be bursting, darling, go on.' She stood in front of the snug door.

'Do I have to?'

'Yes, go on, darling, I'll put the lights on. It'll only take you a minute.' Hattie sulkily thumped off down the stairs. Tess flicked on the light in the snug, and shot over to the fireplace. Christmas cake. Christmas cake with the hangover from hell and a stomach turbulent from oysters eaten at one o'clock in the morning. She and Mark had attempted to tiptoe around the house bringing out presents from various hiding places, but they kept falling over each other and laughing.

'Oof!' Mark said, as she tried to step over him lying on the floor, her arms full of presents for Ollie and Jake. 'Whose idea was Barbie's castle?' On the box it had looked fantastic, a baroque pink mansion with lots of turrets and flowery window boxes and shutters which opened and closed. It was only at half past one they had opened the box to check everything was there before Tess wrapped it, to discover it came in 1.2 million pieces. 'I'll never do this tomorrow,' Mark said, sorrowfully. 'Correction. I have no intention of spending all of tomorrow fitting plastic pieces together.'

'Well, you'll have to do it now,' Tess said, giggling. Which was why they had both sat up until almost three owlishly trying to click interconnecting bits of walls and floors together with decreasing amounts of success until at least the basic structure was assembled. Mark sat back on his heels. 'Thank Christ for that,' he said. Tess delved into the box and brought out a plastic bag containing roughly two hundred and fifty tiny flowers which needed sticking onto green stems for the window boxes. 'I don't think so, do you?' Mark said, lobbing them behind the sofa.

Tess heard Hattie's feet coming back up the stairs. Hurriedly, she grabbed the glass of whisky, and downed it in one. She took one look at the cake, burped, and thrust it behind a cushion. Then she reached behind the tree, stepping carefully over the presents, and flicked on the lights.

Hattie stood in wonder by the door. The multi-coloured fairy lights shone onto the mound of presents, each little bulb reflected in the shiny green, gold and blue wrapping paper.

She sighed. 'He really came.'

There was a noise behind them. Tess turned to see Mark, who put his finger to his lips. He was naked, apart from a towel wrapped around his waist. He bent down, and wrapped his arms around Hattie from behind. 'He came for you,' he said, softly. Hattie, without looking, reached up and wound a finger into Mark's hair.

'He is in real life, isn't he?'

'Of course he is.'

'Shall I wake the boys?' Tess stood up. 'It's just about getting light.'

'Yeah, why not.'

Tess turned to go up to the boys' room, pulling her dressing gown more tightly around her. Mark carried Hattie gently over to her presents.

Chapter Fifteen

'I'd have his babies any day.'

Nicki leant sideways, whispering into Tess's ear. They were sitting in a tight semicircle in her tutorial group. Tess shot her an appalled look, but not before Michael Frost, their tutor, paused in what he was saying to give them his most quizzical smile.

'Would you like to repeat that for the benefit of the entire group?'

'I said,' Nicki intoned quite clearly, 'I would have your babies any day.'

'How incredibly reassuring,' he said, without missing a beat. 'I will bear it in mind in case I tire unexpectedly of the present Mrs Frost. Anyway, as I was saying, the period of the Impressionists was an extremely active one both politically and morally in French society. The role of the woman . . .'

Tess suppressed an urge to laugh. She had never met anyone like Nicki, who really didn't care what anyone thought about her. Tess felt she was the most liberating woman she had ever met, and she was beginning to see just what a sheltered life she herself had led. Nicki had three sons she had raised herself in a tiny council flat. After her husband left, she made ends meet by working in a shop while the children were at school, but once the boys were old enough to let themselves in and out of the flat and make a meal without setting fire to the place, she had determined to try to get the one thing she had longed for most in life – an education. So she had funded herself, by working in a bar every evening and at the weekends, to take a three-year History of Art degree, and had now decided, because she enjoyed studying so much, she would go on to take an MA. Her MA was being funded by Hackney Council, under a new education scheme for single mothers.

She was incredibly bright and could easily have gone to university first time around, but, as she quite cheerfully said, women of her class and background were hardly encouraged to try for university. Her mum was a single mum too, and really it had been a blessing when Nicki's husband pushed off, because he was a bit unpredictable when he drank. She was better off on her own, and all her children – the eldest two were now away travelling – were confident, adventurous and adored her. Tess thought she was brilliant. Mark thought she was a disruptive influence because she drank pints, smoked roll-ups and tried to make Tess more subversive.

Tess rationed the amount of times Nicki was allowed to come round to the house, because she did rather take over and tell Hattie all kinds of inappropriate things, like how pretty she would look with her ears pierced and had she ever thought of a nose ring? Plus the fact Tess was doing everything possible at the moment not to annoy Mark or make him feel that her course was in any way intruding.

Every morning as she set out for college, gathering up her files, books and papers, he would look up with the air of the truly abandoned. This morning he had said, 'Will you be home this evening?' and when she said no, she had to go to an evening lecture and could he pick Hattie up from Clara's, he sighed wistfully. Tess was bending over backwards to try to ensure the course didn't interfere with their lives, but of course it did – she had to leave at eight o'clock to get to the nine o'clock morning lecture and that meant either she or Mark had to take Hattie to Clara's first before school, all ready with her packed lunch and her book bag. The boys assumed an air of martyrdom but had in fact become much better at getting themselves out of bed, dressed and breakfasted, before going to school.

On the whole it worked pretty well – apart from the fact that Tess felt she was being run ragged. She was so determined not to let her studying affect the family that she found herself ironing at two o'clock in the morning and loading the tumble-dryer at six a.m. Fortunately Mark also worked late at home, so she felt justified about sitting up until all hours with the laptop on the kitchen table – they had first of all intended to share Mark's PC but that simply didn't work, as he argued her essays and research were taking up too much space on his hard disk – yeah, right, Tess thought – but the reality was he felt it was his computer and he didn't want to share it. So she had gone out and bought a laptop with an interest-free loan. She loved the laptop – it was like her little electronic friend, so responsive, so efficient and above all, so silent. It never sighed and looked martyred and it gave every appearance of being pleased to see her when she opened it up each day. Nor did it hunt about in its sock drawer first thing in the morning, sighing, before pulling out two ill-matched socks, one of which usually turned out to be Ollie's or Jake's. Nor did it ring her as she sat in a tutorial, saying was it six or six thirty it was supposed to pick up Hattie, whereupon she would hiss that it was actually five thirty and Clara had to go out that night because she had a parents' evening. And because Tess was nearer to home than Mark, consumed with guilt she would slide out, leap into a cab and run breathlessly into Clara's, to find Hattie's minder standing in the hall with her coat on.

Despite all the rushing about, however, she felt ten years younger. She felt so much more alive, positively bursting with all the information she was taking in. It was like seeing everything in her life with new eyes and it forced her to be so much more focused. Before, she felt she had been blundering about, her mind on a million things at once. Now, when she worked, she had to concentrate and blot everything else out, including Mark. The work was both mentally exhausting and yet hugely satisfying. She had decided to specialize in the work of the female Impressionists, with her biggest module concentrating on the works and life of Berthe Morisot. Finishing an essay gave her the greatest thrill of achievement, and it was wonderful to know she could still produce the goods – she had got firsts for both of her last essays – and that her brain hadn't melted into a kind of amorphous blob, only capable of remembering when to pick up the dry cleaning and whether Hattie had taken her recorder music to school.

Tess felt as if she was trying to run two lives. On the one hand there was Mark, home, the children, their social life and a great heap of things that needed doing. On the other hand was university, Nicki and her other friends, the need to study and be completely on her own. Neither life took to each other, and she occasionally wondered if it was all worth it, especially when she sat at her laptop, head in her hands, trying to concentrate, while Hattie banged on the door of the kitchen and said she was having a nightmare about giant ants and did she know that Ollie and Jake still had their television on at eleven at night? Mark tried to be interested in what she was doing but she could patently see through him that he thought it was a waste of time, and she had to carefully tiptoe around his hurt feelings if she rejected his proposal of a meal out because she was too busy. He said next time he'd book an appointment.

In the first few weeks, she had tried to get home every lunchtime. She drove back like a mad thing, threw herself out of the car and then spent three-quarters of an hour galloping around the house, flinging clothes into the laundry basket and loading the washing machine while she mopped the front of the microwave with the other hand. Then, one lunchtime, Nicki had taken her firmly by the arm.

'You,' she said, 'are not going home. You are coming with us.'

So Tess found herself sitting in the union bar, feeling absurdly old and appallingly neglectful. All the things that needed doing at home. The dishwasher needed emptying, they had no milk or bread, what were the children going to have for tea, what would she and Mark eat . . .

'Half a pint of lager?'

'Er – OK.'

So she had two half-pints of lager and a ham sandwich. And heard Nicki's life story and speculated about Mr Frost's sex life. And, hesitantly at first, talked about her plans for the future. Plans she hadn't, as yet, discussed with Mark because the subject of her future teaching career was something of a verboten subject.

'What does Mark think?' Nicki asked. 'Men usually hate women going back to education. They're scared it will reactivate their little brains and make them realize what fools they've been spending their lives picking up socks and trudging round Tesco.'

'Mark isn't like that,' Tess said, quickly. 'He's been

very supportive. He's Australian,' she found herself adding, bizarrely.

'Even worse,' Nicki said, shaking her head. 'Chauvinistic.'

Mark was convinced that Nicki was a lesbian whose sole purpose was getting Tess into bed. It provoked a row one night while Tess and Mark sat in the kitchen and the boys watched TV upstairs.

'Just because she doesn't have a man hardly means she is a dyke,' Tess said, trying not to laugh. 'Why do you always think that a woman without a man should be regarded with suspicion? Women do not need men to define themselves.'

'Oh for God's sake, Tess, what kind of crap is that? God save me from this loony liberal feminism,' Mark said, gloomily.

'Don't be such a reactionary,' Tess said.

'Did you really call me reactionary?' Mark looked at her in amazement. 'You always used to be on at me for not being conformist enough. Look, I'm just a bit suspicious about the way this woman seems to want to – to – devour you. She rings here all the time. She was even round here last weekend, traipsing about in that ludicrous hat with earflaps like some kind of mad llama. Can't we just go back to normal and have some kind of family life on our own without you always having to rush off to some lecture, write an essay or fill the house with nutters? Can't you see? Nicki is a fruitcake and she's only doing this course because she hasn't got anything else in her sad life. She's feeding off you. Are they all like that? It kind of confirms everything I have always suspected about mature students. They are all escaping from something, if only their own loneliness.'

'Oh, for God's sake, Mark. That is a ludicrous generalization. I have met more fascinating people on

162

this course than I have met in the past fifteen years. You are beginning to have a very blinkered outlook, you know. Nicki is not a fruitcake. She is a very bright, interesting person.'

'Interestingly full of cherries and candied peel,' Mark said, grinning.

'I thought you'd admire someone like her. Someone who has made their own way in life and has refused to bow down to the establishment. Or are you the establishment now?'

'I could admire her,' Mark said, 'if she wasn't in my house all the time drinking my drink and telling my eight-year-old she ought to get her stomach pierced. And what,' he said, picking up a newspaper in two disdainful fingers, 'is this?'

'It's the *Guardian*.'

'Since when did this house subscribe to the lovely liberal *Guardian*?' he said.

'Tell me you are teasing me.'

'Yeah, but it's so typical, isn't it? You have never read the *Guardian* in your life, saying it was a patronizing self-congratulatory organ for the chattering classes of Islington who are more obsessed with house prices and education than the bloody *Telegraph* readers, and here you are buying the damn thing and ingesting its subversive communist invective.'

Tess started to laugh, and poured herself another glass of wine. 'Even you,' she said, 'could not call a New Labour-supporting newspaper dangerously communist.'

'Well, it's all part of the downward spiral, isn't it?' he said. 'You'll stop shaving your armpits next. You'll be taking Hattie on feminist self-awareness courses in Hackney and forcing the boys to read Germaine Greer . . .'

'Why,' Tess said, 'do you always have to make fun of me? Why do you have to focus on the negative sides –

or what you perceive as the negative sides – of what I am doing? Can't you see that I am really enjoying myself, really enjoying this course and feel more fulfilled than I have for years?'

'Fulfilled?' he said, looking at her beadily. 'Wherefore fulfilled?'

'Fulfilled in the sense that I am finally using my brain and I stand the chance, if I pass this course and then get my PGCE and use it to get the job I want, of actually doing something of which I can be proud. Something I can look back on and think, "I did that with my life." Don't you understand? You just take it for granted that you have this career which gives you a reason for getting up in the morning. I have loved being at home with the children, and looking after you, but surely you can see that it isn't the same? Can't you see that you can hardly look back over your life and say, "I was a great mother, and boy, did I keep the house tidy"?'

'Why not?'

'Well, could you imagine looking back over your life and listing your achievements as "Great Father"? If anyone asked you what you were most proud of, what would you say? Would it be, "I brought up three children," or "I am a director of a big wine firm"? Can't you see? Work defines men, so why shouldn't it define women? We aren't some different species, with lower expectations, who feel things differently from you, and don't mind achieving less. I feel just the same as you about the family – I adore them, but they aren't who I am.'

Mark looked at her for a long moment.

'Actually,' he said, 'if I could list "Great Father" as you put it, then, yes, I would be very proud, prouder of that than anything else. And one of the reasons,' he added, slowly, 'I married you was because I thought you knew about families. I didn't. And that you had the right values and could show me what to do and how to be a good parent. Now it feels as if none of that has been very important or held any real significance for you. What you are doing now is the important bit, isn't it?'

He pushed the wine glass away from him, and stood up.

Tess sat with a sinking feeling in her stomach. This was going wrong. What she had wanted to convey to Mark was the importance of what she was doing for her own sanity; she needed to get him on her side so he would put up with the odd inconvenience to his life. And it was so rare for Mark to reveal himself. He loathed talking about his own family, and he had never been one for introspection or analysis of his emotions. Deep down, Tess knew that the very normality and security of her family had been one of the things that drew him to her, but wild horses would not have dragged such an admission from him before. He used to tease her about being anally repressed by the strictures of her childhood – no eating in the streets, no elbows on the table, put your hand over your mouth when you cough – and yet now here he was trying to argue that she was throwing it all away.

'Don't be so ridiculous!' she said. 'We were just discussing this. It isn't an argument. Mark, please. Sit down. Finish your wine.' She reached out to take his arm. He pulled it away.

'I'm going to bed.'

Without a backward glance, he walked up the stairs.

'Don't be so childish!' she called after him. But he had gone.

She sat back against her chair and reached for her glass. Why was everyone conspiring to try to make her feel guilty? The boys were just as bad, packing their own sports bags in a martyred way, asking if she possibly had time to wash their kit. Only Hattie was her supporter – she thought it was great her mum was a student, like her. They did their homework together sometimes, on the kitchen table, and Hattie helped her out with the long words. She was getting heartily sick of having to apologize for being out of the house, as if she needed permission. Really, Mark was incredibly selfish. Just because it inconvenienced him a little it had, necessarily, to be a bad idea. He wasn't making the slightest attempt to see how much she was enjoying it. He couldn't see anything from her point of view any more.

She was not going to go upstairs and apologize. Not this time. She had spent most of their marriage apologizing. She couldn't bear them to go to sleep without making up after a row, and invariably she would get into bed and wind herself round a sulking Mark, saying, 'I'm sorry, it was daft.' And Mark, who could never resist her, would turn and say, 'I know, I was stupid too,' and they would kiss and make up and make love, and in the morning the row would be gone.

Tonight, she didn't feel like compromising. He had said some unforgivable things while she had been entirely rational. All she had wanted to do was make him see that there was a purpose to what she was doing, it wasn't just a whim, and he had to take it seriously. For God's sake, he had been leaving them for weeks at a time for years, and she had never given him any drama, or made scenes about his absence. How dare he castigate her for not being there and disrupting their family life. Welcome to the club, she thought, crossly.

A small voice drifted down the stairs.

'Mum?'

'Hattie. I'm down here.'

'Why were you and Daddy shouting?'

'It was nothing, darling. We just had a bit of an argument.'

Hattie appeared down the stairs, wearing her favourite new blue and white flowery nightgown, a soft fleecy affair which fell almost to her feet. Behind her trailed Kissamoose, his head banging on each stair. Hattie's hair was tangled into ringlets, her face puffy with sleep. She rubbed a small hand across her eyes.

'Where is Daddy?'

'He's gone up to bed.'

'He isn't going away, is he?'

'Of course not. Daddy wouldn't go away without kissing you goodbye.'

'You should be nicer to him.' Hattie came and climbed onto Tess's knee, resting her cheek against Tess's. Tess pulled away and looked at her, surprised.

'Do you think I'm not nice to Daddy?'

'You're just so busy,' Hattie said, making a heart shape in a drop of wine spilt on the table. 'You're not as nice as you were. Daddy gets very tired. Do you have to do all this work and be out all the time?'

'It isn't as easy as that,' Tess said, holding her tight. 'I have to finish my course, darling. It's important to me. It's like you having to finish your schoolwork, and Daddy having to go to his office and do his work.'

'But Daddy says it isn't real work you do. I think being with us is more important,' Hattie said.

'I think you ought to read the *Guardian* more often,' Tess said, tipping her off her knee. 'Come on. Bed.'

Chapter Sixteen

The phone rang just as Tess was trying to get out of the front door. She had the door keys between her teeth, Hattie's book bag under one arm and the folder which held all her notes and an essay which had to be handed in today in her shoulder bag, which had irritatingly swung down onto her elbow. She had foolishly offered to give the boys a lift to school because it was raining and someone – Jake, probably – was tooting the horn at her to remind her that they were in serious danger of being late for assembly.

'Hell and blast,' she muttered, as she tried to stop the door slamming with Hattie still inside. Hattie had decided at the last minute, as always, that there was something vital she needed from her bedroom for her day at school – a hairband she'd borrowed from her best friend Georgia or a necklace she just had to show her form teacher – and had gone haring back up the stairs at the very moment Tess needed her to leave.

Tess snatched up the phone, extending a leg to make sure the door didn't slam shut. 'Yes?' she barked. If this is someone trying to sell me double glazing, they're dead, she thought.

'No need to shout.'

'Sorry, Margi, it's just kind of a bad time. I've got the

boys in the car and they're late and I'm late and Hattie's late. What is it?'

'I need to see you this evening.'

'Why?'

'Just – look, it's too complicated to explain over the phone. Can you get out for half an hour? We could meet at the wine bar on the triangle. You know, the one with orange chairs like mushrooms.'

'Can't you come here? I'm not sure what time Mark gets back tonight and if I ask the boys to babysit again there might be a riot.'

'It would be a bit tricky.'

'Well, could I bring Hattie to you?'

'Tricky again. Just bribe them with something, will you? It won't take long.'

'You sound worried.'

'I am. Don't panic, it's not life-threatening, or anything like that. It's just a bit, well, awkward.'

'Can't you tell me now? You've got me all worried. You're not pregnant, are you?'

Margi snorted down the phone. 'God, no! But thanks for thinking it might be possible. I'll meet you at eight – if you've got any problems, ring me on the mobile. I'll be in court most of the day but you can leave a message. OK?'

'OK.' Tess hung up.

'Hattie! Unless you come downstairs immediately I am leaving without you.' There was a long wail from upstairs.

'I can't find it!'

'Can't find what? I'm serious, Hat. Five seconds and counting.'

'I can't find my stone!'

'Your what?'

'My precious pearl stone. I need it for Show and Tell. I promised.'

'Oh GOD.' Tess dumped her bag by the telephone

table and bounded up the stairs two at a time. Hattie was sitting in the middle of her bedroom floor, having upended every pot in her room.

'What a mess, Hat. I'm really sorry, but we're never going to find it. Take something else.'

'Like what?' Hattie said, tearfully.

'Like this – ' she cast about the room for inspiration – 'like your shells. You can tell everyone about Cornwall and our holiday.'

'It's a bit late,' Hattie said, dubiously.

'It's brilliant, Hattie. Recognize brilliance when you hear it. Get down the stairs.'

Ollie's voice floated up. 'Is anyone taking us to school today? We'd have been quicker on the tube.'

'Just coming,' Tess called back. She picked Hattie up and hugged her. 'You can make a wonderful story out of them. Do you remember that morning, when we swam, and you found the turquoise shell on the beach and Mummy thought that she'd lost you?'

'I remember,' Hattie said, eyes shining. 'We swam in the sea and it was really cold and I thought I'd lost you in the water.'

'Bit the other way round, darling. Never mind. Come on.'

'I've only got half an hour. Jake says he's promised to go round to Nick's to play War Hammer or some ghastly violent thing and Ollie says he needs to practise his piano and he can't because Hattie keeps playing chopsticks at the other end. Go on, what is it? You sounded very mysterious on the phone.'

'This.' Margi reached down into her handbag, and placed a mobile phone on the table.

'It's a mobile phone, Margi.'

'I know it's a bloody mobile phone. Read the message on it.'

Tess gingerly picked up the phone. She felt incredibly disloyal, reading someone else's message. It said, 'Jk sys he ds wt 2 shag u.'

Tess dropped the phone on the table. 'Who – who sent it?'

'Nick, apparently,' Margi said, briskly.

'Have you spoken to Francesca? It is Francesca's phone, isn't it? Not Georgina's?'

'Yes,' Margi said. 'So I suppose I should be thankful for small mercies that it is my sixteen-year-old who is the object of so much lustful attention as opposed to my thirteen-year-old.'

'But you joked about Jake and Francesca – I mean, you knew they messaged each other.'

'Oh for Christ's sake,' Margi said, angrily. 'There's a big difference between them messaging each other about the latest episode of *Friends* and moaning about how vile their parents are, and practically making assignations to shag each other!'

'How do you know it's my Jake?'

'How many Jakes do we know?'

'There might be someone at the boys' school near Frankie, someone we don't know . . .' Tess said, hopefully.

'Do you think it's very likely?'

'No,' Tess admitted. She sat back in her chair and looked about her. She felt stunned, and rather sick. Her child, her boy, her fifteen-year-old son wanted to sleep with a girl. Well, of course he did, but it was quite another matter seeing it in black and white. Ergh. She shook herself. Maybe she was being incredibly naive. Maybe all boys talked about such things, of course they did, but it seemed extremely careless to go about sending text messages on the subject. But then they probably didn't expect beady-eyed parents to read them. Tess suddenly had an overwhelming feeling that she ought not to react to this. That she ought not to face Jake with it. It hadn't been intended for her eyes, or for Margi's. She was sure it was harmless, just chest-beating, being big and saying things they did not mean.

'What are you going to do?' Margi demanded.

'What did Francesca say?'

'She said I shouldn't have been reading her messages. Then I got the usual tears and she slammed her bedroom door. When I eventually managed to persuade her to open the door and let me in she was mortified, and said it was the first time she'd ever had a message like that and they never talked about anything like that normally, it was all just fun and stuff about homework and people they knew.'

'Was she embarrassed?'

'Of course she was embarrassed. I was fucking embarrassed, for God's sake, and I'm forty-two. Forty-one,' she added, hurriedly.

'I'm not sure what I can do,' Tess said, slowly.

'You'll have to talk to him. He's only fifteen, Tess. Under age. Really, you know, you do piss me off sometimes. Ever since you started that course you've been walking about with your head in the clouds as if nothing else matters. Jake's on the verge of juvenile delinquency, for heaven's sake, and you're acting as if he's just been caught having a fag behind the bike sheds. This isn't something which is slightly naughty. You have to react. You have to *do* something.'

'Like what?'

'Talk to him, at least. Find out if he meant it. I know one thing's for sure, this phone is going back and that's the end of it. And I'm afraid no more babysitting at your house, either.'

'What do you think he's going to do?' Tess said, crossly. 'Rape her?'

'Will you get real! You go around thinking, oh, this can't possibly happen to me because I'm so nice and my family is so nice and we live in a nice house in a nice area but there is no nice way of putting this. Your son is sending messages, OK, through a friend, to the effect that he wants – no, intends – to sleep with my daughter. Do you want me to talk to Mark about this? I might get more sense out of him.'

'No, don't do that,' Tess said, hurriedly. 'He'll kill him. Leave it to me.'

'You have to stop protecting him, you know.'

'What?'

'Jake. He's been getting up to God knows what, according to Frankie.'

'What on earth do you mean?'

Margi reached across the table and took Tess's hand. 'Nothing, I'm not sure. He is a lovely boy, Tess, but maybe you and Mark had better keep a closer eye on him. That's all I'm saying.'

Tess shook her hand free. 'Will you for God's sake tell me what you're implying? Do you mean drugs?'

'I have no idea. Really, I haven't. Frankie just said she'd heard some rumours but she may well have said that to deflect attention from the phone message and to try to get herself out of trouble.'

Tess looked at her watch. 'I have to go,' she said. She reached down to pick up her bag from underneath the table. 'Thanks for telling me. No, I do mean that. At least I will when I stop feeling this bad about it. I'll have to talk to Mark first, then I'll let you know what's happened. I promise all this will stop. And could you ask Frankie exactly what she's heard about Jake? It's really important.'

'I know. I will. I'm sure it's nothing, just silly rumours.'

Tess bit her lip. It did occur to her that this entire discussion had not questioned as to whether Francesca had led him on in any way, and it was Jake who was being painted as the villain here – hence these mysterious 'rumours'. No friendship was ever so strong that it could be put before the lioness defending her cub, by whatever means. After all, Francesca had been just as feverish a text-messager as he had. Who knew what she had been saying to him? She quickly decided, however, that this might not be the best time to open that particular can of worms.

When she got home, Ollie and Hattie were lying in front of the TV, watching *The Flintstones* on Cartoon Network.

'Where's Jake?' Tess said, casually.

'Dunno,' Ollie said, without looking up.

'I think he's upstairs,' Hattie said.

Tess walked up the stairs, thinking hard. The sound of loud music came from the boys' bedroom. Jake had obviously decided not to go and play War Hammer. His current passion was garage music, which Tess was trying to like, without success. The door was half closed. She gently pushed it open.

Jake was lying on his back on his bed, his eyes closed. He was wearing an absurdly baggy pair of jeans and a huge baseball top. His favourite red boots lay where they had fallen off his feet. He had a large hole in the toe of one sock.

'Jake?' There was no response.

'Jake!' Tess said, more loudly.

'Uh-huh?' He grunted, and opened his eyes. Tess reached forward and turned the music down on his ghetto blaster. She sat on the edge of his bed.

'What?' His eyes were slightly unfocused.

'I thought you were going to Nick's.'

'Couldn't be arsed – sorry, bothered.'

'Are you OK?' she said, unable to resist reaching forward to smooth down the front of his hair, which was sticking up at an absurd angle. He flinched away. His skin was sweaty.

'Yeah, fine. What is this?'

'I just wanted to see you. Look, I'm sorry I haven't

174

been around as much as normal. I've been so busy. We hardly seem to have any time together any more.'

'That's fine. I know you've got your work. That's cool. What's the big deal?'

'No big deal,' she said. 'Have you done your homework?' He grinned at her, so beautiful, his face far too mature for his age. He looked about eighteen. 'Nag, nag. Yes, I have. And I am currently relaxing with my favourite popular music, if that is all right with you.'

'Sure. Um, Jake?'

'What?' he said, his eyes closed once more.

'Is there anything going on between you and Francesca?' His eyes flew open.

'Francesca who?'

'Don't be silly. Francesca Francesca.'

'Why?'

'No reason.'

'Don't be absurd, Mum,' he said. 'She's old enough to be my mother.' He smiled at her wickedly. 'Kind of.'

The sound of discordant music could be heard from the snug.

'Mum!' Ollie yelled. 'Will you tell Hattie to get off my piano?'

'Night, then.'

'Night.'

'Are you sure there's nothing you want to tell me?' she said, pausing at his bedroom door.

'What, that I'm wanted by the law, a crack addict and have a harem of willing young girls who want my body?'

'Jake!'

'No,' he said, laughing. 'I haven't.' Then he put his headphones on and closed his eyes. He lay back on his bed, with the face of a fallen angel.

Mark laughed too.

'It's hardly a laughing matter. Margi was furious.

How would you feel if someone sent Hattie a message like that in eight years' time?'

'Bloody livid,' Mark agreed. 'But how do we know she hasn't been leading him on?'

'Exactly what I thought, but I could hardly put that to her. Anyway, the point is it appeared to come from our son who apparently goes about telling girls he wants to shag them.'

'Sounds quite normal to me.'

'You weren't shagging at that age, were you?'

Mark reached across the kitchen table and stroked her cheek. 'I love it when you say words like that. Your cheeks go all red. And no I wasn't shagging, as you so charmingly put it, at fifteen. Unless you count on my own.'

'Mark, you have to take this seriously. Either you, or I, are going to have to tackle him.'

'I thought you spoke to him tonight.'

'I didn't talk to him properly about it. He didn't look very well, and he was very sleepy. I couldn't face it, to be honest. You ought to talk to him about things like that. You're a boy. Have a manly chat about responsibility and all that.'

'But you're his mum. I thought it was mums who did birds and bees.'

'I think we might be just a tad late for the birds and bees conversation, don't you? I would imagine Jake could probably tell us far more than we ever knew. Even Hattie's done contraception at school.'

'Has she?'

'Well, she asked me what a condom was the other day.'

'What did you say?'

'I said it was a large bird found in South America.'

Mark hooted.

'Well, for God's sake, it's all moving too fast, isn't it? I blame TV. Even the *Nickelodeon* stuff aimed at Hattie has teenagers talking about sleeping with each other. Margi says that Georgina's magazines have letters like, "My boyfriend wants oral sex but I think we're too young, love Carly, aged 12." Where will it stop? They'll all be bored of sex by the time they're sixteen and the entire human race will grind to a halt because no-one can be bothered to do it any more. There isn't much mystery left, is there?'

'Do you really want me to talk to Jake?'

'I think you should. Be forceful. I'm sure he doesn't really have any intention of actually doing anything, he's just showing off. But frighten him a bit, could you? I want him to respect girls, not swagger about talking about shagging them.'

'I'll do my best. Does it have to be tonight?' Tess looked at the clock. It was after ten.

'Nope, leave it until tomorrow. Anyway, I don't want Ollie involved. I'm sure he has nothing to do with this and he's such a gentle soul I don't want him caught up in any of this nonsense.'

'OK. Do you mind if we get an early night? I've got to be off first thing. I need to set the alarm for six.'

Tess suppressed a groan. She really needed to get some lecture notes typed up tonight.

'Do you mind if I work for a while? I won't wake you when I come up.'

Mark frowned. 'Just for once,' he said, 'it would be nice to go to bed with my wife. Do you really have to work tonight? Can't it wait?'

A retort rose to Tess's lips. If Mark had an urgent piece of work to finish there was no way he would leave it until tomorrow, nor would she instruct him to put it off because she wanted him to come to bed. He had also developed a really annoying habit of standing behind her when she was working on the laptop in the kitchen. When she said, 'What do you want?' he invariably said, 'Nothing,' and then hung about behind her, emanating boredom and willing her to finish so she could focus her attention on him. Men were very like children, she thought – they couldn't bear not to be the centre of attention, nor could they bear to think that you had something you wanted to do more than talk to them. The handful of times she had closed down her files with a resounding sigh and followed him up to the snug, she had found him lying on the sofa watching television rather than sitting alertly poised ready to engage her in meaningful conversation. So now she was far more brutal and usually said, 'Push off.'

But tonight she said, 'OK.' Tonight would not be the best time to have the how-much-time-do-you-have-to-spend-on-that-thing row. Although Mark was trying desperately to be fair and even-handed about how much time the course took up, Tess knew that it was a battle within him. What underscored everything was his weaselly feeling that it didn't actually earn any money and was therefore not massively beneficial to the family good, it was somehow just for *fun*. He hadn't dared to actually come out and say this yet, but Tess was waiting for the moment he did voice his real objections. Then she might just have to leave the house – but not before standing heavily on his feet.

She was loading the dishwasher when her phone started to bleep. Surprised, she picked it up from its resting place on top of the dresser where it was plugged in, recharging for the morning. The message sign flashed. She pushed the message receive button.

The screen said, 'Fancy a shag?'

It was very hard, she thought, going up to bed after turning off all the lights and double-locking the front door, being the only adult in this house.

Chapter Seventeen

The wind caught Ollie's kite, sending it higher and higher. Tess had happily agreed to help him fly it, that Saturday morning, mainly to get out of the atmosphere of the house. It was an absurdly blustery day, so windy Tess and Mark had been woken in the night by the rattling of the pane in their small dormer window. Mark had managed to go back to sleep but Tess had lain awake for what felt like hours.

Problems, problems which seemed manageable in the light of day, crowded into her brain not single spies but in bloody great battalions. It was now almost Easter, and Mark's Christmas bonus had wiped out their overdraft but the boys' fees and her tutorial fees had plunged them back into the red. She loathed being in debt -- undoubtedly a hang-up from her childhood. Mark was worried too, but wouldn't talk about it. Talking about money always made him bad-tempered, and Tess avoided it whenever possible. Anyway, she was very much the taker at the moment, so she didn't have much of a leg to stand on.

In a vain attempt to sort out their finances, she had picked a financial consultant at random from the Yellow Pages. As soon as he walked through the door – and she had insisted Mark be home from work early to meet him – she knew it was a mistake.

He was a portly grey-haired man squeezed into a cheap, tight suit, sweating slightly and mopping his face with a handkerchief. He was also a quarter of an hour late, and for all of that time Mark, who was never on time for anything himself, had paced up and down saying, 'Where is this bloke? Tess, I had to miss a really important sales conference for this. You know we don't have any extra money to invest so what is the bloody point?' She had been hissing at him, 'Well, at least he might be able to tell us how to move our overdraft around more effectively,' when the doorbell rang and her face froze into a welcoming smile.

While she made Mr Hall a cup of tea, Mark glowered at him across the kitchen table. He looked increasingly nervous.

'So what,' he said, licking his lips, 'do we feel is the priority here?'

Tess said, 'School fees,' and Mark said, 'Investments.' They looked at each other and Tess managed a brittle laugh. 'What my husband means,' she said, while Mark kicked her under the table, 'is that we would like to set up a few, small, investment policies once we have sorted out the main issue, which is how to pay the school fees.'

'May I suggest,' he said, reaching down to pull out a sheaf of papers from a fake leather briefcase, 'a few little measures I have jotted down after you so kindly gave me a few facts and figures over the phone? I have calculated,' he said, with an oily little smile, 'that once your boys have finished school – and university – and taking the liberty of assuming your daughter will attend a private secondary school as well – you will have spent something in the region of a quarter of a million pounds.'

He sat back, happy to be the bearer of such devastating news.

'Bollocks,' Mark said. He sounded very Australian.

'I'm sorry?'

'These figures,' Mark said, scanning the first sheet in the sheaf, 'are complete bollocks. You are trying to scare us into buying policies. That,' he said, jabbing his finger at one set of calculations, 'seems to assume growth at around six per cent. Are you really telling me that we are about to experience inflation at six per cent?'

Mr Hall coughed nervously. 'It is always as well,' he said, 'to look on perhaps the most pessimistic side so one is not taken unawares.' He smiled at Tess, having decided that if he was to sell anything today, it would be through her. She smiled back at him hesitantly. Poor man. Mark was about to close in for the kill. She pressed her foot down on his.

'So what do you suggest?' she said, pleasantly, ignoring Mark's glare.

'What I had thought,' he said, 'was perhaps an endowment policy. If you put a lump sum into a scheme each month, from say next month, you would have enough to cover your little girl's secondary school fees and the cost of university for all your children.'

Mark exploded. 'Are you completely mad?' he said, forcefully. 'Everyone knows that endowment policies are the biggest con the financial world has ever seen, and yet you are seriously suggesting that we put large amounts of money into one of the most high-risk policies that currently exists. May I see that piece of paper?'

He took the printed sheet out of the man's shaking hand. His eyes rapidly scanned the page. Then he paused, and smiled.

'I see,' he said, in a dangerously pleasant voice, 'that this policy would award you a very substantial commission.' He threw it contemptuously down on the table. 'This,' he said, 'is a pile of shit.' Tess glared at him. Did he have to be so rude?

'Well,' blustered Mr Hall, 'I have alternative suggestions. What about a loan? If you took out perhaps a twenty-five-year loan you could draw down from the capital to keep yourselves afloat when these costs are highest – yet spread the burden over a greater number of years.'

'And pay massive interest charges into the bargain,' Mark said. 'I think you have just confirmed something which is now pretty clear in my own mind, that the cheapest way of borrowing money is either through an extended mortgage or simply using an overdraft at the bank.'

'But what about PEPs?' Tess said. 'Or ISAs, or whatever they are now?'

Mark laughed. 'I kind of think we're not into that stage of financial planning, are we?'

Mr Hall made one last stand. 'What about pensions?' he enquired.

'I have an excellent one through my work,' Mark said, 'thank you.'

'But your good lady wife?'

'Doesn't have a job – at present,' Mark said.

'I'm studying,' she said, defensively. 'I will be starting a career the year after next.'

'However she could still be putting money into a private pension scheme. It all helps, you know, Mr James, in the long run.'

'As and when we decide we need a pension for Tess, I don't think we shall be calling upon the services of your firm, Mr Hall. In fact, if I may be so bold, you have been less use than a chocolate teapot. Now I need to get back to work.' He stood up, and disappeared up the stairs.

Tess sat, embarrassed. Mr Hall began collecting his papers together.

'Rather a short-sighted view,' he said, almost to himself.

'I'm sorry,' Tess said. 'He can be rather, um, impetuous.'

'So I see. Shall I show myself out?'

'If you could,' she said, smiling wanly at him. 'Thank you for coming, anyway.'

That jibe about not having a job had hurt. She started at the sound of Mark's footsteps on the stairs.

'What a little twat,' Mark said.

Tess, to his astonishment, burst into tears.

'What the hell is the matter with you? You can't have been upset by that useless git.'

'The matter,' Tess sobbed, 'is that you just *disregard* me in front of other people. How do you think I felt when you talked all over me and wouldn't give me a chance to say anything, as if I was some little wife who didn't understand the complexities of our financial position?'

'No I didn't,' Mark said, in a reasonable voice. 'I just pointed out to him that he was a wanker who was trying to screw money out of us we don't have. I didn't patronize you at all. You are so thin-skinned these days. You go around with this bloody force field around you saying, "Don't you dare patronize me because I am bleeding Boadicea and I always have to have the last word and run everything because I am a WOMAN." You never used to be like this. We used to discuss things. Now I feel like you're some kind of loose cannon, charging about making daft decisions like getting that twit in here to con us when we're managing perfectly well without any help, thank you.'

'But we're not managing, are we?' Tess sobbed. 'We're horribly in debt and you don't seem to care. I can't even get you to look at the bank statement. For God's sake, Mark, we're hugely overdrawn again and I see no way on God's earth of paying it off.'

'You could get a job,' he said, calmly.

183

Tess put her hands flat on the table and looked at him furiously.

'Oh, that is the perfect answer, isn't it? I could get a job and give up my course which is a complete waste of time, isn't it, me just poncing off to university every morning to indulge my little whims while you have to struggle through the hell of commerce to bring home the family crust. Why the hell can't you appreciate that I am doing this so that I can get a better job, a well-paid job, which really will make a difference to our situation?'

'Do you really think that having a bloody MA or whatever the hell it is, is going to make such a huge difference to the money you're going to be able to earn? I'm sure you could walk out now and get just as good a job, you don't need endless qualifications. If you are so seriously worried about my inability to support this family properly then perhaps you could go back to Sotheby's and pick up where you left off. Don't give me that cant of having to suffer for the long-term greater good. You do this course because you love it and it gives you a chance to fart about with no-hope lunatics like that bloody Nicki woman and pretend you're a student with no ties again. It's all about shirking responsibility, isn't it, Tess? You were bored, so you said, with looking after the children at home with only a part-time job so you wanted a chance to escape, and you're trying to dress it up into some great sacrifice you're making for the family good. Don't you ever stop to think that I am working myself into the fucking ground to enable you to have that nice life you scorned? Don't make me laugh, Tess. You're doing this entirely for yourself and it is you who has put us into this mess.'

'It's not the money, is it?' she shouted. 'It's the fact that I'm doing something for myself, something you can't control and don't even bother to understand!

What really pisses you off about all this is not the fact that I'm not earning any money, it's the fact that poor little you has to make his own dinner occasionally and load the washing machine and take Hattie to school or Clara's or actually take some responsibility for what happens in this house rather than offloading everything onto me. What really makes you mad is the fact that you have to *do* something for a change!'

Mark looked at her coolly.

'Sometimes,' he said, 'I feel like I don't know you any more. And I am really tired of these bad moods.'

Then he walked out of the kitchen and, moments later, Tess heard the front door slam.

Chapter Eighteen

' "I don't think there has ever been a man who treated a woman as an equal and that's all I would have asked, for I know I'm worth as much as they." Berthe Morisot, notebook, 1890. Discuss.' Tess stared at the words she had just written at the top of an A4 sheet of paper as an essay title. Mr Frost had set her the task of examining the overt – and more subtle – prejudice Berthe had faced. She hoped to crack the bulk of it this afternoon, snatching precious time for research in the library.

Around her, rows and rows of heads were bent over notepads and open files. On the wide wooden tables files, scarves and bags were piled at random. Occasionally someone would get up to wander to the shelves, browse and take out a book. The silence of the library was broken only by the low voices of the staff at the far end of the room, scanning books in and out, a noise muffled by the high serried rows of bookcases. There was a persistent hum of computers, a thick electronic murmuring punctuated by the sound of muffled laughter, then 'Ssh.'

Tess, her neck swathed in a woollen red scarf, a gift from Margi, was almost indistinguishable from all the other students. Her thick blond hair was pulled back at random into a bulldog clip to stop it falling into her eyes, and on the slim wrists revealed by the heavy blue ribbed polo-neck Gap jumper rolled up to her elbows were a series of cheap bracelets, some gifts from Nicki, who adored buying junk jewellery, one belonging to Hattie that she had rather fancied, and the rest Tess had bought herself from the antique stalls she and Nicki occasionally browsed in during free periods, at the junk market near the university.

She had forgotten how much she liked wearing jewellery. When the children were young it was so impractical, it snagged in their hair, they grabbed necklaces and earrings as babies, choking her, hurting her ears. So she had simply forgotten about putting it on, only occasionally wearing a neat pair of earrings or a bracelet if she and Mark were going out anywhere remotely smart. Most of her old jewellery had been lost, played with by Hattie, or broken. When she first met Mark she had liked to wear long earrings, fun, cheap stuff. But then, with marriage, she had lost the urge to say, 'Look at me.' She no longer had any time, or need, for attention. Today, she found she liked to adorn herself. She wanted to be a little outrageous.

It was only when she raised her head to look at the clock – she mustn't be late to pick Hattie up from Clara's – that any difference from the other female students was apparent. It was in the eyes, crows' feet radiating from the corners, her lids heavier, the lines underneath a faint cobweb. Here, in this peaceful, industrious haven, she felt not so very different. Just a different set of priorities, different decisions to make from the other students – what they were going to do that evening, whether it would be the bar or a club, should they eat out, which band should they see? Carefree lives making carefree decisions, with only themselves to think about. Tess instead had the routine of her life at home, the routine from which life

187

here, now, was an escape. But its demands did not cease, the rules could only bend, not break. Uniforms still needed to be washed. The kitchen still needed to be tidied, food bought, clothes dried, ironing done, books and games kit to be found. The children had adapted to the bending of their routine quite well but there were complaints – Hattie said no-one had listened to her play the recorder for ages, Ollie couldn't find his piano music and Jake sulked about there being no-one around to give him a lift to Nick's because it was raining and he couldn't be bothered to walk.

She was finding it possible – just. Food could be bought in her lunch break, Clara could be flexible if she had a late lecture and the boys hadn't actually burnt the house down yet heating oven chips. And untidiness hurt no-one. Once the dust was an inch thick, it didn't get much worse. She was careful to keep her files and books tidied away, in a cupboard she had cleared in the kitchen, because she had no study and the children would have spilt apple juice or Ribena over them if she left them out on the kitchen table. Between her and Mark now existed a truce, an entente cordiale. She didn't have the time or energy for fighting, and they had learnt to make space for each other, to agree calmly to minor changes of schedule, to be flexible about who should pick up the children, where and when. It was rather like being a couple comfortably divorced, but living in the same house. They talked amicably when they met in the kitchen, often preparing their own food. At night, they slept companionably, on far sides of the bed. They had not made love for over three weeks.

Opening one of the textbooks spread out in front of her, she mused that what she enjoyed most about her new days was the way in which people treated her. She was simply Tess James, like any other student.

Nobody's wife or mother. No-one had any pre-conceived notions about her, she did not feel she had to fit into any role. And for that, she had to find a personality, and chat about things unconnected to her normal life – what she thought about stories in the news, politics, the theatre, art. She had forgotten the intensity of these discussions and at first she had been on the periphery, during lunchtimes in the pub, or waiting for tutorials to start, too hesitant to find her voice. Gradually she forgot herself, and found she did still have opinions. Nor did she have to think before she opened her mouth. She found herself taking a much more vivid interest in the world outside her family, her close friends. It was as if she had been looking down a narrow tunnel, bounded by the beliefs of everyone else around her. Now she could see much further into the distance.

Sometimes she tried out university arguments on Mark, later, at home. But more often than not she met with a stone wall. Nor did he want to meet any of her university friends. He said meeting Nicki had been quite enough, thank you. He would say, 'Look, I'm tired. I have been on the phone to California all day and right now all I want is a glass of wine and *Inspector Morse*. I do not wish to discuss the selling-out of the Labour Party, or the antediluvian influence on cubism or whatever.'

She had started going to the theatre again too, thinking, hell, why not? When she and Mark had first started dating they had gone together, but it wasn't really his idea of a great night out. He hated having to sit still for three hours surrounded by other people, no matter how engrossing the play, and more often than not he fell asleep. And she could never relax, constantly wondering if he was bored. It took all the fun out of it. Now she went occasionally with Nicki, and really enjoyed it, even if the play was crap. It was just great to be able to sit there and not worry if Mark was enjoying it too. Why did women always think about what men were feeling, and worry if they were happy, when men so rarely did the same for them?

How would you have coped, Berthe? she thought, smiling to herself at the image. She shook herself. She must get on, Clara had a dentist's appointment for her own child at half past four. But then Berthe had a nurse and later a governess to care for her child while she painted, she didn't have to rush home for the childminder's. Even then, she must have felt there was a resentment at this occupation of her time, an activity unbecoming to a woman of her society, class and background. Nor would she have been expected to have a political voice, despite the turbulent nature of her period in history. She must have had to bite her lip, too. Berthe did not look like a woman who would enjoy biting her lip.

The essay title cut to the heart of Berthe's life – how could she reconcile her life as an artist with that of being seen as a good wife and mother? What had been more important, art or motherhood? Flicking through her reference books, Tess read that one of Berthe's teachers of the time, Guichard, warned her mother that if she allowed her two daughters – Berthe's sister Edma was also an artist – to be allowed to develop their talent and eventually display their work at the Salon in Paris, it would cause an 'outrage' in society. The decision, he warned, would be 'momentous' for the family. To her great credit, Berthe's mother knew that their talent was too great to stifle, but that, in the mid-nineteenth century, they also needed to marry well. Tess smiled. How Berthe must have argued against being 'marriage fodder'.

Carefully, Tess wrote, 'What Berthe faced, as did so many other women of her generation, was that she was brought up, having been born into a wealthy family, to acquire as many skills as she could – art, languages, appreciation of literature, music. Yet these qualities were viewed as mere commodities for the marriage market, rather than talents to be appreciated for their own merit. They would simply make her more attractive and interesting to a man. They were not skills in their own right, merely enticements with which to snare a man. A woman could only be decorative, entertaining and amusing – a diversion, not an effective member of society.' It was this inequality against which Berthe railed, Tess thought, especially in the light of her enormous talent. She began to write again. 'In the novel of the time, *Lélia* by George Sand, she wrote, "We bring them (young women) up like saints, then we hand them over like fillies." To be married was the only way of gaining status, security and respectability.'

Tess sat back and thought about that one. How much had changed? Of course women had their own careers, their own lives, their own money – but what was the question most often asked of a young woman: 'Anyone on the scene?' Women in their thirties still felt under pressure to find a man, get a man, persuade someone to marry you so you could have children and become an accepted member of society. We are all still fillies, she thought. Educating ourselves to be sold at auction to the highest bidder. And what happened to women like Margi, perfectly happy on her own with her two daughters, free to do exactly as she pleased? They were pitied, talked about in hushed voices, plans were made to find them new men so they would be complete and acceptable once more. Being a single woman was still to ring a bell and shout, 'unclean'.

Berthe had resisted the urge to marry just anyone until she was in her thirties – very late for women of her day, her mother must have despaired – but then she had been, for many years, in love with the painter

Manet. He had painted her, she fell in love with him, but he was married. He had mistresses too, but Berthe was too high-born to throw herself away so cheaply. So she married – at Édouard's own suggestion – his brother, Eugène. He was a serious man of forty-one, a writer, witty and good company, but dogged by ill health. In marrying him, she said, 'I am facing the realities of life.' Hardly a grand passion, Tess thought, although she undoubtedly did come to love him. Not a bad bargain. She married a man who was way ahead of his time in that he was prepared to support her and encourage her talent, and was more than happy to look after their daughter, Julie, while she worked. OK, so he was no George Clooney, but he did seem to love her and give her the firm base she needed.

Tess paused and chewed her pen, sighing. She had no great talent. She was never going to be a world-famous artist or a wonderful writer, but she was sure, so very sure within herself, that she could be a good teacher. She felt the passion of her interest so keenly, she knew she could transmit that enthusiasm to others. And how satisfying it would be, to feel that in whatever small way she had made a difference to someone else's life. Would Mark be her supporting cast? Hardly. He was too much of a leading man himself. It was hard, she thought, in a marriage, to have two main characters both fighting for the spotlight. Someone had to stand in the wings, and applaud.

'Despite her acclaim,' Tess wrote, 'she had but one personal exhibition in her lifetime. Although her work was widely displayed, she was fêted and often written about, she still failed to gain anything of the fame of her male contemporaries. And, in death, she became all but invisible. She strived, in a way that so many women today could emulate, to maintain with a fighting spirit her devotion and belief in her own talent, and her place in the art world. She recognized the strictures placed upon her, the patronizing comments, the shock at her daring to exhibit alongside men – yet she was always true to herself, and much of that was thanks, in part, to the devotion and support of her husband, Eugène. He recognized just how important this side of her life would always be and he was nothing but steadfast in his support and love for her. And in painting her daughter, she brought together so brilliantly both her talent and her love for her child. No man could allow the strength and independence of her daughter to shine through so wonderfully as in the portrait of a teenage Julie, *Julie Daydreaming*. I have no doubt that for Berthe, her love for Julie was just as strong as her love for her art. As she wrote in the last entry in her diary, as she was dying, "My little Julie, I love you as I die; I will still love you even when I am dead; I beg you not to cry, this parting was inevitable. I hoped to live until you were married . . . Work and be good as you have always been; you have not caused me one sorrow in your little life. Do not cry; I love you more than I can tell you." '

Tess laid down her pen, and a sympathetic tear fell onto the open page.

Chapter Nineteen

The house stood on the outskirts of the village, in a slight dip after a bend in the road. Hattie and Mark sang along in the car to Hattie's new Britney Spears tape. Mark had insisted on driving, although he had a fierce hangover. Every time he opened the window to have a cigarette, all the children shrieked in the back that they were freezing.

'It'll kill you, Dad,' Ollie said.

'No it won't,' Mark said, flicking the stub out of the top of the window. 'The stress of bringing you lot up will.'

'Ouch. Fat Ollie's sitting on me.'

'No I'm not.'

'How much further?'

'Not long.' Tess turned to smile at them. She had insisted they all dress relatively smartly to see the house. Hattie looked adorable in a new denim skirt with red tights, and a striped woolly jumper, her hair pulled back into a grown-up-looking ponytail. The effect was only slightly marred by a Peruvian hat with earflaps given to her by Nicki, which made her look like a minute Deputy Dawg. Ollie was wearing a navy sweatshirt and cords, which made him look rather preppy, and Jake – well, at least Jake had agreed to take off his baseball cap and was wearing his least baggy jeans. Mark annoyed him intensely by calling them his amazing pantaloons. He was sitting, silent, staring out of the window.

Tess was worried about him. He seemed almost depressed, if a teenager could be depressed. There was a sadness about him, a melancholy as though the world was against him. His habitual expression was one of – grief. This was the only way Tess could describe it to herself. She knew she was driving him mad by saying constantly, 'Oh, do cheer up,' and he would flash her a fake smile, before his face resumed its expression of blank acceptance. Surely his life couldn't be all that bad. Things had calmed down at school, he was doing reasonably well and seemed on course to achieve moderate success in his exams. But the only time he ever seemed animated these days was when he came in late from school, and he would talk nineteen to the dozen, raid the fridge and then go and sleep on his bed until Tess had to wake him for tea. He seemed to be withdrawing, pulling himself into some private world where she and Mark could no longer reach him. A gulf had appeared between them, with her, Mark, Ollie and Hattie on one side, and Jake across from them, quite alone battling the demons that appeared to plague him.

Mark said the best way to deal with him at the moment was to ignore him, and that this latest even more uncommunicative phase would pass. But Tess couldn't just leave him out there, alone, she needed to hug him and pull him back, give him warmth and make him feel loved. But he didn't seem to want their love any more, as if he was searching for another form of love which would better suit his needs, and would accept him for what he was without asking him if he was all right all the time. When she quizzed him and forced him to answer her he would say angrily, 'Look,

Mum, I'm fine. I just need you to leave me alone, OK?'
So Tess did leave him alone, reluctantly, but she hated
it. She was scared he would drift so far away from
them he might never come back.

Ollie was such a cheerful, uncomplicated soul but in
many ways this made things worse for Jake, who must
have felt he was endlessly being compared with his
little brother. Ollie was doing so well at school, so
popular with his teachers and consistently top of his
class. He was also proving to be a promising cricketer –
Jake's sport, rugby, which had been his saving grace,
also seemed to be being neglected for whatever pursuit
now took up most of his spare time. Tess had been
alarmed to realize he had missed two Saturday training sessions at school in a row. He had set out to go –
she had washed his rugby kit and packed his bag for
him – but then his sports teacher had rung her on the
second Saturday to say he hadn't arrived for either
session. Jake refused to discuss it until Mark had
become so angry that he had said furiously, 'Look, I
just wagged off and met Nick, OK? It's no big deal, is
it? I'm bored of rugby. Now get off my back, will you?'
Mark was so busy at work he had let it go, but Tess
sensed a storm coming.

Tess had seen by the look in Mark's eyes that night
that he was very close to taking hold of Jake and
shaking him, to force some kind of response. She knew
exactly how he felt – there were times when she
too wanted to grab him, and force him to look at her,
force him to communicate. Silence was his deadliest
weapon, and he used it skilfully.

It had taken her hours to smooth Mark down. He
had said that if this continued, he might not be able
to stop himself from hitting him. Tess flinched, and
resisted the urge to say, 'Not again.' Even now, over a
year and a half later, that memory was still too raw. So
she said instead that would solve nothing. She was

terrified Jake would leave home. He hadn't threatened to as yet, but he was such a big fifteen-year-old she was sure he could look after himself, and after all Mark had left home too when he was only three years older. But then he hadn't had a loving family to protect him. But then her loving family didn't seem to be making too much of a difference, did it?

Jake still showed no signs of wanting to be part of the family. He watched TV on his own in the bedroom, he ate with them around the kitchen table without saying anything, and he even refused to join them for a family outing to Planet Hollywood to celebrate Ollie coming top in his Easter exams. For his birthday, he had refused to do anything at all.

Tess had offered to take a group of his friends to the skateboarding bowl at Battersea and give them the money for a pizza on their own afterwards, but he had said that birthdays were stupid. Tess realized that buying a cake with candles was a little foolish, and hadn't bothered. Then he had come in from school, said, 'Don't bother with the cake, huh?' and gone and sulked in his room. Hattie had cried, because she'd made him a wobbly fairy cake on her own and wrapped a present in lots of crinkly paper for him, and he hadn't opened it until she forced him to much later. And Mark had teased him at dinner, saying, 'It's the incredible non-speaking man,' and when he did ask Hattie to pass the butter for his jacket potato Mark said, 'The boy speaketh! It is a miracle!' and Jake had pushed his chair back wordlessly and gone up to his room. Tess was furious with Mark, who replied he was fed up with all of them having to humour Jake all the time as if he had some kind of terminal disease, and then he stormed off in a huff too.

The house sat back a little way from the road. Tess had read and reread the estate agent's details, hoping to instil in herself some vestige of enthusiasm. Mark's renewed interest in moving to the country had come out of the blue. One night he had come in from work and placed the details on the table in front of her, as she worked on the laptop. He hadn't said anything.

'What?' she said.

'Just look.'

She looked. It was a four-bedroomed farmhouse, still currently a working farm but the existing outbuildings would be demolished following the sale. There were two acres of land with the house, with more land available 'by separate negotiation'. It was described as being in a state of 'some disrepair' and there were no internal photographs. She sat and looked at the brochure for a long time. Was this Mark's way of trying to bridge the gulf that was gradually, peacefully, opening up between them? She would have to react to this. They couldn't just drift on as they had been doing. Good move, she thought. Round one to you.

'The estate agent,' Mark said, over dinner, 'said we could expect twice what we paid for this house.'

'But he hasn't seen it.'

'I told him where it was and how many bedrooms we had. I also said it was in good nick.'

Tess snorted. 'Good nick! It's falling apart. We've hardly done anything to it since we moved in.'

Mark looked impatient. 'The point is,' he said, 'that this,' he tapped the details, 'would cost us much less, and we'd have enough left over to pay off the overdraft and have some left for renovations. Come on, Tess, it makes sense. It gives us a chance to give the kids a fresh start, gets them out of the city and if I'm prepared to commute, what's the hassle for you?'

'The hassle,' Tess said clearly, 'is the fact that I still have to finish my MA and then secure my placements for my PGCE. How on earth can I do that living in the depths of rural' – she squinted at the front page of the brochure – 'Buckinghamshire?'

'You could commute, like me. Or maybe you could put it on hold for a while. Or choose a different university, one nearer. It doesn't have to be the Courtauld, does it?'

'Yes,' Tess said calmly. 'It does.'

'Well, you'll have to commute. We'll just have to add the cost of a nanny into the equation, won't we?' Tess shot a look at him. His face was entirely innocent.

'I will agree,' she said, 'to look at this place. But there is no way I am going to commit myself as yet. It's such a huge step. What about schools?'

'I've thought of that,' Mark said, proudly. 'Charles from work only lives six miles away. He says there's an excellent boys' day school nearby which would suit them. It's cheaper than St Peter's.' His eyes gleamed.

'And Hattie?'

'Hattie is eight. She's hardly likely to mind moving from one school to another at this age, is she? I'm sure there are some excellent village schools nearby.' He reached forward and took her hands. She looked down, surprised. It was the first time he had voluntarily touched her for weeks. 'Please, Tess, please. Can't you see I really want this? I want some fresh air, I want to bring the kids up out of all this crap we read and hear about every day and I want to be able to spend my weekends doing something productive, rather than sitting cooped up in this henhouse with no room to move. It would be good for all of us. Talking of a henhouse, you could have hens.'

Tess sat, thinking. This would need to be handled tactically. She smiled.

'I don't want hens. Why would I want hens?'

'Fresh eggs.'

'You can buy those from the supermarket,' she pointed out. 'All right. I'll come and see it. As long as you accept the fact that I am not giving up the course and you will have to help me and be nice about getting home on time and sharing responsibilities. OK?'

'OK.'

Jake howled. 'Where? The middle of nowhere? Why?'

'Your father thinks we need a change.'

'He means he needs a change. What about school? What about my friends? What will there be to do?'

'Daddy says I can have a pony.' Tess spun round.

'What?'

'Daddy says,' Hattie replied innocently, twizzling the hair of Princess Barbie around her fingers, 'that if we move to the new house he will buy me a pony.'

'Typical,' Jake said. 'And what will I get?'

'A motorbike,' Mark said, walking into the kitchen, ducking his head. 'When you're old enough,' he added hastily, seeing the furious expression on Tess's face.

'This is just bribery, isn't it? And what does Ollie get?'

'I don't want anything,' Ollie said, quickly. 'Really, I don't.'

'I think we're jumping the gun here,' Tess said. The whole family, with the exception of Ollie, frowned at her.

'We haven't even put this house on the market and who on earth is going to want to buy it?'

'It's a lovely house,' Hattie said. 'It's got my pink bedroom.'

'What about Nigel?' Tess said. They all turned to look at Nigel, who was dribbling over his breakfast on the floor. He looked up at them, alarmed.

'He's hardly a country cat, is he? He's hardly ever seen grass, let alone cows. He'll be persecuted by all those rough country moggies. They'll call him a cissy townie cat and bite his ears.'

Hattie's face worked as if she was going to cry.

'Nice one,' Mark said. He took hold of Hattie and gave her an enveloping hug. 'Mummy's just being silly. Nigel would love it. He'd have lots of room to roam about and think of all the mice he can catch.'

'Country mice,' Tess said spitefully, 'are very fierce.'

'I think that's enough of that, don't you?' Mark said, as Hattie's mouth opened to let out a loud yowl. 'Nothing is decided yet, we're just going to have a look.'

Yeah, right, Tess thought.

And the exterior of the house was appealing, she had to admit. It was a red-brick Georgian house, with a big white door in the middle and windows either side. They climbed out of the Discovery and stood in the muddy driveway.

'Isn't it great?'

'The window ledges are rotten,' Tess said.

'Just show a little enthusiasm, will you?' Mark hissed in her ear as the estate agent, who had been waiting by the front door clutching a brochure of the house, approached them. Hattie had climbed out of the back, and Tess could now see that she had put on her special pink suede party shoes Tess had bought for her at vast expense from Daisy and Tom.

'Yuch,' Hattie said, squelching one foot into a large ridge of mud. Tess leant down to pick her up, and Hattie swung her legs forward so that both muddy shoes brushed against Tess's new olive green French Connection jacket.

'Thanks, Hat,' she said.

Ollie had climbed obediently out of the car, and was standing close to Mark. Jake still sat slumped in the back. Tess opened the back door a fraction. Mark was talking to the estate agent.

'Jake, come on.'

'Do I have to?'

'Yes, you do. We've come all this way. Put that down.'

'Why?'

'Because it looks rude.' She reached forward to take his GameBoy. 'Please,' she said, quietly, 'just be nice. Dad's promised to take us out for a meal later, on the way home.'

'Wow,' Jake said. 'Big deal.'

'Out!' she hissed.

Mark, Ollie and Hattie had already gone into the house. When Tess reached forward to open the gate, the latch partly came away in her hand. Jake laughed.

'You're wrecking the joint already. This is like, weirdsville.'

'You watch too much *Scooby Doo*,' Tess said.

The concrete path to the front door was cracked, with healthy-looking weeds growing between the gaps. There was a kind of border by the wall immediately to the left of the gate, but it was hard to see where the grass stopped and the border began. It merged in a muddy blur, and Tess couldn't spot any discernible plants, apart from an ancient and spindly rose.

The garden rose in two tiers towards the road. Tess could see that at one time it must have been professionally laid out, as there were some pleasing old stone steps leading up to the next tier, with tilting stone pots on either side. Four round rose beds had been carved out of the lawn, but they were full of weeds, the heads of the roses bearing but a handful of early buds. Altogether the garden had a sad, neglected air, as if it had been put to sleep hundreds of years ago and needed reawakening. She felt the first stirrings of interest, but told herself firmly to stop. She didn't want to live here, they couldn't afford it.

She looked about her. The nearest house was about two hundred yards away, just visible over the tops of some gnarled fruit trees in an orchard to the right of the house, their branches barely flecked with blossom, as if by a light snowfall. The house she could just see was a much smaller cottage, with a low, thatched roof. It also looked rather decrepit. The wind, still chilly for April, caught her jacket and blew it open. She pulled it around herself, and walked into the hallway.

The first thing that struck her was the smell – it was a smell she hadn't encountered for many years, and it catapulted her back to childhood. She closed her eyes. What did it remind her of? She breathed in deeply and then it came to her, the first house she had lived in with her parents, a narrow, terraced house. She had flowery wallpaper in her bedroom, which had peeled away over a small fireplace, and there was a patch of brown spreading upwards. It was cold in the room, when her mother didn't light the fire, and the smell was there. It was damp, of course, and something else, a mustiness, stale air as if trapped, imprisoned in a lifeless building. Her heart, for an unaccountable reason, began to beat much faster. She felt afraid.

She shook herself. This was ridiculous. You couldn't be scared of a house. It was only because the decoration was so dingy, the lighting so dim and the air so stale that she felt this odd sense of menace, of being in the wrong place, as if the house didn't want her. She had a very strong urge to turn and walk out of the door.

'Tess! Come and look at this!'

She followed Mark's voice into the kitchen. There was a step down into the room, and Tess had a strong urge to clamp her hand over her mouth, the damp smell was so overpowering. Mark was standing next to a vast black range.

'Isn't it brilliant? It's in full working order, look!' He opened one of the doors, and a shower of rust fell to the floor. Inside Tess could see what looked like a small furnace.

'It's solid fuel. So cheap! Just think – all you do is pop coal in in the morning and it's alight all day. No gas, no electricity. Amazing.' Tess looked at him in wonder. He wasn't serious. He couldn't be serious.

But he was. The agent led them from room to depressing room – plaster hanging off the walls, light fittings drooping, held in place solely by ancient wiring which spilled out of the walls like intestines, and a carpet so bald it had actually worn away in places.

'Just look at those floorboards!' Mark enthused. 'We'd take this right off and sand them, wouldn't we, Tess?' She gave him a weak smile.

'What a marvellous idea,' the agent said. 'Now if I can just show you the upstairs . . .'

They obediently followed him. Every stair creaked. Hattie clutched Tess's hand.

'This is a bit of a spooky house, isn't it?' she said.

'Not really, darling. It's, it's – oh God, look out!'

The banister, which was decorated with elaborate twirls of wrought iron, suddenly gave way. One of the central whirls plunged to the floor in the hall, bounced twice and rolled towards the front door. Tess sagged back against the wall to the right of the staircase.

'Mark,' she said, breathlessly. 'Hattie could have leant against that.'

'I do agree,' the estate agent said, 'that is one area which might need a little attention. Now let me show you the bedrooms.' Tess caught hold of Mark's arm.

'It's a death trap,' she hissed. 'It's only a matter of time before we're all killed.'

'Don't be so negative,' Mark said, smiling at the agent. 'I know you're determined to hate it, aren't you?' he said, sotto voce.

'I am not,' she hissed back at him, but he had gone.

'Cool views,' Jake said, looking out of the bedroom window at the back. And even Tess had to concede that the view was spectacular, over rolling farmland, the horizon vast, the sky so open.

'What a big sky,' Hattie said. It was a cold, cloudy day, but suddenly, as they looked, a beam of light pierced the thick grey cumulus, and shone rays of light onto the fields below. It was like a golden hand reaching down to earth.

'Look, Mummy! There's a rainbow!' And there was – a proper rainbow, so clear you could see every individual colour, a rainbow you could see all the way to the moment it touched the ground, not lost behind buildings as it would have been in London.

'It's so beautiful,' Hattie said, wistfully. 'Can I touch it?'

'You can never reach the end of a rainbow,' Ollie said. 'It's a mirage.'

'What's a mirage?'

'Something you can't ever reach, stupid,' Jake said.

'And these are the fitted wardrobes.' The agent reached forward to try to open one of the doors. It was stuck.

'Shall I have a go?' Mark said, and heaved on the old mahogany door.

It gave way suddenly, and piles and piles of old newspapers fell out.

The agent coughed. 'The old gentleman who lived here was something of a hoarder,' he admitted.

'What happened to him?' Tess said. 'Does he still live here?'

'Oh, no. He farmed here alone after his parents died. Then he died, quite suddenly about two months ago.'

'Where did he die?'

'Oh – here. In that bed, in fact.' They all turned to look at it in horror.

'Spook-ee,' Ollie said.

'Gross,' Hattie said.

'Shall we move on?'

*   *   *

By the time they walked out, Tess was desperate for fresh air. She could admit to herself that the house had possibilities, but it would need so much money spent on it. It would certainly need rewiring – the wiring looked lethal, and the circuit box in the kitchen appeared to have been designed by Heath Robinson. The range that Mark was so keen on would also have to go and be replaced by an Aga – a big expense, certainly, but there was no way she was going to stoke that fire in the morning. There was rustic, and there was obscenely rustic. Hang on, she thought. I am almost making this a fait accompli. I do not wish to live here. I do not wish to spend my life looking out of the window at mud. I want Starbucks. I want Harvey Nichols. I want the Conran Shop. I want to be able to purchase polenta whenever I feel the need. I want to be able to nip out and buy a café latte and watch the world go by, and shop in Regent Street at Christmas and say 'ooh' at the lights. I want to take Hattie to the Rainforest Cafe for lunch and I want to see the latest plays and dream about buying a double-fronted house on the Common. I Do Not Want To Live Here. Anyway, the children would be bored stiff.

'Mum, this is just so excellent,' Ollie said, his eyes shining behind his glasses. 'There's a rope swing in the orchard and an old tree house. Come and look.' He took her hand. Together they squelched through the mud to the gate of the orchard.

'And there's a hen house,' Ollie said, shyly. 'We could have hens.'

'They'd be eaten by the foxes,' Tess said, quickly.

'Not if we locked them up at night. Oh Mum, please. This house is just fantastic.'

Tess turned, shading her eyes from a sudden glare of sunlight. By her feet, she noticed that a few primroses had flowered. She never noticed primroses at home.

She looked out over the view at the back. The garden ran to a rickety post and rail fence, and then there was a small paddock, which was currently bordered by extremely unattractive breeze-block farm buildings. But beyond, the land fell away, into a series of rolling hills. As she watched, the light from the sun moved lazily across, and for one glorious moment the hillside seemed burnished with gold.

Mark stood next to her.

'Look,' he said, quietly. Tess followed his gaze. Hattie was leaning against the bottom of one of the fruit trees, examining with an expression of wonder a fat bud of blossom. Above her, a pair of legs dangled. They were wearing Jake's trousers.

'You can get higher!' said Ollie's voice. The legs disappeared, and the tree began to shake.

'Get down!' Tess yelled. 'It might not be safe.'

'Oh, leave them,' Mark said. 'Just let them play.' He put his arms around her shoulders, crossing them over her chest. She leant against him.

'Can't you see how much they'd love it here? It would be better for them, wouldn't it?'

'Hmm,' she said. 'But what about everything that needs doing?'

'Cosmetic,' Mark said, airily.

'Cosmetic! More like open heart surgery. You'd have to practically gut the place inside.'

'You're thinking about it, aren't you?'

'No,' she said firmly. 'I am not. It is a bonkers idea and I will have no part of it.'

'Excellent,' Mark said. 'Now come and see the place I'm going to have for my workshop.'

'But you don't have any tools.'

'Not yet, I don't,' he said.

Chapter Twenty

'You cannot leave. I won't let you.'

'Nothing's final, Margi. We're just testing the market, to see how much we could get for the house if – and this is a big if – we do decide to sell.'

'But that's more than halfway to selling. You're bound to sell your house. It's lovely.'

'No it isn't. It's a pigsty.'

'Maybe it could do with a little redecorating but hey – it's a house and it's nearish the Common. It'll sell. Oh, Tess. Who will I talk to? I won't have anyone I can ring up and have a really long moan at and not worry if I'm boring them by going on and on.'

'Thanks.'

'No, I mean it. Do I bore you? Yes, of course I do, but I don't care and that's why we're such great friends and oh, Tess, Tess, you cannot move out to Mudsville Manor or wherever it is. You'll take up hunting and start saying tally ho and grow your hair into a bob and buy a velvet hairband and start wearing flat shoes and have no taste.'

'Not everyone who lives in the country has no taste.'

'How can they have taste? They live there surrounded by mud and they prefer walking to driving about in cars and there's insufficient concrete. I won't have anyone to drink cappuccino with. I'm sorry, but you're not going.'

'Come on. You have Vanessa.'

'I'm only friendly with Vanessa because you are.'

'No!'

'Oh, Tess, even you Miss Nice As Pie have to admit that she is a snobby cow. And what happened to our invite to St Jean de fucking Luce? That got jettisoned, didn't it, in favour of bloody Lucienne I'm married to Oscar who's just sold his company for twelve million. Not much female solidarity there, was there?'

'Yup, but you accept that about Vanessa, don't you? You accept the fact that if she gets a better offer you're chucked. It's almost part of her charm.'

'Not to me. Look, I've had a fantastic idea. Why don't you let Mark move in with the children and you stay here during the week? You can live with me! Think about it – it's brilliant! If Mark thinks it's so easy to get an au pair then he can live there with her and she'll sort out the children and you can carry on with your course in London and just see them at the weekends. You'll probably get on better with your children if you only see them occasionally. Think novelty factor. We're expected to spend far too much time with our kids. There ought to be some kind of compulsory gap year for parents, when their offspring hit the worst of the teenage years. On that subject, how's Jake?'

'Much better,' Tess said. 'Speaking. You know, opening his mouth and communicating with words. It's rather a revelation. I think it was the thought of moving that did it. Mark has been so much happier, and the whole atmosphere in the house feels different. I suppose that's the main reason why I'm going along with it. To make everyone else happy.'

'But how do you feel?'

'I don't honestly know,' Tess said, slowly. 'It's rather like sitting in a boat and being caught by the tide, and not quite wanting to be swept along but feeling that you don't have any choice, and to row against it would prove too arduous.'

'That doesn't sound awfully like the forceful new Tess.'

'I know. This sounds completely ridiculous, but I feel almost as if I'm disappearing again. When I started the course, it was as if the clouds had parted and I suddenly knew who I was. It was rather like losing yourself for fifteen years and then you turn a corner and meet yourself and you think, yes, that is the person I am. I know her. I even like her. Every morning during that first term I woke up feeling such a zest for life – I know that sounds corny – but I didn't wake up and think, "Book bag, rugby boots, post telephone bill," I thought, 'Essay, notes, money for lunch," and although it doesn't sound wildly exciting the point is that they were all things for me, not things for other people. And for the past fifteen years I have spent my life doing things for other people, not me. What really does worry me is that having found that woman again, I'm not entirely sure I can let her go.'

'But that's what marriage means, isn't it? Having to say goodbye to who you were.'

'But you got out – you divorced Martyn. And a lot of that was because you were fed up with living your life through him, wasn't it?'

'Kind of. But more the fact that if I'd had to live with him for just another day I would have had to kill myself. Or him. No joke, Tess, I really did feel that I had all but disappeared. You say that you had lost sight of yourself, but with Martyn it had got to the point where I was scared to say anything. Me, scared! I found that even before I opened my mouth I was weighing up what I was going to say and how he would react, as if I couldn't think for myself. It was like walking on eggshells, he was so permanently bad-tempered, and he was dragging me down with him. I cannot tell you the relief of being on my own. I stayed with him so long because of the girls – I kept thinking, "He is their father and they love him," so it was up to me to cope with the fact that he was never happy, didn't even seem to like me much, and stay with him for them. But eventually I realized that they were old enough to see I was living a lie and they were beginning to pity me. It's so hard to have any dignity when you are constantly apologizing for your own existence.'

'But it hasn't been easy, being on your own.'

'Nope. But it's been a bloody sight better. I sometimes wonder, you know, if it is possible for men and women to live together any more. I mean, marriage is hardly a natural state, is it? Our mothers had to – their husbands were a meal ticket. But when you live with anyone for a period of time, you go off them, and if you're forced to live with them, positively bound to them, the strain is phenomenal. And the thing is, women are no longer forced to take all the rubbish that men throw at them – they don't need men, they can earn their own money and look after themselves, so why do they need some lazy man who expects to be waited on hand and foot? It isn't natural, you know.'

'But the alternative is lonely. Come on. And anyway, not all men are like that. I know some perfectly good ones who share absolutely everything in the house and are kind and communicative.'

'But do you fancy them and could you be married to them?'

'No,' Tess admitted. 'They're really boring.'

'And you aren't lonely, anyway, when you have children,' Margi said.

'My mother wouldn't agree,' Tess said. 'Her view is that you should stay together through hell and high water and that of course men are tricky to live with, but you have to humour them because of that, they are the father of your children, and if you play them right you can live your own life by a kind of evil subterfuge. Her argument is that women have lost the skill of handling men. We aren't prepared to compromise enough any more.'

'But why should we handle them?' Margi said crossly. 'They're not bloody fish. Why should we pander to all their whims and stroke their egos and put up with their bad temper just because they have sperm and throw us the occasional kind word. If I had my time again I'd have artificial insemination. Like a chicken.'

Tess laughed. 'But what about love? What about the fact that a man and a woman can love each other and if they can stay married, come hell and high water as my mother would say, there is a wonderful purity to their relationship. Don't you think that the most beautiful thing in the world is to see an old man and an old woman together, walking down the street, holding hands?'

'Nope,' Margi said. 'I would think she has spent a lifetime of compromising and probably wants the old bugger dead.'

Tess hooted.

'No, really. If any woman spends any time on her own she realizes just how blissful life can be. Men just suck up our time in pointless effort.'

'So why do we fancy them?'

'Primeval instinct. Gut reaction. There's nothing wrong with wanting to sleep with them – I mean, I, for one, could not countenance sleeping with a woman – could you? All that chatting. You'd be so busy talking about your new calf suede boots from Harvey Nicks you'd never get into bed, would you? At least with men there's nothing to talk about, so you can get straight down to it.'

212

'I talk to Mark.'

'Do you? Do you properly, as easily as you talk to me?'

'Yes. No,' Tess admitted, slowly. 'I do sometimes find, yes I do, that I have to think of specific things to talk to him about and sometimes when I'm driving home in the car from school with Hattie I catch myself practising conversations with him. And all the things I want to talk about, you know, like the children and how they're doing at school and the things I've been studying that day at university and whether we should repaint the kitchen before we sell, I know he finds boring and sometimes it's kind of hard to find a compromise, isn't it? So I have to lead him into conversations and sometimes he goes along with it and sometimes he doesn't. And every night he's home I say, "Did you have a good day?" but he never really tells me, it's only occasionally he opens up and tells me about work and I really love it as he's so funny, but most of the time he can't be bothered because he says he's had a whole day of it and the last thing he wants to do when he comes home is tell me about it. He says that when he comes home all he wants to do is relax, but conversation isn't about relaxing, it's about making an effort. And when I tell him about my day I know I'm boring him and he doesn't give a toss. Being able to interest each other simultaneously is like waiting for two planets to collide. I'm sorry, am I boring you?'

'What? Is that the time?'

'Thanks.'

Chapter Twenty-one

The mobile line crackled, and then broke up.

'What? I can't hear you. Say that again.'

'Dr Williams says we have to go and see him.'

'Oh, why, Mark? I'm frantic. I have to get this part of the thesis finished this afternoon. I've arranged for Hattie to stay at Clara's especially and the boys are both going to friends. I can't just drop everything and go running to school.'

'Do you think I can? I had a board meeting this afternoon, but he's insisting. He says it is very urgent. Sorry, Tess, but I think we have to go.'

'What time?'

'I'll meet you there at three.'

'Did he say anything about what it's about? Any clue?'

'Nope, just said it was urgent. It was him, too, not his secretary.'

'Oh dear,' she said.

She closed the document she was working on, and shut down the laptop. She had nearly finished it, a piece of work into which she had poured her soul. She really enjoyed writing something of length and depth, like this – it was like stepping into another world in which there were simply her fingers on the keyboard, an urgent rush to set down the vivid thoughts, images, facts and feelings which crowded her mind. She could shut out all else, entering this parallel world, a world in which nothing else had any relevance, not even the need for worming paste for Nigel. And when she finished she was so tired, not physically tired, but mentally satiated and content. Nothing else in her life had given her this feeling, and it was like a drug, a compulsion. If she could not study now, or the children or Mark came in and interrupted her, it was impossible to connect and she felt jolted, irritated by their demands and voices.

Increasingly, she caught herself thinking, 'What would Berthe do in this situation?' The woman was becoming her touchstone, which was a bit spooky because she was dead. But she was a useful barometer. Most of the time Berthe advised her to get a life and stand up for herself.

Tess was currently trying to find out which galleries were exhibiting her work, which was tricky because so many of her great paintings were still in private collections. It would be an uphill struggle, but she hoped to persuade the current owners to release them, maybe just for one major exhibition, if she could find someone to help her. She was becoming increasingly excited about the idea of persuading a major London gallery to put on a special exhibition – she was sure Bruno would help with his contacts, and it would be relatively easy to attract publicity.

Women appeared to have come such a long way, she thought, but they haven't really. Not in their hearts. She thought very little about Jake on the way to school. She thought a great deal about herself and her dreams, and Mark. And felt guilty for thinking about herself at all.

*   *   *

'You're late.'

'I had to finish some work.'

'I've been hanging about for ten minutes. Come on.'

I'm pleased to see you, too, Tess thought.

In his study, Dr Williams sat gloomily, with the countenance of a judge about to place a black triangle on his head. He rose to greet them, after they were ushered in by his secretary, who seemed close to tears.

'I am afraid there has been a very worrying development,' he said.

'Fighting again?' Mark ventured. He was unusually pale.

'Worse, I'm afraid.' He leant towards them.

'I'm sorry, but I'm going to have to put this bluntly. Jake has been bringing drugs into school. And selling them to other pupils.'

'What?' Mark roared the word. Tess closed her eyes. Of course. Of course that was what it was. How could she have been so blind?

'What kind of drugs?' she heard herself ask, in a remarkably calm voice.

'Pills of some kind. Ecstasy, or the latest version of it. A form of amphetamine. Not lethal, of course, but potentially pretty dangerous.'

'Of course.' The money. No wonder he had money. He had been buying drugs somewhere, from someone, and bringing them into school to sell and all the time he had probably been taking them too, the over-excitement, the rapid talking, the sudden urge to sleep, his sweating face. And all the time they had thought it couldn't happen to them, that this was something that happened to other children, other families, not nice children who went to expensive private schools and lived in houses just off the Common in Clapham. It was here, it was now.

'And?' Mark said. Tess looked at him. His face was

216

set into an expression she had never seen before. It was rage, blind rage. Her instant reaction was that she must protect Jake. Mark would kill him.

'I am very much afraid,' Dr Williams was saying, 'that we can no longer keep him here. You do understand? He is a boy who has an awful lot to offer but I am afraid that this time he has overstepped the bounds of what we can accept. We have a clear rule that any child found selling drugs is expelled.'

'Does he know?'

'He knows that I am speaking to you, of course. And I am sure that he knows what the penalties are. There is an additional factor.'

'What?' Tess said, in a trembling voice.

'We have an obligation to call the police. They may decide to bring criminal charges.'

'Oh my God.' Mark reached out and took her hand. And held it hard.

'Where is Jake?'

'He's downstairs, in the senior common room. His tutor is with him.'

'Do you need to call the police now?'

'That has been done. They will be making contact with you at home shortly. I hope – and I am sure this is little consolation – they will not bring charges. Only a small amount was involved. The other boys involved have been suspended.'

'Not expelled?'

'They were not dealing, Mrs James. I know it sounds unfair to Jake, but there is a difference.'

'Can we see him?'

'Of course. It would be better if he went home now, before the end of the school day. All his things have been collected together. His tutor has them. I really am very sorry. If you need a reference for another school, I'll be glad to provide it. I'm sure this was very out of character.'

*　　*　　*

Jake stood at the far end of the room. His head was down, like a hunted animal waiting for the final shot. Tess could not bear to see him like that. She murmured to his tutor, made sure they had everything. His tutor called him. Jake walked towards them and Tess reached out for him.

'Don't touch him.'

Mark's words echoed through the long room like gunshot. Tess looked at him, horrified. Jake flashed a glance at her. It was one of pure fear. She reached out and took his hand. Boldly, she looked up at Mark.

'Come on,' she said. 'Let's go home.'

In the car, no-one spoke. It was a relief to pull into their resident's parking space, a relief to have something to do, in unloading the car of his school bag, his games bag, his hockey stick, boots, Barbour coat he needed for wet weather, wellingtons for walks in the grounds. She found herself wondering what they would do with his uniform. It would do for Ollie, if they didn't move after all.

Inside the house, she made a pile of everything at the foot of the stairs. Jake stood helplessly by her.

'I—'

'Don't say anything.' Mark's voice was low, and tight, and threatening. Tess put her hand on his arm. Every muscle was bunched tight, hard.

'Go downstairs,' he said. Tess looked directly at him.

'You cannot solve things like this,' she said.

'I have let you take the soft approach for long enough,' he said, calmly. 'And I am afraid that being civilized does not appear to have worked.'

Tess stood for a moment at the top of the stairs. There was nothing she could do. She turned to Jake. He said, very clearly, 'Go on, Mum.'

218

She did not hear the blow. But she heard Jake's footsteps, running up to his bedroom, and Mark following him. Then the door banged, and there was silence.

She sat at the kitchen table. She felt as if she had been told of a sudden, unexpected death. There was the same sense of loss, and desolation, and incomprehension that life continued, as if she was alone, a fixed point of total madness surrounded by meaningless normality. She had failed him. Mark had failed him. He must have been crying out, he must have been desperate to do such a thing. He was not, she refused to believe, bad. He *wasn't* bad. She knew him, she had given birth to him, she had seen him as a child, a happy child, wayward, yes, but so funny, so clever and bright and sharp and somehow all that promise had turned into a child who wanted to rebel and hurt them. Why? It had to be their fault.

What felt like hours later, she heard Mark's footsteps. She stood up as he walked into the kitchen. His face was as white as a sheet. He sat down at the table. Then he crumpled forward, and buried his face in his hands. Tess moved to him, and, hesitantly, put her hands on his shoulders. Then she leant forward, and rested her head against his hair.

'I hit him,' Mark said softly. 'I vowed I would never do that again and I did.'

'Where is he?'

'In his room. Leave him. We talked – a little – I said he had to understand why I had to do it and how much he had let us down. You do see, don't you, why there was nothing else I could do?'

Tess felt the words forming in her mouth. She was about to say, 'Yes, I know,' and soothe him. Then she thought, But I don't believe that. I think the worst possible thing in the world you could have done was hit him, and alienate him from the people who love him. He has just been rejected by his school, and now you have done the one thing designed to drive him away from us, too. She paused, and drew away from him.

'I'm going to see him,' she said.

'Just leave him,' Mark said.

'No.'

'Tess, for God's sake. Don't be stupid. You'll only make things worse.'

'Let me decide,' she said.

Jake was sitting on his bed. In his arms was an ancient bear, the bear that had slept with him night after night in his cot when he was a baby, the bear which had moved with him into his first bed, and which now spent most of his time on the crowded window ledge, wearing a school tie and a baseball cap. She hadn't seen it for a while. Jake held him close to his chest. He was staring into space, rocking backwards and forwards. He did not look up as Tess entered the room. There was a vivid red mark across his cheek.

Tess sat down carefully next to him.

'I thought you'd lost that.' Jake looked down at the bear.

'Nope,' he said.

'Ollie will be home soon. What do you want to do?'

He looked up. 'Not bothered.'

'We ought to tell him.'

'He'll know.'

'Why, Jake, why? You know how stupid drugs are, we've talked about it often enough. You know drugs are for losers, you've said so yourself. You don't need money. You have everything you need here, with us. Why did you do it? Was it for a thrill? Did you hate school? Please, please, Jake, I am just trying to make some sense of it.'

'Make some sense of it so it can all be neatly packaged away and you and Dad can go back to your normal life and everything can go on as normal.'

'I suppose so. What is so wrong with that?'

'Because no-one listens to me! No-one ever takes into account what I am feeling and I'm always made to feel that I'm the bad one, I'm the naughty one who does everything wrong compared with blameless Ollie and lovely Hattie. Do you have any idea what it's like? What it's like to grow up as some kind of pariah and I know, I just know, that you and Dad love them so much more than me, so what the hell does it matter what I do with my life? I'm not as clever as Ollie, I'm never going to make it, am I, make you proud of me? So I may as well just go off and screw myself up because at least that way I can have some fun. I'm really glad they caught me, Mum, I wanted them to, just to see the look on their stupid faces. I hate that school. I hate those teachers with their sneering faces and the snobbery and the expectations, of course you'll go to university and of course you'll get a good job and end up in the City or wherever and you'll marry some posh boring girl and have two point four children and end up as fucked up as you and Dad. I don't want it, Mum. I want something different. I feel' – he hit his chest, hard, with his fist – 'that I am different. I am different from everyone else. So different from every-one else in this family and I can never, never fit in. You don't want me. You never have.'

He stopped, panting, and turned his back on her.

Oh God, she thought, is that what he really feels? Jesus. What a mess we have made. She put her hand on his shoulder.

'You cannot think that,' she said, gently. 'You are our firstborn. Of course I love you all the same but you are special. I have known you the longest. I know you best. This isn't you, Jake. I don't – no, I can't –

believe this is how you really feel. Maybe the other two are easier' – Jake snorted – 'but that doesn't mean either of us love you any the less for it. We just thought it was a phase, a teenage thing. I had no idea you felt like that. How can I make it up to you?' I am a mother, she thought. I ought to be able to make this better. But I don't know how.

'It isn't you,' Jake said. 'It's Dad.'

'What?'

'Dad has no time for me. He used to take me to football and rugby but now it's all Ollie and his cricket. We used to watch TV together. He doesn't have time now, or he's working. He's always too busy or he isn't even here. When he does look at me it's as if he hates me. I just fuck everything up for everyone. There's no point to anything. I dread waking up each day and I dread going to sleep. You don't know what I dream about, Mum. I must be really sick. I hear you and Dad shouting at each other and I know it's about me. Dad wants me just to go away.'

'We don't row about you. That isn't it at all. Dad loves you so much.'

Jake was silent.

'We've all been a bit tied up this year, you know that.'

'It isn't just this year. It's been years. I don't think I can live here any more.'

'But where could you go, darling? Be reasonable. You have to stay here, we have to go on from this. We can find you another school.'

Jake laughed derisively. 'Oh, no. I've blown that one. Dad made that very clear. No more expensive education for me.'

'That's not true. Even if I have to, I will find the money for a good school for you, and I will personally force them to take you.'

Jake smiled at her. 'You would, wouldn't you?'

'Too bloody right I would. But one proviso.'

'I know. No more drugs.'

'Ever. I mean that.'

'Not even the odd smoke?'

'Jake, that is not funny. Now come down and have a coffee.'

'No.' The blood, which had returned to his cheeks, drained. 'I'll come down when Dad goes. OK?'

'OK. But you have to sort this out between you. I can't do it for you.'

'I know,' Jake said. 'But I think it's his turn to apologize.'

'You know what this means, don't you?'

'What?' Tess stood with her back to Mark, putting the kettle onto the Aga.

'We have to move. There's no other school for him here. He'd be even worse at the comp. Anyway, it will get him away from all these temptations and whichever little bastards sold him the drugs in the first place.'

'Do you really think that is the answer?' She swung round to face him.

'Yes,' Mark said coldly. 'I do. And it's about time you toughened up, Tess. If I find you've been making up to him and softening everything I have said I will be so bloody angry I cannot hold myself responsible. What has been lacking here, Tess, is discipline. That is what he needs.'

'No, he doesn't,' she said. 'What he needs is love. Your love.'

'Oh, for fuck's sake! Save me the touchy-feely university approach, please. He thinks he can get away with doing whatever he wants and we will always forgive him because that is how you have brought him up and you will always cover up for him.'

'And you?'

'Oh, no. You can't drag me into this one. I have always said he needed a firmer hand but it was you saying don't thump him, that's the stupid backward Australian way, let's do it the nice British middle-class way and we'll talk him out of it. Well, it's worked brilliantly, hasn't it? He's been expelled for selling drugs. I'm sorry if that is a little too blunt for your delicate *Guardian*-reading sensibilities but it is the plain fact of the matter. And now we are going to deal with this my way. There is to be no going out until we move. No seeing his friends. No football matches, no cinema, no hanging about the shops. He will stay here, where we can watch him, he will keep up with his work – I'm sure St Peter's can help – and then, when we do move, I am going to find the toughest bloody school I can and there will be no more of this indulgence shit. When I think of the way he has spoken to you over the past year I cannot believe how we have allowed him to get away with it. But no longer.'

'You're wrong.'

'What the hell do you mean?'

'I mean you're wrong. About all of it. One of the reasons he has been behaving so badly is because we have been ignoring him. We have treated him as the outsider, the villain in this family. Ollie and Hattie have had everything in the way of attention, Jake very little. If you lock him up now, and ostracize him, you will simply drive him further and further away. What you need to do right now is go up and talk to him and show him that, whatever he has done, you love him and you can trust him in the future.'

'No.'

'Sorry?'

'No. I am not going to do that. I am not going to be told how to treat my own son. It is about time that what I say goes again in this house. And we are moving. That is final. Now I have to go back to work. And leave him alone, Tess. Let him just sit and think about what he has done to this family.'

'You are so wrong,' she said. He shook his head wordlessly, in despair, and left.

Chapter Twenty-two

Jake lay with Francesca on her narrow single bed. The teddy bears and other cuddly toys she had insisted on keeping, despite the recent redecoration of her room in Sixties style, with lava lamps and lilac walls, had fallen to the floor. Dido sang mournfully on her CD player. The door was locked, although Francesca knew her mother wouldn't be home for at least another hour.

'Where do they think you are?'

Jake tightened his grip of her hand.

'At the library,' he murmured, softly. Francesca laughed, and, leaning on her elbow, gazed at him. He lay on his back, staring up at the ceiling. Hesitantly, she reached up to trace the outline of his lips. Almost roughly, he pulled her to him, and kissed her. He held her more tightly, so their bodies were almost indivisible. He draped one leg over her, forcing her closer to him.

'Look,' he murmured. 'We fit.'

She drew back slightly, and looked at him. Her heart was beating very fast, and yet she felt curiously peaceful, as if this moment could go on and on for ever. If I died now, she thought, I would be happy.

'What are you thinking?' he said.

She smiled up at him, her eyes huge in her pale face. 'I'm thinking that I cannot bear to see you go.'

'Don't. Don't say that now. Not when we have another hour.' He put his hand under her chin, and tilted her face to his. Then he kissed her slowly, and delicately, all over her eyelids, her cheeks, until his lips rested on hers.

'You don't mind, do you?' she said, quietly.

'No,' he said. 'It's too risky anyway. I think that would be the last straw for my parents. My dad would fucking kill me.'

'So would my mum.'

'Do you want to?' Jake asked.

'What do you think?'

'Have you? Ever?'

'No.'

'You are the first person,' he said, 'I have really loved. Apart from my mum.'

'What about your dad?'

'Hardly.' His hand reached up and rubbed the faint mark, still visible.

'I don't blame you,' she said. 'I don't love my dad. He's a bastard. He thinks he can buy our love.'

'How often do you see him?'

'Every couple of weeks. He gives us loads of things, as if that will make up for it.'

'What does your mum think?'

'Oh, she hates him. She always has.'

'They're useless, our parents, aren't they?'

'They didn't show me much of an example,' Francesca said. 'I don't think I'm ever going to get married. I don't want any child to feel as bad as I did when Mum and Dad split up. It's OK now, just, but it was so awful at the time. You're lucky your mum and dad are still together.'

'I dunno. They're rowing a lot. Mostly about me,' he added, with grim satisfaction.

227

'That's because you're bad,' she said, smiling at him.

'How bad?'

'Oh, very bad.' She leant her head against his shoulder. He rested his mouth against her hair. It smelt clean, and soft, of shampoo. It felt innocent. His arms tightened around her. 'I'd like to sleep like this.'

'We better not. Mum would come home.'

'We can pretend. Can't we?' And he kissed her slowly, until she was no longer sure where he ended and she began.

Chapter Twenty-three

Mark's voice, from just above her head, was full of muffled enthusiasm.

'There's so much potential up here! It's fantastic.'

'What can you see?' Tess called.

'Lots of straw and – yuck – bats' droppings, I think. But there's plenty of headroom and I'm sure this ceiling will come down easily.' He banged his feet hard on the floor, and a small shower of plaster drifted gently down onto Tess's head, like snowflakes.

'Can I come up?' she called.

'Yup, but be careful. The ladder is very rickety.'

Tess gingerly placed one foot on the bottom rung of the crumbling wooden ladder which led to the hayloft, situated directly above the kitchen. She agreed with Mark that the kitchen was too small, but she was not quite sure if she could face the thought of having the whole ceiling taken down. There was already so much chaos everywhere, she didn't think she could stand much more. It was like living through the Blitz. There was nowhere to sit down, all their furniture was shrouded in dust sheets like bulky ghosts and everything was covered in a fine layer of builders' dust, so there was absolutely no point clearing up. Tess felt bilious from living on a diet of Chinese takeaways, burgers, and fish and chips from a van that stopped in the village every Thursday night. The children seemed to think it was great, but Tess felt as if she would never be clean again, inside or out.

Very gently, she heaved herself up through the trap-door opening. The air was musty, and the old beams hung with cobwebs like canopied curtains. She stood upright, taking great care to stand on a beam rather than the floorboards.

'Look at this!' Mark said. He held up a Players cigarette packet. 'Ancient!' he said happily. 'And this – a newspaper from 1942.'

'Incredible,' Tess said.

'You don't seem very enthusiastic. Tess, no-one has been up here for years. It's history!'

'No it isn't,' she said. 'It's derelict.' Then Mark put his foot through the ceiling.

They had been in the house for precisely five weeks, and for all of that time they had been unable to have a bath, as the old one was so corroded Tess banned everyone from getting in, for fear of contracting tetanus. She sensed people moving away from her as she sat on the train on her way to university. She felt surrounded by an almost visible fug of odour. Mark insisted that there was an optimum level of dirt to be reached and after that you didn't get any dirtier. It was like dreadlocks, he said, having had these in his travelling days. You reached maximum grubbiness and then your hair actually started to repel the dirt. Both Ollie and Jake thankfully could shower at school, and Hattie also now had the facilities to have a shower after games, so they hadn't quite reached the radio-active stage Tess felt she was approaching. She had a wash in the hand basin every morning, but it was hardly the same as a long, delicious wallow. She'd begun to dream about having a bath and steaming power showers. The only answer seemed to be to take the children to the local municipal swimming baths and shower there. But, oh dear. Tess was no snob but these baths were simply not clean. Their nearest swimming pool in London had not exactly been a cornucopia of luxury, but at least it had toilets which didn't stink.

The first time Tess had gone shopping in their nearest market town she couldn't believe her eyes. It was like the land that time forgot. The town was built around a small market square, but instead of having the sort of thing you would expect in a reasonably prosperous rural commuter town, like antique shops and inviting cafés, it had a wool shop with a cross-looking toy sheep in the window, a shop which sold car aerials and a pre-McDonald's fast food restaurant with smears of grease on the windows. OK, so of course the shops wouldn't be London, but she had hardly expected them to be like this.

After slogging up and down looking for a deli-catessen – and failing – she took Hattie into the one coffee shop she could find which didn't have Formica tables. It was very dark, and there didn't appear to be anyone serving.

'Hello!' she called loudly. A boy aged about ten appeared.

'Could we have a coffee and a Coke?' she said.

'I'll ask me mum,' he said.

It was five minutes before anyone reappeared.

'Yes?' a cold-looking woman, clearly his mother, said from the doorway into a kitchen.

'I'd like a cappuccino and a Coke,' Tess said, nervously. 'Please.'

'Coffee?'

'Yes, cappuccino. Thank you.'

'We don't have that.'

'Espresso?'

'No.'

Tess was beginning to enjoy herself.

'Café latte?'

'No.'

'Mocha?'

'No.'

'Frappacino?'

'No.'

'Do you sell Coke?'

'We do.'

'Coke, then, and a filter coffee. What a lovely place you have here.' The woman looked at her suspiciously. 'So airy and light.'

Hattie leant forward and tugged her mother's arm violently.

'Do we have to stay, Mum? It smells.'

'That'll be the dog,' the woman said.

They turned to look. An ancient retriever lay next to an electric fire, with only one bar working. It looked up at them piteously, and thumped his tail.

'He's only just had his operation and it's still a bit weepy,' the woman said.

'I don't think we've time for a drink, Hattie, do you? Many thanks. Goodbye.'

'Margi. Come and get me. I can't find anywhere that sells a decent cappuccino and there's no-one to talk to and every time I go out I get dirty and we have no hot water and I haven't had a bath in weeks. It's supposed to be healthier in the country but I feel like I'm coming down with the plague.'

'Well, don't ask me to come and rescue you. I don't do mud. How are the family coping?'

'Happy as clams,' Tess said. 'Jake appears to actually like his new school, Ollie is possibly the brightest child ever to attend the same school and is therefore fêted like a minor god and Hattie has been made form captain.'

'And Mark?'

'Mark has discovered his primeval self. His natural element seems to be mud. From first thing on a Saturday morning to last thing Sunday night he is out there, striding about wearing a lumberjack shirt, moving great mounds of earth and planning walls and hedges.'

'What about you?'

'I stay in and huddle by the fire, trying to tap on my laptop with freezing fingers. It's just so cold even though it's June. The new radiators haven't arrived yet although the boiler is in, thank God, and the second-hand Aga we bought for a song keeps packing up. I am trying to work with gormless workmen in and out of my study all the time carrying pieces of piping and calling me missus, not to mention playing the radio very loudly. And don't ask about the couple who came round yesterday to have a good nosy.'

'Go on.'

'Jeremy and Loopy – I'm not joking – and their teenage daughter Kerame. I thought she might provide a bit of female company for Jake, but blimey. She's at some smart weekly boarding school, thin as a rake and clearly anorexic, and so neurotic she couldn't get two words out. She just stood there pulling her jumper down over her hands and looking as if she was about to burst into tears while her parents told me in the kind of voices that sound like they're permanently constipated how much fun she has living here and what a wonderful social life there is for teenagers in the village. They live at the manor house – honestly, they're no more country people than we are, they used to live in Fulham – but they've just bought their way into the whole thing, you know, Range Rover covered in mud, hunting, clip-on Labradors, all that stuff. They went on and on about how the Master of the Hunt is their great friend, and did we know him, as if we would. Loopy asked me if I rode and when I said I didn't she made this strange screeching noise and said it didn't matter, because I soon would because if I was going to meet anyone who was anyone I had to ride. Then Mark engaged Jeremy in some incomprehensible conversation about land and making haylage and what types of fencing were the best and did he think we should drain the paddock and all I wanted to do was lie down on the floor and sob. I'm so bored. Please, please come and stay so I can have a normal conversation that isn't about the best way to hang a five-barred gate.'

'I will once you get hot water,' Margi said, dubiously. 'Is there any form of heating?'

'Open fires at the moment,' Tess said. 'Very romantic until you have to clear the bloody things out and get covered in soot, and most of them smoke so you sit there wondering if it's better to be smoked herring or frozen fish.'

'What a wild time you're having.'

'Oh, it's riotous. And you know that wonderful high-speed rail link Mark went on about? Well, it actually takes an hour and a half, unless it stops for half an hour for no reason, and it takes me twenty minutes to drive to the bloody railway station in the first place. An hour if you get stuck behind a fourteen-year-old driving a tractor down the middle of the road.'

'How often do you have to come in?'

'I'm down to twice a week at the moment and the rest of the work I'm supposed to do from home but most of the time I'm so bloody cold I can't face it. It's much easier to get the train in and work in the library. More civilized, too. Actually, that's a point, it would be easier to meet you for lunch in London. Anyway, what was the vital thing you have to tell me before I bored you with life on Cold Comfort Farm?'

'Handbag is pregnant.'

'What? How?'

'What do you mean, how? Through sexual intercourse with my ex-husband, of course. I mean, she's twenty-four. She'd only have to brush up against him at that age to be up the duff.'

'Do you mind?'

'I do, actually. It's one thing having your husband living with someone almost half your age, it's another thing to have them starting a new family with them. How are the girls meant to feel? He's their father, for goodness sake, not someone else's. On the surface Francesca was all bubbly and won't-it-be-lovely-to-have-a-little-sister-or-brother and then I found her in tears in her bedroom. It's almost as if he's saying you're not good enough as a family, I want a nice shiny new one.'

'How do you feel about it?'

'A bit shaken up, I suppose,' Margi said slowly. 'What it does is underline the finality of our lives, we are the old family, past history, bring on the new because ours failed. I didn't mind him sleeping with her – sex is a commodity, it's cheap, isn't it – but having children with her is altogether different. I guess it means that he must love her. They may even get married. Oh, imagine, Tess. My girls dressed up like fairy bridesmaids to attend the wedding of their father to some trollop eight years older than Francesca with whom their father is sleeping. It isn't Topsy and Tim, is it? It isn't exactly the way to give your children good family values, it's like saying families don't matter, if it goes wrong, whoops, don't worry, another one will be along in a minute, like a bus. Not much longevity, is there? Or permanence.'

'But you don't want him back, do you? You've never let the girls think he might come back?'

'God, no. I just feel rather – and this is really silly – rejected all over again. He's starting off on this brand new life and all I have is my old one.'

'But you love your life. You're always telling me how much happier you are now he's gone.'

'I know. But I'm bloody lonely too, sometimes, Tess. Don't make Mark feel too bad about making you move, will you?'

'Why on earth do you of all people say that?'

'Because he sounds happier than he has been for ages and it isn't a lot to ask, is it, just to like it there?'

'It is, actually,' Tess said. 'This sounds mad – and for God's sake, don't tell anyone, not even Vanessa – but I think the house hates me.' Margi yelped with laughter.

'That's it. You've gone too far. Now I am seriously worried about you. What does your tongue look like? Who is the Prime Minister?'

'Shut up. I know it sounds a crazy notion,' Tess said. 'But I can't settle here. I can't find peace – I know that sounds loony – but in the old house at least I did feel I belonged there. I don't feel I do belong here. Hang on. Hattie, if you throw that at Ollie one more time I will take it off you. There are just so many decisions I need to make, about decorating and all that stuff – and I just can't find any enthusiasm to get on with it. I feel like I am being buried alive. It's driving Mark mad. He's striding about being Mr Happy from Happysville and I drip about looking suicidal. The boys' school is all right but God, Margi, Hattie's school. The village primary only went up to eight, which was no use, and the combined school from eight to eleven had really huge classes. So we've had to ask Mum and Dad for help and they're paying for her to go to this prep school six miles away. It's a fabulous building and she loves it, but the other mums – archetypal country smuggies, four-wheel drive de rigeur, coffee mornings, staff v. parents netball matches, you know the kind of thing. I can't find anyone I like and I'm all on my own with no-one to play with. I feel incredibly dislocated and unreal. It's a bit of a nightmare, in all honesty.'

'Stop bleating,' Margi said. 'I'll come next weekend.'

Mark was not exactly thrilled at the prospect of Margi coming to stay. He tended to view her as a bad influence on Tess – but not as bad as Nicki – because she was so forthright about being happier on her own. And Mark's current obsession was that Tess wasn't trying hard enough to make new friends here. He argued that he'd made friends already, mostly through the local pub, and surely there were some mothers at either the boys', or Hattie's, school who must be OK. The undercurrent was that she was deliberately trying to sabotage any attempts to be happy and fit in. He pointed out that this was going to be their life for a very long time and she ought to make more of an effort instead of rushing back to London at every opportunity.

When he said this, Tess's heart sank. Of course she could see the beauty of the landscape, but once you'd sat and looked at it for a bit there was nothing else to do. You couldn't engage landscape in meaningful discussion. She could throw herself into decorating the house once the plasterers had finished and they could paint, but what was the point if hardly anyone was going to see it? Mark said that was a ridiculous attitude and lots of their London friends would love to come and stay for the weekend, and they would soon find couples here they both liked. Tess pointed out that although the house was bigger, they still only had four bedrooms and so where were all these guests going to sleep now that the children had annexed a bedroom each? Mark said maybe they ought to think about an extension, and Tess had to sit down she was laughing so hard. Extension? When they'd already had to borrow another huge lump sum to pay for the renovation work and their mortgage was now bigger than it had been on the house in Clapham and all Mark's confident financial calculations meant absolutely nothing? And now she was stuck out here how on earth was she going to find a well-paid job? Mark replied that he'd never thought she had any intention of teaching anyway, she'd only done the course to spite him because he didn't want her to. Tess replied that if that was the level of his respect for her then he could go and live in his horrid new workshop which was a half-renovated cow byre with an earthen floor.

But she had to admit he did look much healthier. She was sitting with the children on the sofa one night underneath Ollie's duvet, watching *Stepmom*, when he wandered into the room and lounged against the door frame. In one hand was a hammer, in the other the power drill that was now welded to him, like Edward Scissorhands.

'Come for a walk,' he said. 'There's the most fantastic sunset.'

'What a romantic you are,' she said. 'But it's cosy in here.' She snuggled down into the warmth. They always watched TV under duvets, it was too cold otherwise. What the hell would winter be like? They'd have to smear themselves in whale blubber to survive.

'Out,' Mark said, grinning. 'What's the point of living in the country if you don't go out into it?'

'I can look at it through the window,' Tess said petulantly. 'Oh, all right. Jake, get your legs off me, will you?' Jake lifted his legs, and Tess slunk out from underneath the cover. Hattie growled as a draught of cold air wafted in under the duvet.

Mark pulled the front door shut firmly behind them. The paint was peeling and he kept meaning to give it a fresh coat. In fact, he positively looked forward to doing it. He had forgotten how much he liked working with his hands, what a sense of peace repairing things and painting gave him. He had done carpentry at school, and he found he could remember most of the necessary skills. He felt happier than he had for years, making shelves for Tess's study, planing and smoothing the wood. He caught himself humming whenever he looked out through the cobwebby windows over his land. His land. There wasn't that much in acreage, but it was as far as the eye could see and it meant a great deal to him. It gave him such a sense of achievement that he could afford to buy all this – well, OK, maybe not afford, exactly – and he could take pride in it, in a way he couldn't with the London house because it was exactly like everyone else's and although it was worth a lot of money in most people's books, it wasn't real money, it was just an inflated amount pushed up by the fact that the house was in the capital. Here, you really got something for your money. He felt rather squire-ish, and there was nothing he liked more than strolling the perimeter of his land at dusk. They must buy a dog. And maybe he would take up smoking cigars. A cigar and a Labrador would be good things for a man to have with him on his late-night stroll around his land.

And it would be so much cheaper, living here, once they had got over the hurdle of renovating the house. Tess said this was rubbish, and she was already spending at least five times as much in petrol ferrying the children to their respective schools and then belting off to get the train, and she had to spend far more on her weekly shop at the supermarket because if they ran out there was no more popping down to the convenient corner shop to plug the gaps. What she had failed to grasp, Mark thought, smoking his imaginary cigar, was the idea of living more off the land. He liked the thought of that very much. They could grow their own vegetables – he was sure Tess wouldn't mind digging the vegetable patch out while he was at work, he would sow the seeds and plant the potatoes, the creative parts that needed more thought and organization. They could keep hens – the children would love that, and it would hardly take Tess any time at all to feed them in the morning before she set out for university. They'd only need cleaning out once a week, possibly. And sheep. Sheep would go rather nicely in the small paddock until they got around to buying Hattie a pony – Tess was being very unreasonable about that. It was unlikely to be much work – all they ate was grass, after all, and she'd soon get the hang of tack and mucking out. Then there was the benefice of nature itself – the apple trees, which would be laden with fruit in the late summer. He might buy a cider press. What a good idea. Tess would only need to peel the apples first, and then they could make wonderful fresh apple juice for the children. The problem with Tess was that she was not thinking the thing through sufficiently. All she seemed to see was more work for her.

Gradually, the house was coming together. The first thing they had had to do was replace the windows, which had been so rotten you could put your finger through the sills. Mark had insisted they get a carpenter to make proper mullioned windows like the originals, and it had cost more but it had been worth it. The facade of the house, which at first had looked sad and neglected, now looked lived in, cared for. The bricks around the windows had been pointed, and any crumbling ones replaced with original old bricks which Mark had found in a pile down one of the fields at the back of the house.

'Doesn't it look brilliant,' he said, taking her arm as they walked down the front path. Tess had pulled up the weeds, and the workmen had laid some old slabs they had found at the back of the stables.

'It was the right decision, wasn't it?'

'Of course it was,' she said, hugging his arm to her.

'You aren't bored?'

'God, no. There's so much to do, and having to go in to university . . . Do you mind the commuting?'

'I enjoy it. It's a chance to get some work done on the train, and it was taking me half an hour from Clapham, anyway. God, Tess, I can't tell you how great it feels at the end of the day to know that in an hour I'll be out of there, out of the smog and crap and all the people, and driving down quiet country lanes into the peace and quiet of the village. It's made me feel like a different person.'

'Jake seems happy,' Tess said, carefully. She stopped and looked up at him. 'His school has been great.'

'He does seem calmer,' Mark agreed. 'We had a good chat about shooting the other day. There's a farmers' syndicate I've been asked to join and . . .'

'When? When did you get asked that?'

'In the pub last Sunday lunchtime. I said I used to do a bit of shooting back in Australia and this old boy piped up and said there might be a place available on the syndicate next season. Quite an honour, apparently. Some people have to wait years.'

'But do you want to do that?'

'What?'

'Go shooting? Go out killing things for fun?'

'Oh for God's sake, Tess, get real. Where do you think supermarket pheasant comes from? Where do you think any meat comes from? This is the country. Animals die so that we can eat. It's part of life's natural circle. Stop coming all liberal with me about it. I thought your father used to go shooting.'

'A bit,' Tess conceded.

'Well, Jake's school does clay-pigeon shooting as one of its sports and I think it would be a good idea if Jake got involved.'

'Take out some of his natural aggression on a defenceless clay pigeon?' Tess said.

'Ha, ha. But it would give him an inducement if he thought he could come out shooting with me. It would be nice if we could do something together.'

'True.'

'Have his teachers said anything about him?'

'So far, so good. You like the head, don't you? He seems pretty down the line. I mean, it isn't going to be as academic as St Peter's, but then thank God he isn't going to end up in a young offenders' institute, either.' She shuddered. The police, thankfully, had decided not to press charges because the amount of drugs involved had been so small and Jake was a minor, but an officer had given Jake a severe talking-to, which seemed to have done him good. He had obeyed their curfew to the letter, and even found time to go and work in the library, before they'd finally moved.

And, at his new school, he was something of a hero. Not only was he streetwise, tough and good-looking, he also had the additional kudos of having been expelled. He had been something of a celebrity from day one, because the news of his past had spread like wildfire through the school, after one of the boys had heard two masters talking about it while he waited outside the staff room.

'Just look at that sunset.'

Ahead of them, just sinking below the level of the horizon, was the sun, still glorious, still glowing so deeply orange it seemed on fire. The light was not blinding, but a gentle amber which rolled over the fields towards them. The sky above was cobalt blue, fading to a dark midnight, so vast, so much wider, higher and encompassing than the London skyline. It made Tess feel very small.

'It's getting rather dark,' she said. 'Do you think we ought to leave the children?'

'Oh come on,' Mark said. 'I hardly ever get you to myself these days.'

They walked slowly down the track at the side of the house, just beginning to dry out, the mud finally hardening into ridges which would smooth out under the lush summer grass. Mollie, who ran the village shop, said Tess soon wouldn't recognize the place. 'Full of flowers,' she said, 'all over the green. And that awful muddy path at the side of your house – it dries out completely. It's beautiful, down there, in the summer, with the wild roses and then the blackberries in late August. It'll be lovely for your three to go picking them, all the village children do.' Tess tried, and failed, to imagine herself picking blackberries with her children. When would she find the time?

'You are happy here, aren't you?' Mark paused by an old five-barred gate, a gate which led into a field containing four large brown horses. They were owned by the local farmer and were friendly if goofy things, pushing each other out of the way and standing on each others' feet to get at the children's flattened hands, proffering carrots and Polo mints. Tess had been rather nervous at first at letting them do this, until Mark intervened and said they would come to no harm, as long as they didn't actually climb in with them. There was a footpath across the field, but Tess hadn't dared use it as yet, because she was worried the horses would spot her as the mother of the beneficent children and come charging across in a mint frenzy.

'Nigel certainly likes it,' Tess joked. He hadn't, at first. They'd kept him in the house for a week, as the cat books suggested, with a litter tray which he spectacularly failed to use. Then they had let him go out into the garden, the children following him from tree to tree, on tiptoe like the Pink Panther. Nigel put one paw onto the muddy grass, shook it disdainfully, and stalked back towards the house. The children leapt out from behind their trees, grabbed him, and carried him squirming and yowling into the middle of the lawn. They put him down and he glared at them angrily, swishing his tail. Then a bird swooped down in front of him. His eyes shone, his plump body went rigid, and silently, steadfastly, he stalked it over to the hedge which ran down the middle of the front garden, dividing it from the old orchard. He forgot about the mud, the chill wind and the strange smells in the thrill of the chase.

From that moment on, Nigel became an outdoor cat. He spurned the comfort of the hearth and the children's beds. He spent his nights stalking the multitude of voles, shrews, mice, rats and small birds which proliferated around the garden, orchard and paddock. He refound his hidden tiger, and one night he had a famous victory over a mothy tortoiseshell tom which had claimed the garden for his own when the old man lived there. He wore his bitten ear as a mark of pride, like a feline *légion d'honneur*. He was having the time of his life, keeping the family well supplied with all the dead furry animals they could ever desire. After a week, he disappeared for three days. Hattie was bereft, but Tess assured her he was just off on a thrilling cat adventure, and sure enough he turned up, grubby, dishevelled and with a coat full of twigs and burrs, meowing at the back door. Then he slept solidly for two days, while Tess poked him occasionally to make sure he wasn't dead.

'Don't avoid the question.' Mark's smile, in the half light, was hesitant.

'Do you want me to be honest?'

Mark turned away from her, and leant against the gate.

'No,' he said. 'I don't think I do.'

'In that case,' she said vehemently, 'what is the point of asking me? All you want me to say is that yes, I

244

absolutely adore it and the children are clearly much happier and it was a brilliant idea of yours and I am a witch for ever doubting the fact that it would be the salvation of our family.'

'Just for once,' he said, turning back to look at her, 'can't you see things from someone else's point of view?'

'But you asked me how I feel,' Tess said, helplessly.

'I know, but surely you can see that everything is better here. Hattie has space to run around and play. She's doing better at school. She's made a friend in the village already, and they can do proper child things like climbing trees and making dens and hunting bugs, instead of lolling in front of Cartoon Network like she used to do all day at the weekend. Ollie is – well, OK, he's Ollie and he would probably be happy anywhere but Jake – he isn't the same boy, is he? He even smiles occasionally.'

Tess held up her fingers, and counted them, one by one. 'So that's you. Happy. Hattie. Happy. Ollie. Happy. Jake. Happy. It's only selfish me, isn't it, the fly in the ointment, the only one not to embrace mud and boredom and isolation with open arms.'

'Oh for fuck's sake,' Mark said. 'Look, all I'm saying is just try. Just try to like it. Just try to like it for a year.' Tess yelped. 'If you still hate it after a year we'll think about moving back.'

'But you have absolutely no intention of moving back, have you?'

He slumped onto the gate, and let his head fall into his folded arms. 'Yes,' he said, wearily. 'I would do it for you because I love you more than anything in the world and I want you to be happy, because if you are not happy then my happiness means very little.'

'So why pile on the pressure about the children, making me feel that I would be doing them out of this idyllic Enid Blyton childhood?'

'Because you would,' Mark said. And laughed. 'Sorry, sorry.' He reached out and took her in his arms. 'Poor Mrs Grumpy. What can we do to make you happy?'

'A glass of wine would be good,' she said. Her smile did not quite reach her eyes.

'Easily fixed,' he said. 'Let's go home, you sad alcoholic.'

Chapter Twenty-four

'Darling, it's fabulous!'

'That's all very well for you to say. You can breathe in the fresh air and then get back into your car and drive back into the land of rocket and hot water and pizzas delivered to your door.'

'You know how much I love you, but I think you are being a bit shallow on this one.'

'Watch out!'

Margi's platform heel, elegantly encased in suede, sank into the deep mud at the side of the front steps.

'Maybe you're right,' she said, extracting her heel with some difficulty. 'Come on, Francesca, Georgina!'

The two girls were sitting in the car, looking about them in wonder. Tess understood just how they felt, because the demolition of the old farm buildings had reached a delicate stage. To the left of the house stood a large barn, which now had a gaping hole in the side wall. It had been used for cattle, with railings along each side, and the old straw on which the cattle had stood was still present in all its muddy glory, at least four feet deep. It had an odour all of its own, an odour Tess had almost stopped noticing. As Francesca climbed out, Tess thought that perhaps open-toed platform sandals had not been the most sensible of footwear.

'Is it always this dark?' Margi whispered, as they walked into the hallway.

'We're having a bit of a problem with the wattage,' Tess admitted. 'If you put anything in more than 40 watts, the whole system blows.'

'Have you thought of getting a new one?'

'This is the new one,' Tess said.

'Ah.'

Like the land around it, the house was not looking its best. They were currently at the plastering stage, so every wall was a dull grey in various stages of drying out. Wires hung out of the walls, waiting for fittings, and as yet the skirting boards hadn't been fitted so there was no point in laying the carpets. Bare floorboards, some of which would be sanded and varnished, did not make the house seem any cosier. With its bare boards and grey walls, it looked rather like a nineteenth-century lunatic asylum.

'At least we can have a proper cup of coffee,' Tess said over her shoulder as Margi followed her down the step into the kitchen. 'I got totally fed up with instant so I went out and bought this Gaggia.' She reached forward, and switched the machine on. There was a flash of blue light and a loud bang.

'Maybe we should go out,' Margi said, looking around the kitchen. It had just been plastered in here too, and the new kitchen cupboards which Tess had recklessly ordered had not yet been delivered. She had decided on free-standing units – an old oak dresser, butcher's block and central unit with chairs and a built-in wine rack, on the basis that she could always take them with her if they left. She told Mark free-standing was much more fashionable than a fitted kitchen.

'Out where?' Tess said. 'There's nowhere to go. Not

within half an hour's drive. We could go into Oxford but it takes three quarters of an hour and the traffic is terrible.'

Hattie, wrapped around Francesca like a baby monkey, was carried into the kitchen.

'Where's Mark?' Margi said, looking about her.

'Oh, he'll be chopping something. His current obsession is chopping logs. It's like living with a manic beaver.' The door banged.

'Margi.' Mark loomed behind her, and she turned to kiss him. How wonderful he looked, she thought. His thick dark hair was standing on end, his tanned face smeared with dirt. He was wearing a fleecy-type lumberjack shirt, open at the collar, over grass-stained jeans, with walking boots caked in mud on his feet.

'Hang on,' he said, holding up blackened hands. 'I need a wash first.' He smelled of fresh air, and wood smoke, and earth.

'I don't mind,' Margi said, and leant forward, kissing him on his cold cheek. 'Whatever have you been doing?'

'I'm pulling up an old post and rail fence. It's completely rotten, the main posts have rotted away under the ground. I'm planning to put in a whole new fence around the paddock. Hasn't Tess told you? We've promised to get Hattie a pony.'

Hattie bounced in Francesca's arms. 'For me! For me!' she said.

Margi looked at Tess. 'Really?'

'I know,' Tess said. 'But we haven't quite decided when, have we, Mark? Because I have an awful lot of work to do at the moment for the end of year exams and I think it will have to be in the summer, if at all.'

'Ignore Mummy,' Mark said, bending down to kiss Hattie. 'We'll get one sooner than that, won't we?'

Margi and Tess exchanged glances.

'I'll just have a wash and then I'll show you round

outside,' Mark said. 'Just wait until you see the views.'

'I'm not sure she's got the shoes for it,' Tess pointed out.

'Oh, she can borrow your wellies, can't she?'

'I'm not sure I do wellies,' Margi said. 'They make my feet look enormous and they don't do a thing for my thighs.'

Tess surveyed Margi's outfit. She looked wonderfully out of place in the chaotic kitchen. She had dressed as she would normally dress on a Saturday afternoon, in a pair of well-cut black trousers, black suede platform-soled ankle boots, and a sharply cut black jacket that Tess knew had cost a fortune, even in the Joseph sale. She knew because she'd been with her when she bought it, and had longed for it herself. But they couldn't afford it because they were saving up for the move.

Margi thought that Tess looked different. She was a little plumper, her hair was longer and her face, which had always been so pale, had more colour. She was wearing jeans, which Tess rarely did, and there was a carelessness about her, as if she hadn't bothered to look in the mirror at all that day. She wasn't wearing any make-up, either – although she seldom wore much, she usually put on some lipstick and eyeliner. Margi was used to Tess being such a head-turner she was rather surprised to see her looking so, well, ordinary.

Jake appeared in the kitchen. He didn't look at Francesca.

'Mum,' he said, 'can I take the puppy out?'

'Puppy?'

'We have a Labrador puppy,' Tess said. 'Archie.'

At that moment, a rotund ball of black fur shot into the kitchen. It had long legs and very big feet, and its legs appeared to be going in four different directions.

The puppy emitted a series of high-pitched shrieking yelps of joy, until Jake expertly caught it by the tail, and lifted it, squirming, into his arms.

'Oh, isn't he sweet,' Francesca and Georgina cooed. Francesca, shyly, lifted a hand to stroke the puppy's flat black head. She lifted her head and caught Jake's gaze. He flushed.

'And whose decision was this?' Margi asked, smiling.

'Mark's,' Tess said. 'He took the children off last Sunday afternoon and came back with Archie.'

'Aren't we lucky,' Hattie said, beside herself with joy. 'He's the loveliest thing ever. He's only done three poos in my room and they weren't runny ones. Mummy picked them up with toilet paper and flushed them away. I want him to sleep in my room but Mummy says he has to sleep in here although he makes a lot of noise, doesn't he?'

'He does,' Tess said. 'And he's scratched the back door which we've just had stripped and he's shredded the tea towels and chewed most of the table mats but we love him, don't we?'

'Ignore her,' Jake said, holding an ecstatic Archie up to his face and talking directly to him. 'She'll come round.'

'How on earth do you manage?' Margi said.

Tess gave her a rueful smile. 'As Mark has to leave at half past six to get into work on time I generally let him out and feed him before I take the children to school and get the train myself. Then we employ Eve in the village to come and let him out at lunchtime by which time he has crapped precisely twice on the floor and chewed the legs of the table. As the children stay at school until six, doing prep and after-school club for Hattie, I go straight from the train to pick them up and then we come home and let him out and feed him, by which time he is completely bonkers at being on his own. It's a bit of a dog's life at the moment but Mark assures me that when I feel the need to go into London less, then life will become easier. Won't it, darling?' she said to Mark, as he walked back into the kitchen.

'I look after him at the weekend, don't I, kids?'

'You take him out in the garden, yes. But you aren't very good at clearing up after him, are you?'

'It turns my stomach,' Mark said, making a face at Margi. 'I can't help it. Tess is much better than me at that sort of thing. Always has been. Nappies as well.'

'It's just a lucky skill I have,' she said.

'Look, bugger coffee,' Mark said. 'We ought to have champagne. This is a celebration. A kind of house-warming. You're our first proper guest.' He wandered off into the living room, which ran the length of the right-hand side of the house, and could be heard rooting about in the cupboard they were using temporarily for drink. There were plans afoot to build a wine cellar for him under the old scullery floor, which Tess was currently resisting on the basis it would mean more builders, more dust and more inconvenience. 'Voilà!' he shouted.

'Come on. Let's drink it outside,' he said, returning with a bottle under one arm. 'Rather a nice little number we've picked up for the supermarkets.'

'What's with the mania for outside?' Margi hissed at Tess, as they all trooped out after Mark.

'Healthy,' Tess muttered back. 'Fresh air is healthy and good for us.'

'But it's fucking cold,' Margi replied, under her breath.

Mark happily pulled the chairs around the wooden garden table he had purchased at some expense last weekend. The pathetic plastic table they had used for al fresco dining in their tiny back yard in London had been dumped, to be replaced by a splendid refectory-style model, which would seat about twelve. Tess wouldn't have minded, but they didn't even have a fully functioning cooker yet, with the Aga's nervous breakdowns, and there was Mark spending a fortune on patently unnecessary garden furniture.

'Look out!' he called. The champagne cork shot past Georgina's ear.

'Can I get my jumper from the car?' she said to Margi, shivering.

'I'll get it for you,' Ollie said, quickly. He had always had rather a crush on Georgina. But she wouldn't look at him. She would only have eyes for Jake, like all the girls. It was very hard being the swotty younger brother of someone like Jake. It was all very well if you wanted to be in favour with teachers, but not much good when you were seeking the approval of your schoolfriends and, lately, girls, who didn't seem to place much store by academic excellence. He must persuade his mum to let him try contact lenses. It was OK for her telling him that glasses were really trendy, and she had bought him the coolest narrow oval pair she could find, which he thought made him look rather like a James Bond villain. But if there was a choice between a boy with glasses or without, they were hardly likely to go for the speccy option, he thought. And, at fourteen, he badly needed to be found attractive. He was sick of being called cute, and cuddly. He wanted to be macho, and dangerous, like Jake. Maybe he should try the moody stare and lose some weight.

'Tess, get the glasses, would you?'

'I'll give you a hand,' Margi said. She followed Tess into the house.

'Are you all right?'

'What?' Tess said, her head in the cupboard. 'Bugger. We've only got four champagne flutes left. Will the girls have some? Or would they prefer Coke?'

'Tess, will you answer me?'

'What?' she said, withdrawing her head and turning to Margi. 'Don't I look fine?'

'You do. You look incredibly healthy. Ruddy.'

'Gee, thanks.'

'No, you look outdoor healthy and more, well, rounded.'

'Fat! You think I look fat!'

'Not at all,' Margi said, hastily backtracking. 'You look great, so natural.'

'Natural,' Tess said, frowning, 'is not good. Natural means uncared for. Ugly. Lacking in the chic department. You think I've let myself go.' Her voice was mocking.

'I don't mean that at all. What I mean is that I am worried you seem to have lost a bit of your, well, sparkle. Zest. All that fierce new independence and jangly bracelets you were going in for. You seem a little – muted.'

'I'm just tired,' Tess said, running her hand through her hair, greasy at the roots. 'I am sick and tired of living in mess and I have no idea how long it's going to go on for. It's fine for Mark, he steams out of here first thing in the morning and comes back late at night, and then all he does is eat a takeaway or whatever I've managed to cobble together on a lukewarm Aga before falling into bed. At the weekends he's outside being Ted the Lumberjack Man and it's only me who's trying to push back the frontiers of chaos and get things organized. That, and trying to keep up with the course, is doing my head in.'

'You could do with a holiday.'

'Oh yes,' Tess said bitterly. 'That I could. But we have no money for a holiday. I cannot imagine we will ever go on holiday again. We can't even afford to go to Cornwall this summer. We have borrowed up to the limits of our borrowing to fund the renovations, we have spent what tiny savings we had and we have tapped all available financial resources from Mum and Dad to pay for Hattie's school fees. I can't ask my mum again, anyway. She gets that cat's bottom sound into her voice, "We would like to help, you know we would, but we're on a pension remember, it has to last us out," as if I'm holding them up like Dick bloody Turpin.'

Margi laughed. 'What about Mark's father?'

'Oh, please,' Tess said. 'Fine, if you want to be in hock to some weird Bolivian arms dealer who will probably turn up in the dead of night and kidnap the children. Mark would never ask him.'

'It can't be all bad,' Margi said, consolingly.

'Yes, it can,' Tess said, brutally. 'What Mark is refusing to accept, with all this champagne celebration, is that we are yet again in debt up to our ears and I can't afford to pay my tuition fees for my PGCE next year and he is implying that it is deeply selfish of me to want to continue when we so urgently need the money for the children's school fees and to keep this leaking roof above our heads.'

'Sell up and move back to London?'

'Yeah, right,' Tess said. 'Over Mark's dead body. Come on. He'll be wondering what we're doing in here.'

They sat out in the garden, and ended up drinking three bottles of champagne, as the sun began to sink over the roof of the house and the bats swooped across the garden.

'Yeow!' Georgina shrieked. 'What was that?'

'A bat,' Ollie said. 'We have lots of them. Aren't they great? Daddy took Hattie and me into the garden late last night with torches and we watched them. It was brilliant. They aren't scary at all.' Georgina made a disbelieving face at him. 'Do you want to see my room?' he asked shyly.

'Why?' she said, looking at him incredulously.

'I've got a PlayStation,' he said. 'Mum got me one for my birthday like Jake's. It's got a game on about vampire bats that take over the universe.'

Margi nudged her younger daughter with her foot. 'Go on, darling.'

'Come on,' Jake said to Francesca, who had a dozing Hattie on her lap, eyelids drooping, thumb hovering on the rim of her lips. 'They're too pissed to feed us. Do you want some chips?'

'Please.'

Jake reached down, and with a practised gesture took Hattie out of Francesca's arms. She clung sleepily around his neck. 'Read me a story,' she said.

'We both will,' Francesca said. They walked together into the house.

Margi followed them with indulgent eyes. She had forgiven Jake.

'No men on the horizon?' Tess asked, once Jake and Francesca had disappeared.

'Zip. Nada. I have resigned myself to spinsterhood. I even caught myself thinking about going to church the other day. You will tell me, won't you, if I grow a moustache?'

'I'll try,' Tess promised. Mark drummed his fingers on the table, bored by the conversation.

'What about food?' he said.

'I had thought we'd all go to the pub,' Tess said.

'They don't like children in on a Saturday night.'

'No nice nearby restaurants?'

Both Mark and Tess snorted. 'Not exactly.' Even Mark had conceded that there was something of a shortage in gourmet food on offer in the nearest restaurants, who seemed to regard melon with Parma ham as dangerously exotic.

'I'll go and get a takeaway,' he said.

'Oh don't roll out the red carpet for me, just because I'm a guest,' Margi said. 'What kind of takeaway?'

256

'Indian. But should you drive?' Tess asked. 'You've had loads of drink.'

'When,' Mark said, getting up carefully, 'have you ever seen a police car on these roads? Anyway, Peter the policeman is always in the Slaughtered Lamb about this time.'

'Isn't he gorgeous,' Margi said, following his broad disappearing back with greedy eyes.

'Oh, try living with him,' Tess said.

'You don't mean that, you sour old thing. I'll have him.'

'I think I do. Anyway, come on. Give me the London gossip. What about Vanessa?'

'Missing you. But she's so busy flitting backwards and forwards between Cla'am and the South of France like some fucking annoying butterfly she says she has no time for anything. I don't envy her at all, of course, I would hate her life. It must be awful trying to remember if the potato peeler is in London or St Jean de Luce.'

'She probably has two.'

'Probably has six, darling. Silver-plated ones. I'm sorry, but without you I can't stick her. She invited me in for coffee the other day but I found an excuse not to go. I think I said I needed to go and clean the toilet. She looked kind of horrified, anyway. It's just without you as a buffer she goes into that carefully hidden poor you living on your own with very little money routine until I want to slap her and point out that at least I am doing something useful with my life instead of pandering to the needs of that vile git. You know, while we were talking he pulled up in his horrible huge car, got out and walked into the house without even saying hello to her. She was really embarrassed. And the girls say that Clemmie is getting so spoilt, wittering on about her French home.'

'Not that you're one to bitch.'

'Of course not. You asked. Anyway, how's Jake?'

Tess felt immediately protective. 'He's fine, doing well at school. He's still a bit moody sometimes but his teachers think he's on line to get good exam results. He's going on about wanting to go to America for university but I'm afraid that's out of the question, there's no way we could afford it. So I think he's going to try for art college, which would be fantastic. What about Francesca?' she said, keen to deflect the conversation.

'Oh, an angel. No trouble at all. It's Georgina who's the horror. I am this complete ogress because I won't let her use the mobile phone Aphid bought her and why do all her friends shop at Kenzo and we don't, and why can't she go out on her own to watch 15-rated films and have a pizza with her mates? I point out she can't because she is thirteen, not fifteen, and then she slams the door, shouts, "Thanks, Mum, for ruining my life," and storms off to her bedroom. It's lovely. Really creates a warm, loving atmosphere. What I really mind is how much time all this drama takes up, I mean, it's all so pointless, such a waste of energy. I wish I didn't have a normal teenager. I wish I had a spotty quiet one who has found Jesus instead of a mini Britney Spears covered in love bites.'

'Not very likely.'

'Suppose not.'

'You know what the problem is.' Margi leant across the table towards Mark, as they sat eating the takeaway. Tess kicked her under the table, but she was too pissed to take a hint.

'You aren't talking to each other enough. That's what's missing. The art of communication. You have to keep all lines of communication open, that's what everyone says about marriage, says me, the marriage expert. Now you like living here. Tess doesn't.' Tess booted her again. Mark's face was set in a sardonic smile.

'Really, Margi?' he said, leaning forward to refill her glass. 'Tell me more.'

'Oh she hates it,' Margi said, waving her fork about wildly. Tess deftly caught a piece of chicken korma before it fell to the floor and was eaten by Archie. 'Loathes it. But she lives here because you want to. And just think of the sacrifices to her career.' Tess tried a pleading look. 'She was doing brilliantly on that course but now she says she might have to give it up. She will resent that,' Margi said, choosing her words very carefully and trying not to slur. 'And then she will resent you for making her give it up.'

'Margi, I don't think this is the right time for this conversation, do you?'

'On the contrary,' Mark said. 'I'm riveted.'

'She has such a fantastic future. She's so bright, and clever. She can't give up now. It's like your job. Would you give that up?'

'That's hardly an option,' Mark said calmly, taking a sip of wine. Margi took a slug of hers.

'But why is it so different? Why is your career so much more important? Tess could have a fantabulous career if she finishes her course. She might become a world-renowned lecturer and give lectures or whatever all over the world. And then you could retire and chop logs.'

'Sounds good to me,' Mark laughed.

'And it is good,' Margi said, nodding owlishly. 'It's Tess's turn, can't you see? She's spent all these years devoting herself to the family and now it's time for her to break out. I've seen such a big change in her. She's much more confident.'

'Stop talking about me as if I wasn't here,' Tess said. 'Look, Margi, I do appreciate what you're saying, but it isn't exactly like that. I am happy here—'

'That's not what you said before.'

'I am happy here,' Tess repeated loudly. 'I just need a bit more time to adjust, and we'll sort out the course thing, won't we, Mark? It'll be fine.'

'But what about money?' Margi said. 'You're worried about that too.'

'Not very,' Tess said, with a tight little smile. 'We'll manage. Margi, don't you think we ought to check the children are in bed? It's after eleven. I put Francesca and Georgina in Hattie's room, and you're sleeping in Ollie's. Come on.'

'Oh you go,' Margi said. 'I want to talk to Mark.' Tess and Mark flashed looks at each other over her head. He made a 'help' face at her.

'Anyway,' Tess said. 'I'm going to bed now. I'm beat.'

'Me too,' Mark said, yawning.

'Oh, don't go to bed,' Margi said. 'I want some more wine.'

'You've had enough,' Mark said, lifting the empty bottle off the table. 'Come on, Margs. You'll feel awful in the morning.'

'Oh, bugger off,' she said grinning at him. 'Don't be so boring. You've got so boring since you moved here.' Tess put her hand under her arm as she staggered slightly, getting up from the table.

'I haven't been this pissed for ages. Don't let the girls see me.'

'I won't,' Tess said, and led her carefully up to bed.

'No en suite?' Margi said, peering round Ollie's room.

'Hardly,' Tess said. 'We haven't even got one bath yet.'

'Good night. I didn't say the wrong thing, did I?'

'No. You were brilliant. Night. Sleep well.'

'So.'

Mark was sitting up in bed, his arms folded across

his chest. 'You loathe it here. Not mildly dislike; not find a little inconvenient, but loathe. I am a mean skinflint who will not pay for your course. I do not talk to you. I am so wrapped up in my own world I cannot see that my wife is deeply miserable.'

'Oh, come on,' Tess said, turning away from him and taking off her jeans. 'She was pissed. I didn't say all that to her.'

'So she must made it all up, did she? For the sake of stirring it. How extraordinary.'

'Look,' Tess said, getting into bed naked except for her knickers, and trying to snuggle into his arms. He pulled away from her. 'I might have said, OK, that I am not absolutely thrilled to have moved but you know that anyway, don't you? We've talked about it. And I have said that I am happy to be here because everyone else is and I am sure that I am going to be able to fit my work schedule around having to commute – just as you do,' she pointed out.

'And what was that about money? Have you really been blabbing to Margi about the fact that we are totally broke?'

'I have not blabbed, as you so rudely put it,' Tess said. 'I told her, quite honestly, that we are a bit on the short side at the moment. Because – ' she cast about for a reason – 'she invited us to go on holiday with her. To France,' she added wildly.

'And you said we couldn't because I do not earn enough.'

'Oh for God's sake!' She drew away from him, angrily, and pulled the duvet over her as she turned onto her side, back towards him. 'Stop being such a martyr. All I said to her was that I was worried about the fees for next year's course and could she think of any grants or anything, that's all.'

Mark reached out and clicked off his bedside light. Tess lay rigidly next to him, wondering if she ought to make some kind of approach. They hadn't made love for ages, not since the first night they'd moved in when Mark said they ought to christen the house. Either he was in bed asleep by the time she crawled up after a late night on the laptop, or he had to stay over in London as he had an early meeting. We're not like ships that pass in the night, she thought. We're like separate continents. There were only a few feet between them in the bed, but it felt like a chasm. How easy it was for a warm atmosphere to chill. How did we used to make up rows? she wondered, bunching the pillow more comfortably under her cheek. Oh, now I remember, she thought. I used to say I was sorry.

Chapter Twenty-five

Tess hesitated. Brie with watercress on ciabatta or smoked salmon and dill on rye? Oh, the bliss of choice. 'I'll have the smoked salmon,' she said, decisively. 'And hold the dill mayo. Rye, yes, please, and a latte.' Gathering up the steaming coffee and sandwich and trying to push the change into her purse, she followed Nicki to the only free table in the busy restaurant.

'God, this is lovely,' she said, taking a dreamy sip, and gazing about the heaving room.

'What?' Nicki said, confused. 'It's a coffee, Tess. Not manna from heaven.'

'You have no idea. It is to me. Look what I bought.' She held up a bottle green carrier bag with Harrods written across in gold lettering.

'A Harrods carrier bag?'

'Don't be silly.' She reached down and pulled out a soft black top. It nestled into the palms of her hands, like a luxurious kitten. 'It's a cashmere Joseph jumper,' Tess said, in hushed tones. 'I have never in my life bought anything from Harrods before, on principle, but I just had to have this.' She held it against her cheek. 'I am so very happy.'

'Don't you think you're taking this retail therapy just

a little too far?' Nicki asked, nervously. 'I mean, wasn't it really expensive? And you have just told me you are very broke.'

'I know,' Tess said, slipping it back into the bag. 'But I am sick and tired of making do. I am not going to give up the things I love doing – like shopping occasionally – just because we are allowed to pander only to Mark's whims and bizarre new hobbies, like killing furry animals. He's even bought a sodding second-hand gun.'

'So you'll be telling him exactly how much it cost?'

'What, this old thing? Margi gave it to me.' She licked the froth off her spoon. 'Anyway, I deserve to celebrate. It isn't every day a girl gets a Distinction. God, Nicki, you have no idea how happy I am. I feel like leaping up and down and shrieking, "I got a Distinction! I got a Distinction!" Do you think I could get a T-shirt printed?'

'Sure, why not?' Nicki said. 'With "Clever Bitch" on the back. I am so proud of you,' she added.

'And I'm proud of you too,' Tess said, quickly. 'You did brilliantly.'

'But not as brilliantly as you.'

'I know,' Tess said, flashing her a grin. 'But we can't all be a genius, can we?'

'Oh, fuck off. So what are you going to do now? What's happening with the PGCE?'

'I have been accepted, I should be filling out forms about work placements but I can't until I hear about the funding from that organization the bursar found for me, the European one.'

'You can hardly plead poverty. Isn't that for sad single mothers like me?'

'Hardly sad. But there is a special fund for art, apparently, which is available to anyone as long as you're a woman. I can't give up now,' she said, her face falling. 'It feels like everything is so close I could touch it, but all the time I am battling this silent opposition from Mark. Half the time I don't even want to go home. I'm not sure I would, if it weren't for the children.'

Nicki looked at her sharply. 'You don't mean that.'

'I'm not sure,' Tess said slowly. 'I just didn't anticipate how much I would care about this – it's almost as if I am having a child taken away from me. I love my new life, and the prospect of what might happen. Sitting on the train, coming here, leaving all that mess at home, is like escaping. I can't spend the rest of my life cleaning the mud off wellies. And what am I going to do over the summer? Mark wants me to get the house decorated, but God, it's so boring. What I really want to do is pack up the car and head off for Cornwall, but guess what, we can't afford it.'

'What do the kids want to do?' Nicki said, through her sandwich.

'I think they'd be pretty happy staying put,' Tess admitted. 'Mark's still on about getting Hattie a pony and they're all in love with that bloody dog. Jake, I don't know. It might do Jake good to have a change of scenery. He seems a bit preoccupied again, which is such a pain, I really thought we'd put all that behind us – I guess he's just worrying about his exams next year. I thought we'd passed the worst, but he's kind of withdrawing again. Anyway,' she said, brightly. 'What about you? What are you going to do now, Ms Nicki Holton, MA?'

'Travel,' she said, grinning. 'I'm going to stay on a kibbutz.'

'No!'

'Too right. Mick invited me out, said there is loads of room and there are other "mature" people out there like his ancient mother. I shall lie in the sun, shrivel up like a prune, pick oranges and work out what to do next, like an old hippie. I might go to Egypt with Mick, that's his next port of call. Apparently we can pick fruit there too. I've never seen the Pyramids.'

'You're so lucky,' Tess said. 'You are so free.'

'My kids are grown-up,' she pointed out. 'It'll come to you. Really.'

'Hardly. I want to do a PGCE and Mark acts as if I want to rip my clothes off and then join the Moonies. If I said I was going to a kibbutz I think he'd have me certified.'

'You know what you ought to do this summer,' Nicki said, taking a large bite out of her sun-dried tomato and pesto on granary. 'You ought to try and arrange that exhibition.'

'Oh, how?' Tess said. 'Ring up the Musée d'Orsay and say, "You don't know me from Adam but I am arranging an exhibition of Berthe Morisot's work. The first exhibition of her work since the late nineteenth century. What do I do? I'm a student. Yes, not from a gallery. How do I plan to fund this exhibition? And insure the safe transportation of her priceless works of art? You've got me on that one a bit. Can I ring you back?" ' Tess mimed putting down the phone. 'Brilliant idea. It'll never work.'

'No, come on,' Nicki said, eyes shining. 'It could work. All you need is someone from one of the big galleries behind you – Tate Modern would be perfect. It's not as if she's an unknown, is it? Lots of people have heard of her, and I think a new gallery would think it's a brilliant idea, a real coup to bring all her works together and hold a retrospective.'

'Stop, stop,' Tess said, holding up her hands. 'A. It will never work. B. I do not have time. C. Mark would kill me.'

Nicki looked at her sternly. 'I thought we'd got past that stage, hadn't we, Mrs James? What husband might say if wife wants to do something on her own?'

'All right. I'll think about it,' Tess said, lifting her coffee to her mouth. Her bracelets slid down against the sleeve of her jumper. 'I will think about it. But I'm not promising anything.'

'You are joking, aren't you?' Mark said. 'I can see it's a great idea, but you don't have time, not with everything we have to do at the house. Now the course is finished I had sort of hoped you might concentrate on us for a bit. Come here, you little bugger.' He caught Archie just as he was crouching for a pee, and carried him swiftly towards the back door. 'You'd need to keep shuttling backwards and forwards to London again, which wouldn't be much fun for the kids. They've hardly seen anything of you recently, with your exams. Not to mention the fortune it's costing us in childcare.'

'They haven't seen much of you, either,' Tess pointed out.

'But that's work,' he said, quickly.

'Of course.'

'Look, I'm not saying no.' Tess looked at him incredulously. 'But I'm not saying yes, either.'

'I think you'll find,' Tess said, icily, 'that yes or no is not actually your decision. It's up to me. As long as I can arrange child-care then there's no reason why I can't take on a project like this.'

'But who's going to pay for it? Please, Tess, be reasonable. We're on our beam ends as it is. And if a gallery wants to put on a Berthe Morisot exhibition it will, it's hardly going to take someone like you to bounce them into it, is it?'

'Thanks for your faith in my persuasive skills.'

'It just seems like a bit of a waste of time, that's all. You've done so brilliantly, and we are all so proud of you, but surely now the time has come to be at home for a while. The kids are so looking forward to having you back. And there's so much to do. So much we can do together.'

'I don't particularly want to spend my summer chopping logs or killing things,' Tess said, with the glimmer of a smile.

'Very funny. I just meant that I could take some time off and we could do the decorating together. We can't if you're running around organizing this exhibition. Haven't you achieved enough for now? You know we really need to talk about next year and money . . .'

Tess cut him short. 'Enough to keep me happy and fulfil my little whim to do something with my life?' she said sarcastically.

'It's hardly worth talking to you any more,' Mark said. 'You seem incapable of listening to anyone else's point of view and you're not taking into account the practicalities. One. We are paying a childminder and the after-school club a fortune. Two. The children break up in three weeks and who is going to look after them? And three, I have bent over backwards to make sure you had enough time to study and come home early when you asked me to but now I really need to be able to get back to normal. This is a really busy time of year for me, and I need your support. It's like talking to a brick wall.' He paused, and looked rather sheepish. 'Oh, and by the way, you can't rely on me for child-care in August anyway. For three weeks, possibly. Sales conference in California and Rupert says it's a three-line whip.'

'And that's fine, is it?' Tess said. 'It's perfectly fine for you to go away for three weeks to enjoy delicious food and wine in the sunshine but somehow I do not have the time to organize an exhibition I care passionately about?'

'Mine,' Mark said, 'is essential. And it is financially lucrative work. Yours is a pipe dream.'

'I would like to speak to someone about arranging an exhibition. A small one. The press office? No, I don't think it is the press office I want. Or maybe it is. Could you put me through?'

'It worked! I'm going to see them next Wednesday. To be honest they'd been thinking about putting together an exhibition of leading female artists anyway, and they said I was more than welcome to get involved, because I have done so much research into the subject. Only they can't pay me, of course. But that's fine, it's a labour of love. I'm to work with their own expert and Berthe is going to have a room of her own just off the main concourse. It's bloody brilliant, isn't it?'

'I am seriously impressed,' Nicki said. 'What does Mark say?' Tess frowned at the phone.

'He doesn't exactly know. Because unfortunately the date of the exhibition in August is going to coincide with his being away but he's going to have to come home a bit early, isn't he? Right, I have to make a list of all the places we need to contact. Christ, not only are there all the museums in France and private collections, there's also Copenhagen, Brussels, Ireland, the Netherlands, Norway, Sweden, America, Canada and even bloody Buenos Aires.'

'I hope they're helping to pay your phone bill,' Nicki said, 'while you're acting as an unpaid researcher.'

'Oh, who cares? This is just the most exciting thing I have ever done in my life,' Tess said.

Mark picked up the phone. 'You want to speak to my wife? I'm sorry, she doesn't speak to anyone unless it's about a female painter called Bert. Do you happen to be the National Gallery? Or the Ordrupgaardsamlingen Collection? You aren't? Fat chance then. Hang on. Tess! It's Margi.'

'What the hell was he on about?'

'Don't ask,' she said. Then, lowering her voice, 'Things are a bit tense at the moment. How are you?'

'Fine, apart from the fact I haven't seen you for weeks and your mobile is permanently engaged. What are you doing?'

'You are not going to believe this, but helping to organize a major exhibition which is going to be attended by just about every art critic from all the heavyweight newspapers in this country and by this time next week I will be on *Woman's Hour*. Talking about Berthe Morisot with lovely Thomas from the Tate who's working with me and a total expert and I am not scared about it, not nervous at all. I feel very calm, and serene, verging on the swanlike.'

'Bugger me, Tess, you have been busy. And what does Mark think?'

'I really wish,' Tess said patiently, 'all my friends would stop asking me what my husband thinks about something I am doing with my life. It's not as if Mark's colleagues say, "And what does Tess think of all this?" when he pulls off a major deal. Just give me credit for being me, will you.'

'Whoo,' Margi said. 'Get the big-head.'

'I feel rather big-headed. I'm also going to be interviewed by several newspapers. To be honest, I mean, who do I think I am? I'm just a student, but they seem to like that. I'm terrified they're going to ask me something I don't know.'

'Wasn't it rather presumptuous of you to approach Tate Modern in the first place?' Jenni Murray looked kindly at Tess over the top of her half-moon glasses.

'I suppose it was,' Tess said nervously, clearing her throat. She wished there wasn't that awful red light over the door to the studio, shining in her eyes. It reminded her more than anything that here she was live on national radio. 'But I felt so passionately about the fact she had been largely ignored by the art world and the balance ought to be redressed. And,' she said, warming to her theme, 'ignored at the expense of so many other male artists simply not as talented as she was.'

'Like whom?'

Tess's mind went completely blank. 'Er – Sisley,' she said. God, how was she going to defend that one? Thank God she hadn't said Renoir. That would have been even worse.

'In what way?' Jenni asked.

'Because I think, as a woman, which I am, of course – '

'Indisputably,' Jenni said, smiling.

'That she, as a female artist . . .'

'I think we have established that conclusively.'

Tess took a deep breath and kept going. 'She speaks to women in a way many other artists don't. I mean, a lot of her paintings were portrayed as simply "domestic", but that is the stuff of our lives, isn't it, putting children to bed, playing with children in the grass, picking cherries (what?). And it is the way in which women in her paintings are represented, so honestly, without all that cod sensuality you often find in male artists of the same period . . .' (Cod? Had she really said cod? What had fish got to do with it?)

'I think that's the first time I've heard the word "cod" used to describe sensuality,' Jenni said, laughing. 'So how on earth did you go about bringing her work together?'

'Very tricky,' Tess said, nodding, then realized that was pointless because no-one could see her. 'First of all I tried to find out where her major works are held, in galleries and private collections all over the world, and then I rang them – with Thomas's help of course, and when I didn't get anywhere I wrote. Another problem is that there isn't any definitive catalogue of her work anywhere, if you can believe it, although three French art experts are working on that at the

271

moment. The response has been amazing – we think we're going to be able to pull together about seventy-five per cent of her work, including some which have never been seen in public before.'

'Now, Thomas Starkey, as I said at the beginning of the interview, you're the director responsible for new projects. Now why on earth has it taken so long to bring these works to the wider public? I mean . . .'

Tess looked down and saw her hands were shaking. They were also very sweaty. God, she hoped her voice hadn't been wobbly. But it had gone really quickly. Too quickly. She hadn't said anything really stupid, had she? Only the cod thing. And she had said absolutely a lot. Absolutely. And nodded. Anyway, it was over.

'And that,' Jenni said, 'is sadly all we have time for on that subject. Now, it's said that the way to a man's heart is through his stomach. Well, as Catherine de Souza reports, it's clear that even today . . .'

Thank you, God, Tess thought, as Jenni gestured they could take off their headphones. Jenni held up her hand to prevent any conversation until she was sure they were into the tape. Then she said, 'Well done. That was fascinating.'

'I didn't sound too nervous, did I?' Tess asked.

'You didn't. Really, you were great. It sounds wonderful. May I come?'

'Oh, God, I'd love you to,' Tess said. 'I'll make sure we send you tickets for the press night.'

'She said,' Tess said breathlessly into the mobile, 'that she really admired what I had done. This is the happiest day of my life after getting my Distinction! Did you hear me? Was I awful? Did I talk gibberish? I cannot tell you how nerve-wracking it is. This red light comes on and you're just paralysed, your mind goes completely blank and when you open your mouth this silly voice comes out like Minnie Mouse on speed . . . and . . .'

'Tess, calm down. You're ranting. I've got the picture. Yes, I heard you. No, you didn't sound like Minnie Mouse. Yes, you did say sensible things. Most of the time. What silly things did you say? Well, you said "absolutely" quite a lot. But that was OK,' Margi added hastily. 'And cod was a bit baffling, but it's a nice, different kind of word, isn't it? It could have been worse. You could have said halibut. Of course I'm coming. I wouldn't miss it for the world. It'll mean I can go out and buy myself an entire new outfit. I'm sorry, but I am not turning up at the debut of your major entrée into the art world looking like a single mother who hasn't two beans to rub together. I am going to shine, darling, in some skimpy little number. Do you want me to pretend to be someone famous? I could try Winona Ryder? Too old? Thanks, I love you too. Yup, bye. My hero.'

Chapter Twenty-six

'How can I come home?' Mark carefully closed the
door to the kitchen, as Hattie, Ollie and Archie slid
down the stairs on a duvet, shrieking and barking. 'I'm
up to my ears. This isn't some kind of freebie junket,
you know, it is a massive conference attended by all
the leading vineyards and buyers. Do you have any
idea just how important that is? This isn't some kind
of whim. I'm not going on purpose to spite you. If I tell
Rupert I have to come home early because my wife is
too busy organizing some kind of exhibition I will look
a complete chump and put myself in danger of being
sacked. Can I put it any plainer than that? Why on
earth is this suddenly a problem? You know what
my job involves.' He opened the door. 'Ollie! If you
do that again you are all going to die. Put the bloody
thing away. No, I don't care how much fun it is. Just
do it.' He closed the door. 'You have always accepted
that my job, by its nature, means that I have to be
away. And yet, now, this has suddenly become un-
acceptable.'

'I am not going to row about this,' Tess said calmly.
'I'm just asking for a little back-up. I need you, Mark. I
really need you to help with the children, just for a
week, because I can book them all in for an adventure

club during the day but there isn't anyone to look after them in the evenings, and I am going to have to stay over in London at Nicki's. There's too much to do. I can't concentrate with the children.'

'Can't you ask Margi to come here? Or Nicki?'

'Margi also works full-time if you hadn't noticed and Nicki is going away to Israel on the Tuesday. Anyway, why should I find women to mop up after your responsibilities?'

Mark sighed, and sat down opposite Tess.

'All I am asking,' she continued, 'is that for just one week you could come home to help me out. You will have already been there for two weeks. How long does it take to order wine? Please. Think of all the times I've supported you. Tell me honestly. Do you ever think twice when you have to go away? Do you ever think, "What am I going to do with the children?" Do you hell. You just assume that, whatever I am doing, I will drop it to make sure I am there to care for them. Well, not this time. I'm not going to be here, and I need you to be me. Just for a week. It isn't a lot to ask.'

'What about your mum and dad?'

'They're going away to Malta. They booked it ages ago. Anyway, for goodness sake, Mark, you're their father! Why is it such a massive deal for you to have to change your working plans? You don't ever notice, but I do it all the time, making arrangements, ringing round desperately, hurtling onto trains like some kind of whirling dervish and panicking that I'm going to be late picking them up. You never feel that, do you? You never have that sick feeling in the pit of your stomach that your child is going to be the last one standing on the steps of the school. Do you ever give them a thought at all when you're at work?'

'Oh, that's hardly relevant, is it?' he said. 'What a ridiculous thing to say. What, do you think that I sit in board meetings worrying about whether Hattie's remembered her pumps or whatever? Oh, come on, Tess. Grow up.'

'But I do!' Tess said. 'I have sat in lectures when I ought to be concentrating thinking, "God, have we got any toilet paper?" And don't tell me that doesn't matter because it isn't real work, and it's nothing to be proud of, even getting a Distinction.'

'Don't give me that bollocks. I am very proud of you. I think you've achieved a massive amount. I just can't see why it has to go on and on and interfere with our lives so much. Where is it all going to end? Are we ever going to get back to normal? Everything's changed. Everything about you has changed. You used to be such a fantastic mother, you always put the children first. Now you have hardly any time for them, when you are here you're always on the phone and you take a damn sight more notice of fucking crack-pots like Nicki than you do of me. It's pretty sad, Tess. I think you ought to stop and take a good long hard look at yourself and what you've become with all your "What about me?" and "What about my needs?" as if you're some kind of sacred cow. It's pathetic and I'm not angry about it, I'm just bored. I'm very, very bored of living with you and listening to the same old shit about how selfish I am when you are the selfish one who is currently making our lives so complicated.'

'Why don't you just leave then?' she said, furiously.

'What?'

'Leave.'

Mark, who had started to get up from the table, sat back down, laughing bitterly. 'Oh, perfect,' he said. 'I should leave, should I? I should leave the children I love more than anything in the world and the house I have paid for and worked on just because you can't cope with a few tough truths. Listen to me carefully, Tess.' He leant forward over the table, his handsome face hard and implacable. 'I will never leave this house. This is my house. This is my home. If you decide that you cannot live here with me any longer because I am so unreasonable, then you can leave. You can fuck off back to London and go and live with Nicki or Margi or whoever and enjoy the freedom you so clearly desire without the irritating fetters of your children and a husband who would like to be acknowledged, just occasionally, for all the things he does for this family, instead of being pilloried as incredibly selfish because he wants to actually get on with the career that pays for all your studying and your little interests. Doesn't suit, does it, Tess? Doesn't fit in with your grand feminist ideals, does it? What you want is to run this family, don't you, take my money and be able to do whatever you want, whenever the fuck you want, with your girlfriends and your art and your theatre instead of having to give time to a boorish bloke who takes up space and would like to make love to you, just once in a while.'

The phone rang. They both stopped, shocked, and stared at it. Without thinking, Tess picked it up.

'Tess, I'm so glad I caught you in.'

'Oh hello, Kathy. They did what? Arranged for Sophie to come and stay tonight? Aren't they naughty. No, she hasn't told me. Hang on.' She walked across the kitchen, opened the door and bellowed up the stairs. 'Hattie! Have you arranged for Sophie to come and sleep over? Why didn't you tell me?' She walked back to the phone. 'No, I'm sorry, she can't. I'm really sorry, Kathy,' she said, trying to keep her voice normal. 'Now isn't a great time, to be honest. Could we leave it until next week? You're sure? Thanks so much. Yes, see you then. Bye.' She turned towards Mark. He looked at her blankly, and rubbed his hands over his eyes. Then he stood up, wearily.

'I've had it, Tess,' he said. 'I'm fed up with all this. I don't have the time, or the energy, to cope with the emotional crisis you appear to be having. Just let me know, will you, when you feel you can be reasonable again. I have to get up at half past five tomorrow morning to get the train into London to do the job which is apparently such an obstacle to your life. Boring of me, I know, but there we are. You have made it patently clear,' he said, in the same awful, dead voice, 'that you no longer find me attractive or desire me in any way. I am going to sleep on the sofa. Tomorrow Ollie is going to have to move into Jake's room and I will have his room. I think we both need a bit of space, to coin a phrase.'

'Don't do this,' Tess said, feeling a terrible sinking sensation in her heart. Why had she gone so far? 'What will the children say? You can't, they'll know that something is wrong. They'll be so worried. We can't drag them into this.'

'You should have thought of that before you started making completely unreasonable demands and telling me to fuck off out of my own house. I'm not some kind of toy, Tess. You can't order me about and think you can get away with it. If you want to play dirty, I can play dirty too. I am not going to make this easy.'

As he went up the stairs, she heard him shouting to Ollie, 'Will you come and move this fucking duvet!' before the door of their bedroom slammed.

Tess sat, for a long time, staring into nothing. She felt too shocked even to cry. She felt brittle, and numb, as if all sensation had left her body. She also felt helplessly out of control. How could a reasonable discussion go so badly wrong? He had taken everything the wrong way, and totally overreacted. She hadn't meant it about leaving. It was the worst row they had ever had, and she had never seen Mark like that – so cold – he had looked at her almost as if he hated her. Had she really changed so much? Was she really so selfish? She couldn't see it. She could only see the things that had happened to her as positive, good things which had made her feel so much happier about herself. Admittedly she hadn't been around at home as much lately, but that was OK. It was good for children to see their mothers engaged in something purposeful which didn't include them. She was right to fight for this, she couldn't just give in. She had been their virtual slave for too long, all she was fighting for was to regain at least some semblance of her own identity. She had lost sight of what she loved, what made her happy, as if marriage to Mark had damped down her own personality, neutralized it to the point where she wasn't sure what she felt about anything any more. All she was doing was finding her feet. Only they were now standing on shaky ground.

She had felt that this confidence was giving her more power in their relationship, but in one fell swoop Mark had taken it all away. Maybe he didn't mean it. She looked at her trembling hands. No. He did. If he said he was going to do something he always did it and he had the courage to see it through. Would compromise work? Should she go to him and say she was sorry, she was wrong, what she wanted wasn't important and of course she didn't need him to come home from California, she would make all the arrangements and cope, as she always had? She placed one hand very slowly upon the table, and pressed it flat. She had always liked her hands, they were slim with long, artistic fingers. But they had changed. The skin, which used to fit so neatly, was wrinkled, in thin criss-cross lines, across the back of her hand and fingers. Over her knuckles, the skin pouched. She made her fist into a ball. That was better, the skin stretched taut, gleaming white. She lifted her hand to her face, and gently rubbed the puffiness under her eyes, feeling the way the soft skin moved under her fingers. She was getting older, no longer able to rely on beauty. What would it be like, to be alone?

She could not stop now, stop everything she had worked for over the last year, especially now she had this one chance to take part in something so fascinating. She had talked about the exhibition on *Woman's Hour*. Would she really have to pull out because her husband felt it was too inconvenient? The idea was ludicrous. Imagine a man helping to organize something like this, and then saying he couldn't be there in the vital week before because he had to go and pick the children up from adventure camp. What lunatic situations we face, she thought. Endlessly having to think about small details, endlessly being made to feel guilty. She would not let him spoil this for her. He was trying to control her life, pulling her back to where he thought she ought to be. She had too much pride to go back now.

That night she slept alone.

Chapter Twenty-seven

They could have walked to Jeremy and Loopy's but the night was chilly, even for July. Tess said she would drive home, she didn't mind not drinking.

They dressed in their bedroom, without saying anything. There wasn't enough room in Ollie's bedroom for all of Mark's clothes, so some had to stay in their room. He left his work clothes – shirts, suits and trousers – hanging in his wardrobe, but piled jumpers, socks and pants in untidy mounds on the floor of Ollie's bedroom. Tess made no attempt to tidy them.

Most of the time she managed to maintain a relatively calm front for the children. Because he was leaving for work so early in the morning it was possible to get the children up out of bed, make breakfast and sort out uniforms, games bags and musical instruments as if everything was normal. There had to be explanations, however, about why Ollie had had to move into Jake's room. At first Tess had tried the 'snoring' excuse. Hattie replied that Daddy had always snored, so why did now make so much difference? At nearly nine, she was as sharp as a tack, fiendishly intelligent and beginning to become wilful. What had been cute precociousness was turning into cheekiness and Tess occasionally had to tell her to just simmer down.

She then said that because she was working so hard at the moment, gearing up for the exhibition, she needed to sleep well and Daddy getting up so early in the morning woke her. She and Mark were icily polite to each other, speaking only in the children's hearing. If Mark caught himself alone in the same room as her, he would walk out.

Sometimes she woke in the night, thinking it must be a dream. But then the empty space beside her told her it was not. Living like this, two separate people who moved around each other but did not touch, was like attempting to live a normal life inside a hideous, distorted play. And Mark looked so tired, and stressed, and unwell. At the weekends he had given up bashing around in his workshop, and the fencing project stood half-finished. Hattie had stopped asking about her pony. There was a strange air about the house, a sense of waiting, as if work had ceased and the ghosts were lying in wait. When he wasn't at work Mark walked, for miles, with Archie. Hattie often asked if she could go with him, but he said no, he was going too far. The atmosphere of the house squashed even Hattie, who was losing her bounce. A worried, haunted look was beginning to creep into her eyes, as the silent gulf between her parents widened.

The atmosphere touched all the children, making them apologetic, even Jake. They stopped shrieking and laughing, too worried about making things worse. None of them knew what they could do to make it better. Hattie tried, drawing both of them pictures which she pushed under their bedroom doors, or left on their pillows, decorated with multicoloured hearts, telling them how much she loved them. Ollie constantly asked Tess if she was OK, and became even more scrupulously tidy. Jake withdrew even further into a place where no-one could reach him.

One night, Mark did not come back at all. Tess lay

awake, staring at the ceiling, willing herself not to care, and sleep, she needed so desperately to be strong, and to be strong she had to sleep. Every fibre of her being longed to hear his key in the lock, the slam of the door. But he did not return, nor did she sleep. The next morning Hattie wanted to know where he was because his bed hadn't been slept in, and Tess said that he had had to stay over in London on business. Hattie rang him on his mobile, and Tess tried not to listen to the conversation. Mindlessly wiping the wooden draining board in the kitchen, she heard her say, 'When are you and Mummy going to sleep in the same room again? Why? I *could* understand, honestly. Please, Daddy. I don't like you in Ollie's room. Ollie doesn't like it either, he hates being with Jake. It doesn't suit any of us, Daddy, and Mummy's sad.' Tess stepped out of the kitchen and made a face at her. 'She says she isn't but she is. Will you be home tonight? When? OK. I'll wait up for you. I love you. When will it be all normal again?'

When the invitation came from Jeremy and Loopy, Tess's first inclination had been to throw it in the bin, or ring and say they couldn't go. But then she thought, I haven't been out for ages. Why not? And at the back of her mind was the insistent thought that if they did go out together, Mark would have to talk to her. It was eating away at her, not knowing what he had been doing for the past two weeks, where he had gone, where he had been that night he had not come home. She felt powerless in the face of all the conflicting feelings she had, and exhausted too, exhausted with staying awake crying and trying to make plans, poring over houses in the newspaper, trying to work out how she could possibly afford to buy or rent a place for herself and the children back in London. She couldn't stay here, even though the children were happy at school and both Ollie and Jake were at a crucial stage in their school careers. Although housing would be cheaper, she would just be so lonely. No, it had to be London.

And then she would sit back, thinking, what the hell am I doing? This is lunacy, like living in a mad nightmare I cannot control. Am I seriously planning to leave the man I have lived with for sixteen years to set up on my own at the age of forty and begin again and be a single mother? She would have to abandon all ideas of her teaching diploma and get a full-time job. She couldn't expect Mark to keep her, and anyway she did not want him to have that power over her. She would sit, calmly making plans about the house and money and her career and thinking she could cope and then it would all break down, and she fell back into confusion and helpless fear. It was like looking into the abyss. She seemed to lurch from one extreme of emotion to the other, and the stress of it made her feel close to the edge. It was only, ever, the children who pulled her back. Without them, she would have thought seriously of suicide as being a less painful option. Then she would think maybe they could try to build some kind of bridge. Perhaps, just perhaps, this dinner party could be a chance to try.

Mark turned his back to her as he was doing up his shirt. It was ridiculous, she thought, after all these years, to be embarrassed at the thought of being seen naked by your own husband. But that would make her feel vulnerable, and she couldn't afford to be vulnerable in front of him.

'Ready?'

She had to admit he looked sensational. The haunted look which had so worried her seemed to have gone, and he looked perfectly normal and calm. Whereas she felt she looked as if she had been put through a mangle. Every joint ached, her eyes were pink with weeping and no amount of foundation could hide how pale and tired she was.

Lately, she had been having the most powerfully violent dreams, dreams filled with images of her and Mark making love, or being forced to watch while he made love to someone else. And the intensity of the way she felt, the jealousy, had been so strong it had woken her up, heart pounding, skin sweating, totally lost and frightened. She hadn't felt in control in her dreams at all, she had felt helpless, and furious, and so lonely. In another very vivid dream she had been standing on the deck of a ship and, looking down, she saw Mark and the children, tiny figures in a sea of people. And they kept moving, getting smaller, and she couldn't see them, they were blurring and disappearing. And then she was running, running down the deck pushing past people, straining to lean over the side, to see them and shout that she loved them, but someone was holding her back and she realized she could no longer see anyone any more. The sense of loss was terrifying. It was the same kind of dream she'd had when the children were little, that they were tiny, thumb-sized, and she dropped them, and lost them, down cracks in the floorboards, and it was all her fault for not taking enough care.

She had thought about what to wear, putting on a dress she knew Mark liked, a fuchsia pink silk dress which stopped just short of the knee, with a bright turquoise silk hem. He liked it because it clung to her body, and he always said that she didn't wear fitted clothes enough, swathing herself for university in a series of big jumpers and long, shapeless skirts. She put on more make-up than usual, smoothing foundation under her eyes in an effort to hide the bags and the puffiness. One good thing, she noted wryly, about being miserable was that you did lose weight. She must have lost over ten pounds, and the dress hung off her, where it used to cling to curves. She smiled at herself brightly in the mirror. Christ. She looked like a grinning skull.

Jake was babysitting, having been bribed with cash by Tess. The three children lounged in the TV room, watching *Blind Date*.

'Be good,' Tess said. 'We're only up the road.'

'You look wicked, Mum.'

'Thanks, Ollie.' She reached out to ruffle his bristly blond hair. She'd given in to contact lenses and let him have his hair cut like Jake. Although Jake, perversely, was now growing his so a long floppy bit dangled in his eyes. It made him look like a poet, Byronic. Ollie's contact lenses, Tess felt, had not been a great success. He squinted slightly, but she could not tell him. He was very sensitive about everything at the moment.

'Bed by nine at the latest for Hattie, I mean it, and Ollie make sure you let Archie out for a wee. Jake, no phoning. You have your mobile, and you put £20 into it yesterday. And no Internet. You left it on last night. Do not touch Dad's computer and if I find anyone has been in the drinks cupboard there will be hell to pay. There's stuff in the fridge. Good night. I love you.'

'Come on,' Mark said impatiently from the door. He held it open to let Tess pass. As he turned to close it, Tess stopped, so she was standing immediately in front of him.

'Mark?'

'What?'

'I . . .' She reached out to touch his shoulder. He stood very still.

'Don't,' he said, distinctly. 'Thank you.' He walked away to the car. All the emotions she had tried to hold onto in his presence, for fear of letting go and embarrassing herself, spilled out.

'God!' She put her face in her hands, and sobbed. He didn't stop.

'If you've finished, maybe we could leave,' he said.

She reached up, and, with a shaking hand, smoothed the mascara away from under her eyes. She swallowed, pinched her side very hard, and followed him to the car.

'I'll drive home,' she said, in as normal a voice as she could muster, once she'd got in.

'You won't get too pissed, then?'

'No, I won't get too pissed. I think I can trust myself.'

At the entrance to the drive, heralded by two stone pillars topped by large circular stone balls, she said, 'Stop the car.'

'What?'

'I said, stop the car. What do you think stop the car means? I can't go through with this. I cannot walk into that room as your wife and pretend to be happy and normal and be nice to people and make small talk when I do not feel that I am your wife and this is all a lie.'

'Fine,' he said. 'I'll go on my own.'

'And how would that look?'

'It will look like how it is. My wife is emotionally unstable and although I appear to be able to manage the fact she is determined to sabotage our marriage, she cannot.'

'I am what?'

'Determined to sabotage our marriage.'

'There's a car behind us, flashing its lights.'

Mark moved off up the drive.

'Don't do this to me,' he said. His voice was very cold, without emotion. 'Don't make me look ridiculous. There are several people going tonight whom I already know, and like. You may not have been able to make friends here but I have, and I am looking forward to this evening. You won't have noticed but I have

287

been working very hard lately and it would be nice to relax without one of your dramas. You started all this, and you are not going to suck me into any more lunacy. I have really had enough.'

'I can't believe,' Tess said, as he stopped the car on the immaculate circular gravel drive, 'that you seriously think I am the one trying to sabotage our marriage. When you were the one who deliberately moved out of our bedroom and have ignored every attempt I have made at compromise and stayed out at night shagging God knows who.'

'Shut up,' Mark said, smiling pleasantly, as Jeremy advanced towards their car.

'So glad you could come,' he said, opening Tess's door. Tess put her head down, and slid out, without catching his eye.

Peering into the gilt-edged mirror in the palatial downstairs toilet, her worst fears were confirmed. Her make-up was smudged, her face blotchy. God, she looked old. She rubbed savagely at her eyes. No wonder he didn't want to stop this. She repulsed him. She ran her fingers through her hair. She'd left her handbag in the car. Fortunately, there was a silver-backed hairbrush with ridiculously soft bristles on the marble table under the mirror, like a baby's brush. What a daft bathroom, she thought. It was decorated in burgundy and white stripy flocked wallpaper, and even the marble table had gilt leaves on the corners, and down the legs. On the walls hung caricatures of Jeremy and Loopy. There was a pencil sketch of Loopy falling off her horse with a caption underneath saying, 'Loops comes a nasty cropper at the oxer.' Oh yock, fucking yock, Tess thought. What am I doing here? She ran the brush through her hair. Immediately, it all stood on end. 'Oh God,' she said, furiously smoothing it down. Now it lay against her head like a swimming cap. She moved the brush towards it again. Her hair leapt to attention. 'Just behave,' she said sternly to it. She ran her fingers through it. It crackled. She ran the brush under the tap. 'Now brush, damn you. You're a brush. So brush.' She pulled it gently through her hair, keeping a sharp eye out for sudden leaps skyward. That was better. Only a little – damp. No matter. Nothing could be done about her eyes, she thought, leaning forward and peering into the mirror, but maybe she didn't look too bad. The redness was disappearing.

Well, that was it. She had tried to make contact and he had thrown it back in her face. As if she was the one who was breaking their marriage. Just who the fuck did he think he was? She would never make herself vulnerable again. Ever. She would play him at his own game, and talk civilly, and pretend in front of other people, including the children, that everything was OK. If he wanted war, he could have bloody war. She would not let him see it was getting to her. To be vulnerable meant you could still be hurt.

She took a deep breath before she opened the door to the living room. There was a smart roar from within, and when she pulled the door open it revealed a scene from Noël Coward, of women in long dresses (long dresses?) and the men in black tie. Oh buggery, buggery. She hadn't read the invitation properly. Mark walked towards her, his face furious. He put his hand under her elbow.

'Why didn't you tell me it was black tie?' he said very quietly into her ear. 'Did you want me to look like a complete twat on purpose?'

'Of course not,' she hissed back. 'It was a mistake.'

'Why is your hair wet?' She did not reply.

'Loopy, how lovely to see you again,' Mark said, politely. And then he moved away to talk to the men, several of whom were in the syndicate he hoped to join.

Tess was left in a sea of horsy women. Blah, blah, they went, about their wretched nags and their hunting and the Pony Club and how good Jemima was getting and why did boys lose interest so quickly, and what was the best kind of feed for the winter months and how to prevent poaching in gateways. It was when a woman so thin she made a line look chubby said, 'Oh, ad lib hay I think, don't you agree?' that Tess realized she would have to move or stab someone. She walked over and stood next to Mark. Immediately, all conversation ceased. Mark looked at her pointedly. 'Would you like another drink?'

'Nope,' she said carelessly. 'I'm fine.'

'I'll get you one,' he said, and holding her firmly under the elbow, steered her back towards the drinks table. 'Stop being an arsehole,' he said into her ear.

'That's not a very good word to use in such company, is it?' she said. 'And I refuse to be pitchforked, literally, into a group of boring horsy women who have not, as yet, asked me one question about what I do or even about my children.' She turned her face away from the other guests. 'They are not interested in me, I am wearing the wrong clothes, I do not fit in, I hate them. I want to go home.'

'You are being so childish. Yes, of course some of this lot should be culled, but I am afraid they are our neighbours and we have to get on with them. Can't you just try to make an effort?'

'No. Not tonight. Can't we go home?'

But he had left her.

Where once they would have laughed about a situation like this – she would have caught his eye above the assembled heads and flashed a look which they both knew meant 'plonkers' – now he was siding with a roomful of strangers against her. She was losing him.

The rest of the evening passed in a painful, silent

blur in which like a consummate actress she nodded, laughed and prevented herself from crying, when all she really wanted to do was lie down and die. Being strong was going to be even more exhausting than being vulnerable. It was like having to encase yourself in steel and not let anything escape.

Chapter Twenty-eight

'Where's Daddy?'

'He's gone, darling.'

Hattie looked up at her, her eyes filling with tears.

'He didn't even say goodbye.'

'I'm sure he came in and kissed you.'

'Did he kiss you?' Tess turned away and began to lift the dirty bowls and side plates from the table, methodically stacking the dishwasher, before hitching it back onto its rails, sliding the bottom rack in and pushing the door shut with her knee. Then she bent down and felt for a dishwasher tablet in the cupboard under the sink.

'I said, did he kiss you goodbye?' Hattie demanded, standing very close behind her.

'No, darling,' Tess said quietly. 'He didn't.'

'Mum, where's my clean shirt?'

'Over the Aga rail. Hang on. You've got some egg on your face. And you've got toothpaste all round your mouth.'

'Ouch,' Ollie said, as Tess licked her finger and rubbed at his face. 'That hurt.'

'But you have to look your best, doesn't he, Mummy?'

'He does. All those prizes he's got to receive. Maybe

292

you ought to take a suitcase in with you,' Tess said, smiling.

'Mum! Shut up.'

'Well I, for one, am very proud of you.'

'Dad isn't, is he?'

'What on earth do you mean? Of course he is.'

'So why did he have to fly out today? The conference isn't for another week, is it? He could have come.'

'He's coming back early, remember. So I can sort out the exhibition.' Hattie and Ollie exchanged glances and made yawning faces at each other.

'Where's Jake?'

'Still in bed.'

'Oh God,' Tess said crossly. 'Ollie, go and get your brother out of bed and tell him that unless he gets up now he is not having a lift to school and he will be put in detention if he's late for assembly today.'

Ollie's feet thumped up the stairs, she heard the door of his bedroom open and then there was a loud crash.

'Oh Christ. What now?' Tess ran up the stairs two at a time. Ollie was standing by the door, looking shocked. 'Jake threw a football at me.'

Right, Tess thought. I've had enough. She pushed open the door. The curtains were still closed, but the bright July sunlight shone through sufficiently for her to be able to make out Jake's mound under the duvet. She stalked over and pulled it back. He was lying on his back with his eyes closed, naked except for a pair of boxer shorts.

'Get up,' she said. 'And don't you dare throw things like that!' She felt tears welling up.

'What's the matter with you?' Jake said, opening his eyes.

'Nothing. I'm just tired of having to chase everybody around. We are going to be late, you have to get up

293

immediately. I mean it.' She pulled the duvet away from him, onto the floor.

'OK, OK. Keep your hair on. Anyway, it doesn't matter much if I don't turn up, does it? Not as if I'm going to walk away with millions of prizes on Speech Day, am I, like Wonder Boy?'

'You can hardly blame your brother for being a success.'

He regarded her dispassionately, raising himself onto one elbow. 'Oh, no. I can't do that. Where's Dad?'

'Gone.'

'Of course. At least I will only have one parent to witness the fact I am the only member of my year not to get an award for something, even if it's some lame book token for endeavour.'

'You nearly got that sports award.'

'Nearly, but not quite,' Jake said, getting up and looking around for his uniform. It was thrown, in a chaotic heap, at the foot of his bed. 'Did you wash my shirt?'

'No,' Tess said. 'I'm sorry, I forgot. Have you heard about the prefects yet?'

'Oh yes,' Jake said. 'I have. And before you say anything, Mum, I am not going to be one, or even a dinner monitor. OK? Conversation over.'

As she drove back from their schools, promising that she would not be late with Hattie for the two o'clock start of the prize-giving, she started to think about what she ought to wear. Some kind of dress, she supposed. And a jacket. She hoped she wouldn't be the only mother there on her own.

She and Hattie sat uncomfortably on the folding chairs in the chilly marquee, Hattie in a pretty flowery dress she hated, Tess in a button-through cream linen dress she had spilt milk on just before leaving. She pulled the flap between her knees, to hide the damp patch. Linda, the mother of one of Ollie's friends, leant towards her. 'Hasn't Ollie done well?' she said.

'He has. I'm really proud of him.'

'No Mark?'

'He had to go away.'

Linda made a sympathetic face. Her own husband sat rigid with boredom beside her, smartly dressed in a pinstripe suit. He took out his mobile, looked at it intently, and then switched it off in a resigned manner. 'When are they going to start?' he said, crossly. Linda picked a small piece of fluff from his lapel before settling her handbag more comfortably on her lap. Tess noticed she was wearing gloves. Tess seemed to be the only mother who wasn't wearing a hat. God. It was like a society wedding.

In front of them, Jake's form filed silently in. All the prize-winners had to sit on special seats at the front, and Jake was by no means the only one who hadn't been given an award, he had been exaggerating. But where was he? She could see his friends, but no Jake. He couldn't be late for this. He had to be here somewhere. She craned her neck, trying to see if he was lurking at the back. But the sixth form had entered, and now the master at the back was pulling the flaps of the marquee closed. Maybe he was ill. Why hadn't the school rung her?

The violin section of the school orchestra screeched into life. Hattie leant back against Tess, sucking her thumb. Tess automatically reached over and pulled it out. Where was he? She tried to concentrate on what the headmaster was saying. The prize-giving went on interminably. 'I need the loo,' Hattie whispered. 'You'll have to wait,' Tess whispered back. One by one the boys trooped up, with pink cheeks, to be shaken by the hand by the Chair of Governors, and handed a pile of books. Hattie cheered wildly every time Ollie had to go up. Then there were poems, and musical recitals, and a speech by the Chair of Governors and all the time Tess kept thinking, What has happened to my son?

'Well done,' she said, ruffling Ollie's hair.

'Brillianto,' Hattie said. 'Now can I go to the loo?'

'Ollie, where's Jake?'

'Dunno. Isn't he here? He ought to be.'

'Hang on a sec. Ollie, can you show Hattie where the loos are?'

She had just caught a glimpse of Jake's form tutor. Smiling and nodding at people as she pushed her way through the crowd, she reached him eventually.

'Excuse me, but do you know where Jake is?'

'Jake? He should be here.'

'I know. But he isn't.'

'He was in the classroom before we left. Wait here a moment.'

He disappeared, and then came back five minutes later, while Tess tried to make small talk to a couple she barely knew. His face was worried.

'We can't seem to find him. Excuse me.'

'I'll try his mobile.'

She walked out of the marquee, and dialled Jake's number. It rang and rang, before clicking onto the answerphone service. That was not like him. He normally answered after just a couple of rings. What the hell was she going to do? All around her parents stood chatting, glasses of wine in their hands, relieved the speeches were over and looking forward to the picnics they had brought with them. Tess had forgotten about that, anyway she really didn't want to sit on her own.

Ollie and Hattie wandered back towards her.

'Have you found him?' she asked.

'Nope. No-one's seen him.'

'Oh Christ. Bloody boy. Ollie, could you look in all

the places he might be, like the Common Room or his classroom?'

After an hour of searching by Tess, Ollie and Jake's tutor, there was still no sign. 'Perhaps he has gone home?' his tutor said.

'How?'

'On the bus?'

'It doesn't seem very likely.'

'I am afraid we are going to have to take some kind of action about this.'

'I know. Only let's just find him first, shall we?'

'Ollie, try his mobile again.'

'No answer.'

Tess clutched the steering wheel tightly. 'Come on,' she muttered, as a tractor pulled out in front of her. 'Oh, get out of the bloody way, will you?'

At home, she wrenched open the door and ran up the steps to Jake's bedroom. It was empty. But hang on. There was his blazer. Thank Christ.

'Jake!' she shouted. 'Where are you?'

'He's not downstairs,' Ollie called. 'I've looked.'

'Look in the garden. I'll do upstairs.'

She ran from room to room. There was no sign of him.

Suddenly, from the garden, she heard an unearthly wail. It was Hattie.

Oh, my God, she thought. She ran down the stairs, almost colliding with Ollie. Together they ran towards the scream. It had come from the orchard. As she wrestled with the latch she could see Hattie standing, looking down, her hands covering her mouth. They ran towards her.

Jake was sitting behind a tree, hunched over. From his wrists dripped a steady stream of blood, staining the grass by his feet, the white cuff of his school shirt.

Tess reached out and pulled Hattie away.

'Take her inside,' she said to Ollie. He looked up at her, horrified, then silently put his arm around Hattie and tried to make her turn. Her body was rigid.

'Take her in!' Tess screamed. Shocked into life, Hattie stepped backwards and allowed herself to be led back towards the house.

'What the hell have you done?'

'It didn't work,' he said, so quietly Tess had to bend down to hear him. 'It's much harder than it looks. I thought it would be easy, but I couldn't do it, Mum. It hurts. It really hurts.' She knelt down and put her arms around him, hugging him so hard. He looked up at her, shocked beyond words.

'Press on them. Hang on.' She jumped up and ran into the house. In the kitchen she wrenched two tea towels off the Aga rail. Outside, she wrapped them firmly round his wrists.

She didn't know whether to take the bewildered Ollie and Hattie with her to the hospital. In the end she had to take them, because she couldn't bear to leave them alone. Together they sat in Casualty, wordless. Terrified.

He was seen immediately. The nurse on the desk said she should have called an ambulance, but Tess didn't know what the correct procedure was for teenagers who had incompetently hacked at their wrists with a blunt razor blade. So she had driven him into Oxford herself, unheeded tears pouring down her cheeks. Jesus. How could they have screwed things up so badly? What kind of parents were they? Nothing else mattered. They had failed. Jake sat, gripping the tea towels, silent, in shock, staring unseeingly out of the window. In the back, Ollie and Hattie sobbed.

*   *   *

'He will be all right,' the junior doctor said. 'Has he ever done anything like this before?'

'No. Never. We've had problems, but nothing like this. Can I see him?'

'Of course.'

The wounds had been stitched. The doctor said they were mostly surface cuts, and would heal very quickly. The mental scars, he said, might take longer.

Tess stood at the end of the bed, and looked down at him.

'Are you going to tell Dad?'

'Do you want me to?'

'No.' He turned his head into the pillow.

'Why did you do it?'

'Why not?'

Tess sat down by him, and put her hand under his cheek.

'I love you.'

'No, you don't.'

'Oh, for God's sake, Jake! Stop acting as if you are the only person in the world who has the right to feel so desperate! Don't you think anyone, ever, has felt like you?'

'You don't know how I feel! You can't see inside me!'

'Yes, I can.' She bent over, and held him. 'You're part of me.'

'I'm not part of anyone. I'm not part of our family. Just a bloody nuisance. And you and Dad are splitting up.'

'No we aren't!'

'Oh, for fuck's sake, Mum, do you think I'm blind? Do you think I can't see what's happening? It's all falling apart, and on top of everything else I can't bear that. I can't bear to see what it will do to Dad.'

'Dad?'

'Yes, Dad. You can't see how screwed up he is, Mum. I've heard him crying.'

'No!'

'I sometimes think I'm the only one who notices anything! You're just too wrapped up in your studying and your exhibition to see what's going on. I'm not going to take my exams. I'm going to leave home and get a job, in London. I don't fucking care what happens to me, I just want out.'

'Please, darling, don't say that. It will be all right. I'll make it all right. You'll see. Give us both a chance.'

'Yeah, right. I think it's too far gone for that.'

She had to leave him to take Hattie and Ollie home. Sophie's mother Kathy said she would come to look after them. Tess had told her that Jake had hurt himself and was in hospital. She left him sleeping, exhausted by the shock. Like a broken child.

'What? What the hell are you saying?'

'Jake's had an accident.'

'What kind of an accident?'

'He cut his wrists, Mark. We couldn't find him and he had come home and, he did it. I'm sorry . . .'

'Hold on. Please. For God's sake. Is he all right?'

'Yes. He's OK. Physically, anyway. He's coming out of hospital tomorrow. He can stay at home but the doctors want him to see a psychiatrist. He wasn't badly injured, he didn't even get near a vein, they're just surface cuts, but Mark, the blood . . . Hattie is beside herself. She found him.'

'I'll come home. Today. Don't worry about meeting me at the airport, I'll get a cab home. Just look after the children, will you? You're not still . . .'

'No, of course I'm bloody not. Do you really think I could carry on with the exhibition when my son has slashed his wrists? Don't be so fucking stupid.'

'Stop swearing at me.'

'I'm sorry. You just don't know what it's been like, finding him, and then the hospital, and he's still so

300

angry. You have no idea what it has been like. It's a nightmare and I feel so guilty . . .'

'It isn't my fault, Tess, that I'm here. I'll see you tonight.'

'I didn't say it was your fault!' she shouted. But he had gone.

She drove to the airport on autopilot, her hands trembling on the wheel. She missed the turning off the motorway, and had to turn around at the next junction, trying frantically to remember which terminal his flight was arriving at. Her brain felt disjointed, as if she had to tell her body to work. She could not co-ordinate her movements. Kathy had said she shouldn't drive, because she looked very pale. Had Jake hurt himself badly? Tess wished to God her parents were at home. She could have told them, and shared this nightmare, and they would have known how to look after Ollie and Hattie, and taken them away so she could concentrate on Jake. It would be quicker if she picked Mark up, they could go straight back to the hospital. After she had dropped the children off with Kathy at home, she went back to be with Jake. She sat with him, while he slept, and watched his innocent face, studying every detail. She might have lost him.

She pressed her hand to her mouth. God, how she needed Mark. Only he could understand.

The news came on the radio, and she forced herself to concentrate, in case there was a travel report. The newsreader said, 'A recent survey has shown that seven out of ten youngsters would prefer their parents to remain in a warring marriage than separate. The survey, by the children's charity . . .' She flicked it off. They had to try again. It might mean giving up her dream, but what was her dream compared to the stability of her children? They had to be the most important thing in her life. A tricky marriage was not

301

the end of the world. Lots of people lived like that – surely they could hang on until the children were old enough to leave and then they could reconsider.

Concentrating hard, she turned into Terminal Three. There were so many lanes to choose from. Where was the short stay car park? Oh sod it, there it was – she swung across a lane and the car behind her blared its horn. Ducking, as she always did driving the Discovery in low-ceilinged car parks, she drove endlessly round until she managed to find a space. There was a quarter of an hour until Mark's plane was due to land.

In the terminal she looked up at the overhead computer screens. The sign next to the California flight was flashing 'landed'. He would be through soon. Oh thank God, please, please hurry. She hated leaving Jake alone, although the doctor had given him a sedative and said he would sleep for hours. As she was turning, she caught a sudden image in the corner of her eye. She felt, rather than saw him.

His brown leather overnight bag was slung over his shoulder, and he was wheeling the big black suitcase they used for long holidays which had a clasp which often stuck and Mark had to bounce on top of it with all his weight to get it to open. It was known in the family as the black hole. His head was turned away from her, towards someone. Tess paused, her hand gripping the shoulder strap of her bag.

He was laughing.

Around her people talked and called to the passengers they were meeting. The tannoy announced that a flight, which had been delayed, was just landing. A small child bumped into her legs, and she put out a hand to steady it. I do not know him, she thought. The man walking towards her, who had not seen her, chatting to a person he had met on the plane, was a stranger. He would arrive, his face suitably composed into worried grief, at the hospital, but here, where he was to his belief unobserved, he had a life quite separate from them.

At any moment he might look up, and see her. She forced herself to move. She turned, and blundered into the newsagent's stall behind her.

'Won't you look where you're going?' an angry woman said, pulling at the hand of a toddler.

'I'm sorry, so sorry,' she said. She could not focus, and she thought she might faint. Breathe deeply, she said to herself. She felt physically sick. She ran out of the concourse, almost into the path of an airport bus. She held up her hand, distractedly, and headed for the car. Mark would get his cab. Her mind raced. She had to get back to the hospital.

Jake had just woken when Mark arrived. They both started when he walked in, his face flushed, full of anxiety. It was real, Tess thought, of course it was real. But he could switch it off, and she hated him for that. He was not consumed, as she was. He reached down and put his arms around Jake, jerking him up towards him. He did not look at Tess. She stood, awkwardly, by the bed.

'I love you,' he said, tears running down his face. 'I love you so much. Don't ever, ever, doubt that.' Jake shut his eyes, his face pressed tight into his father's shirt, tears sliding through his closed lids.

Tess looked at them. They did not need her. She went home to Ollie and Hattie.

Chapter Twenty-nine

I am strong, she said to herself, over and over again as she drove home. We no longer matter. How I feel does not really matter. What matters is Jake, and making him well again. The image of Mark's laughing face played over and over again in her mind. The innocent loss, the final and definitive loss of love, of belief, of trust.

Mark got home late, after Hattie and Ollie had gone to bed. Hattie had tried to keep herself awake to see him, but she was too exhausted by the shock and strain of the past two days. Tess too longed for sleep, but knew it was unlikely.

When Mark came in, she was clearing the kitchen. One by one she put the plates away, wiped the table and the top of the Aga, straightened the post she hadn't had the time to open on the dresser. He stood behind her, and put his arms around her.

'Thank God,' he said. She stood very still. 'He'll be OK. What did the doctor say it was? A cry for help. It's worked, hasn't it? He's certainly got our attention.'

'Is that what you feel?' She could hardly bear to talk to him. 'That it was an attempt to get our sympathy?'

'Yes,' he said. 'I do. It is the ultimate form of manipulation.'

'I don't know you,' she said. 'I don't know you any more.' She hadn't meant to cry, and thought that all emotion had been exhausted. But the tears fell anyway.

'What the hell do you mean?' He took his arms from her.

'I mean that in a while, once Jake is better, I need to go away, somewhere, on my own.'

'What for?'

'I just do.'

'Oh, cut the fucking drama, will you? What the hell are you talking about? For Christ's sake, Tess, surely what this has done is make us both realize that we cannot carry on like this, so selfishly wrapped up in our own problems without noticing the effect it is having on the children? What the hell do you need to be on your own for? What we need to be now is together, and try to work something out.'

I know what I have lost, Tess thought. I have lost truth. He cannot see it, because he does not know. I cannot make my life a lie, not even for the children I love more than anything in the world.

'You may be right. But I need some time on my own to decide if that is going to be possible.' Now I am lying, she thought. Enough.

'Why do you have to go?'

'Jake, get off my clothes. Because I just do.'

'Is it because of me?'

'Will you stop thinking that everything in this bloody house revolves around you?' She waved at him to get off the bed. 'I won't be gone for long. I just need some time to think.'

Jake looked at her fearfully.

'It'll be fine. Dad will be here, he's taking a week off.'

'Are you two OK?'

'Of course,' she said, bending her head over her suitcase. She must not cry. 'I need to sort out what I want to do next year, and make a few plans.'

'OK.' He looked at her hesitantly. She smiled at him. He looked fine, his face was tanned, he was almost babyishly keen to please. The awful scars were beginning to fade and that terrible day was a memory, the raw pain softened by the passage of time. Only Hattie still had nightmares.

The children would be fine, she said to herself over and over again as she headed down the motorway. But Hattie had a birthday party tomorrow, and she'd forgotten to buy a present and card, and she wasn't sure if Mark knew where Georgia's house was. Nope, she had to let go. He had to find out how to cope. Hattie would remind him, she'd already put her purple velvet party dress out, and selected which shoes she wanted to wear.

Tess craved the sea. She wanted to sit at the edge, look out towards the horizon and plan what she was going to do in a place which filled her with peace. She could think there.

Halfway to the cottage, it began to rain. Not gentle drops, but a heavy, pelting rain which made her put the windscreen wipers on double time. She slowed her speed.

It was dark by the time she arrived at the cottage, and as she closed the door behind her, and breathed in the smell of musty air and sea, she wanted to weep from the familiarity. She flicked on the lights. Everything was just the same, the bookcase which ran the length of the hall, full of books for holiday reading, Gerald Durrell, Mary Renault, and dog-eared copies of Dickens and Steinbeck. Opposite, on the bureau, lay the visitors' book, open at the last page. She stopped to read it. 'Had a fab time. We walked to Polperro in an hour. I found a dead jellyfish on the beach. This is the best holiday ever, Sam, aged 8.'

The children should be with her, but she had to do this on her own. They could come next summer, the four of them. She carried her case in from the car, and then ran herself a deep, hot bath. Afterwards she slept as she hadn't slept for months in the wide double bed, the bed she had last shared with Hattie.

Chapter Thirty

She was falling. Falling towards the sea, reaching out to try to stop herself. And then her hand caught hold of a branch, and she hung, swaying, over the rocks beneath and she could hear Mark's voice shouting, 'Let go. I'll catch you.' So she let go but she was falling faster and faster and he did not catch her.

She woke with a start, her heart pounding. Where on earth was she? She touched the heavy old-fashioned bedspread. The cottage.

She drank her morning coffee leaning against the Aga in the kitchen. The house felt chilled: Margaret the housekeeper had explained she hadn't put any heating on this week because they hadn't been expecting anyone. It was getting colder, this first week of September, there was no sign of the Indian summer of two years ago. Tess agreed with her the weather was disappointing, but assured her she'd be OK. She didn't know how long she'd be staying. A couple of days, maybe the week. No, the children weren't with her, she needed a break on her own. They were at home, with their father.

After breakfast she set off for the beach. She had planned to walk the coastal path to Polperro, about three and a half miles away. It was a tricky path, over steep hills and valleys, with some alarmingly narrow ledges with a sharp drop to the sea. A fine rain fell. She liked the rain. She didn't want sun, it would make her think of being on holiday with the children. Hattie pretending to sunbathe, wearing bright pink speckled sunglasses and lying still for exactly two minutes before she jumped up again, bored. Mark, surfing with the boys. She smiled at the memory.

It made perfect sense to be here. She lifted her face to the wind. It was so clean, so fresh. She was almost at the stile. She paused, and slowly climbed over. Am I mad to do this? she thought. The pieces of her life would never fit together in the same way again. It did not frighten her. She felt stronger, and calmer, than she had for the past two years. It had taken everything she had gone through to bring her to this place.

She caught her breath. The sea was as she had never seen it before. The water was a fierce slate-grey colour, not the deep blue she remembered, and instead of the flat calm she had expected it was rolling, angry, foaming, every rock met with a roar of spray. The gulls wheeled, catching the wind, crossing each other, wings outstretched, crying into the air. Above the sea the rain became a fine mist, blown like shoals of tiny fish, and overhead the clouds were a heavy, leaden grey, fading up to high white cumulus, angel clouds. She watched, so still, eyes open, a camera, passive, recording. The anger of the sea caught her and filled her with joy.

She crunched down onto the beach, and stood at the shoreline. Wave upon wave rolled in, leaving a thick residue of white froth, like foam, which was caught by the wind and hurled skywards. The beach was covered in debris from the raging tide, pieces of wood, seaweed, shorn-off bits of thick plastic, bottles, gloves, rope. No treasure, but the detritus of modern life, cheap flotsam. She was quite alone on the beach –

it was too cold for anyone to sunbathe, too windy and dangerous for anyone to surf.

Walking back up towards the path, she paused, and sat down on a rock. Tucking her hair behind her ears, she looked up at the sky. The impenetrable storm cloud had cracked, and, through it, there was a sliver of blue, a beautiful blue, like the wing of a kingfisher.

Chapter Thirty-one

Hattie's eyes had never been fearful. But nothing in her life was a certainty any more.

'It's my fault, isn't it, for not being a good enough girl and leaving my bedroom in a mess and breaking the toilet window?' She held a Barbie in her arms, and she pulled and pulled the doll's hair.

'It isn't you. It's Mummy and Daddy.'

'Where will Dad live?'

'He's renting a flat in London, Jake. Near his work.'

'Who will make his tea?' Hattie said.

'He'll have to do that on his own, for now.'

'He hasn't got a bread board,' she said.

'He'll buy one. Don't worry, darling, Daddy will cope.'

'No, he won't. He doesn't know how to make things. He burns everything he cooks and he doesn't know how to make a washing machine work.'

'My love.' Tess knelt down in front of Hattie. 'He'll learn very quickly. It isn't rocket science.'

Ollie stood very still, leaning against the dresser.

'So we have to move.'

'I think so, yes. We can't afford to live here on our own.'

'Where will we go?'

'Back to London. Or Cornwall.'

'Why Cornwall?'

'There is a job there, a job I might apply for, lecturing at a further education college.'

'No more private school, then.'

'I'm sorry, no. To be honest we couldn't really afford it anyway.'

'How can Daddy read me my bedtime story if he isn't here?'

'He will come and see you. And you can go and see him.'

'That's not the same!' Hattie shouted. 'It's all wrong! Can't you see? Families are supposed to stay together, not break up into little pieces. It's all broken and it's all wrong!'

Ollie, whose expression had been detached, crumbled. The tears ran down his cheeks. He reached forward to hug Tess. 'We love you, Mum.'

'I know,' she said, holding his arm, tears coursing down her face. 'I'm so sorry we've failed you all like this.' She wiped her eyes with the back of her hand. 'But I couldn't help it. You know, for all of you, I would have saved it but I couldn't.'

'That's not what Dad says.' They all looked at Jake.

'Dad told me he wanted you to stay but you insisted on leaving.'

'Do you believe him?'

'I don't know.' Jake eyed her warily.

'The trouble is,' Tess said carefully, 'I'm not in love with Daddy any more. And he doesn't love me.'

'But you can't say that.' Hattie was howling. 'Mummies love daddies and daddies love mummies! That's why they make us! Because they love each other. You told me I was made out of love and now you say it isn't true!'

'I know, but sometimes mummies and daddies stop

loving each other. We loved each other when we made you, really we did.'

'But you can't switch it on and off! It's all a lie then, isn't it?' Hattie said, the words coming out one by one, in between sobs. 'It's all one big lie and I'm not going to believe anything in my life ever again. If you can stop loving Daddy then you can stop loving me, too, because love doesn't mean anything.'

Ollie had written an essay for his new school's magazine. He had settled in very well, considering, and was delighted when he had been asked to be the editor. The piece he decided to contribute was called 'The Journey'. In it, he wrote, 'As we drove to school we went past a forest and I imagined how my family had branched out like a tree, and my mum and dad had been the trunk which had held me up. Now I felt like I had been struck by lightning, and I had been torn in half. As I remembered how lucky I had been I felt ashamed of myself for how I had always wanted more and that a drastic thing like this had made me realize how selfish I had been.'

Postscript

Jake was sitting in the new cyber café in Fowey, emailing Francesca. He stopped for a minute, looking out at the brightly coloured little boats in the harbour, rising and falling as the tide ebbed and flowed against the secure walls. On the tanned wrist which rested on the keyboard was a bracelet of twisted love beads. Some of the beads had fallen off, leaving bare patches of thread. When he moved his wrist, the beads slid together.

'It feels like we've all failed,' he typed, in his clumsy two-fingered fashion. 'I've been thinking about it and I feel like to be a part of a whole family, a real family, is the only truth. As soon as you break that, then everything around you gets smashed up. We're lucky, I suppose. We still have Mum. And a tiny bit of Dad. But who does Dad have? He doesn't have anyone, just this crappy timeshare family. I hate seeing him in his new flat. I've told Mum I don't want to go any more. I feel so bad, so bad I can't sleep sometimes, thinking about him trying to be normal, but he can't, he's just destroyed. Mum isn't happy either. She says she is, but I know she isn't. It does my head in. I can't wait to get away and be on my own. Sometimes I think I can never forgive Mum. I love her, but I will never forgive her. They broke what little truth I had. Does that sound mad? Maybe I'm just crazy without you.

I really love you. Hey, maybe we'll get it right?

Kisses and a lot more,

Jake.'

THE END

HOMING INSTINCT

Diana Appleyard

When having it all just isn't enough . . .

It's time to start thinking the unthinkable . . .

Carrie Adams, successful television producer, mother and wife, is about to return to work. Baby Tom has fallen in love with the new nanny; six-year-old Rebecca isn't too keen, but hopes the nanny will at least be better organised than Mummy. Carrie meanwhile is desperate to reinvent herself from housewife to svelte career woman.

Because this is what today's women do, don't they? They're smart, successful, glamorous wives and perfect part-time mothers. They can be brilliant at work *and* brilliant in bed. Carrie lives by the maxim that working full-time is no problem as long as she has the right child-care, and has never doubted for a moment that this is her path in life – until reality begins to hit home. She isn't happy, the children aren't happy, and husband Mike – until recently trying desperately to be a New Man – is now becoming more and more detached from family life. She begins to think the unthinkable. Perhaps, just perhaps, she doesn't *have* to do all this . . .

'A FABULOUS, FUNNY NOVEL . . . THIS WONDERFUL BOOK IS ESSENTIAL READING FOR MOTHERS TRYING TO DO IT ALL'
Daily Mail

'RUTHLESSLY AND HILARIOUSLY FRANK'
New Woman

'A BRILLIANTLY FUNNY READ'
Woman's Realm

0 552 99821 4

BLACK SWAN

A CLASS APART

Diana Appleyard

Class? It doesn't exist any more, so we're told. We're
not supposed to be conscious of subtle class
differences. We no longer look down on people
because of their accents, their education or the car
they drive. Or do we?

Lucy Beresford knows her middle-class family thinks
she's married beneath her when she gets together with
devastatingly sexy Rob. He's gorgeous, he's thoughtful,
he's clever – but he's undeniably working class. Her
parents cannot believe that she would choose him
above Max, her so-suitable former boyfriend – who is
truly one of us. Gradually the differences between Rob
and Lucy – at first so unimportant – begin to loom
large, as they argue over how the house should be
decorated, how the children should be educated, and
whether the evening meal should be 'dinner' or 'tea'.

In this funny, contentious and brilliantly observed
novel, Diana Appleyard scratches the surface to reveal
the petty snobberies which still exist in most of us,
and which make Rob and Lucy . . . A Class Apart.

0 552 99822 2

BLACK SWAN

PERFECT DAY

Imogen Parker

Can one day change your life?

If we were a song, what song do you think we would be?

On a perfect spring morning, Alexander catches an
early train into London, but he never reaches work.
Instead, he spends the day with Kate, a waitress he
has met the previous evening, a woman so unlike
anyone he has ever known, she makes the world
shimmer with possibility.

Such a perfect day, Nell takes her child Lucy to the
seaside, hoping that the sea air will blow away the
doubts she has about her life.

As Nell ponders why falling in love is so different
from loving someone, Alexander allows himself to
imagine leaving his old life behind and starting afresh.
And by a strange turn of fate, there's an opportunity
to do just that – if he chooses to take it . . .

0 552 99838 5

BLACK SWAN

A SELECTED LIST OF FINE WRITING
AVAILABLE FROM BLACK SWAN

14721 4	TOM, DICK AND DEBBIE HARRY	Jessica Adams	£6.99
99821 4	HOMING INSTINCT	Diana Appleyard	£6.99
99822 2	A CLASS APART	Diana Appleyard	£6.99
14764 8	NO PLACE FOR A MAN	Judy Astley	£6.99
99734 X	EMOTIONALLY WEIRD	Kate Atkinson	£6.99
99860 5	IDIOGLOSSIA	Eleanor Bailey	£6.99
99854 0	LESSONS FOR A SUNDAY FATHER	Claire Calman	£5.99
99687 4	THE PURVEYOR OF ENCHANTMENT	Miraka Cobbold	£6.99
99836 2	A HEART OF STONE	Renate Dorrestein	£6.99
99840 0	TIGER FITZGERALD	Elizabeth Falconer	£6.99
99910 5	TELLING LIDDY	Anne Fine	£6.99
99795 1	LIAR BIRDS	Lucy Fitzgerald	£5.99
99759 5	DOG DAYS, GLENN MILLER NIGHTS	Laurie Graham	£6.99
99890 7	DISOBEDIENCE	Jane Hamilton	£6.99
99883 4	FIVE QUARTERS OF THE ORANGE	Joanne Harris	£6.99
99867 2	LIKE WATER IN WILD PLACES	Pamela Jooste	£6.99
99940 7	SHOPAHOLIC ABROAD	Sophie Kinsella	£6.99
99737 4	GOLDEN LADS AND GIRLS	Angela Lambert	£6.99
99938 5	PERFECT DAY	Imogen Parker	£6.99
99909 1	LA CUCINA	Lily Prior	£6.99
99872 9	MARRYING THE MISTRESS	Joanne Trollope	£6.99
99780 3	KNOWLEDGE OF ANGELS	Jill Paton Walsh	£6.99
99723 4	PART OF THE FURNITURE	Mary Wesley	£6.99
99835 4	SLEEPING ARRANGEMENTS	Madeleine Wickham	£6.99
99651 3	AFTER THE UNICORN	Joyce Windsor	£6.99